I0685258

FIELDS OF SHADOW AND GLORY

1863: THE CIVIL WAR CRUCIBLE

BROTHERS IN PERIL TRILOGY
BOOK THREE

Elizabeth Ann Boyles

Copyright © 2025 by Elizabeth Ann Boyles
All rights reserved.

No part of this book may be reproduced in any form or by any electronic or mechanical means, including information storage and retrieval systems, without written permission from the author, except for the use of brief quotations in a book review.

This is a work of fiction. Any references to historical events, real people, or real places are used fictitiously. Other names, characters, places, and events are products of the author's imagination, and any resemblance to actual places, events, or persons, living or dead, is coincidental.

Published in the United States by Promise House Publishing, Colorado Springs, CO
Library of Congress Control Number: 2025911763
ISBN: 978-1-7345011-5-5 (Paperback)
ISBN: 978-1-7345011-9-3 (Ebook)

Scripture quotations are from the King James Version of the Bible.

Cover design by Kim Killion/The Killion Group, Inc.

Dedicated to My Former Students through the Years
Living in many different places
But united in God's love

CHAPTER 1

Late January 1863, San Francisco

"There she is. Ready to bowl us over." Tom Ballard stopped his younger brother and pointed out their prettiest traveling companion, Sara Ogawa. She waited for them in front of a tailor's shop halfway down the block, holding two packages.

"Guess the seamstress concocted what she wanted." Terry sounded about as enthusiastic as when he'd had to swab the merchant ship's decks. "Don't know why you're so fired-up. She's not gonna look like a whole new person in a Japanese kimono if that's what she's got."

"True enough. She'll be as good-looking as ever." Tom grinned at Terry's sour look as they headed down the sidewalk. But his brother was right in calling him out. Without a doubt, calamity would come knocking if his admiration slid into a relationship they could never have.

Tom wove around several pedestrians, then jerked to a standstill. Two scruffy sailors were talking with Sara, practically in her face.

One man's hand snaked out and took her right arm. Then both men yanked her forward as she clutched her packages.

Tom took off, ignoring the grumbling people he passed in a blur. Seconds later, out of nowhere, a hand grabbed his shoulder. He whipped around, only to find his brother gripping him.

"Hold on! Think!" Terry let go. "She would've fought to get loose if there weren't a gun. Maybe two."

"You're right." Tom shot a look at the sailors leading Sara away. "Then we'll have to blindside them. They won't expect jiu-jitsu moves from either me or graceful Sara. Come on!" He set off again, staying far enough back to avoid detection, with Terry keeping the fast pace beside him.

The ruffians hurried Sara past the Chinese stores and stalls on Dupont and then onto Pacific Street. San Francisco's notorious Barbary Bay district lay ahead. Aware the men could have allies among the ne'er-do-wells, Tom kept his eyes out for a policeman. But not one was in sight.

After a block of seedy saloons, brothels, and a barely-disguised opium den, the two brutes halted with Sara in front of the entrance to an alley. One man kept a hold on Sara, and the other pivoted, eyeing the crowded sidewalk. His gaze passed over Tom and Terry without pausing. If the men had seen either of them in the past, their new clothes likely disguised them. Wool trousers and waistcoats were nothing like the get-ups they had worn onboard the ship they'd arrived on.

Not wanting to get too close, Tom pulled Terry toward a boy selling *Daily Alta California* newspapers. He paid a penny and took the paper in time to glimpse their quarry disappear into the alley.

Tom stood next to Terry, peering into the alley's gloomy passageway, full of drunks, toughs, urchins, and a few white-haired elders. "Can you see them?"

Terry shook his head.

Fear for Sara slugged Tom's chest. "We can't have lost them already!"

Keeping to the heavy shadows of the run-down buildings and overhanging balconies, they hunted for any sign of the three. Two girls—the kind their folks back home railed against—called to them in front of a hole-in-the-wall pub, no doubt identifying them as easy pickings.

"Not customers. Not now anyway." Tom winked to keep their cooperation. "But can you help us out? We're looking for a pretty Asian friend—about as pretty as both of you—and two shabby sailors who could do her a lot of harm. They came this way, not five minutes ago."

"Forget the lost darlin'," one said. "I can you're my sort of fellow." She glanced at a man standing in the doorway behind her, then leaned forward, showing curves. "Any men," she murmured, "who're a threat to your friend would hurt us if we blabbered, don'cha know?" Tilting her head, she squinted at a nearly invisible passageway leading off from the alley. "But come back after you finish your business," she said in a throaty voice after straightening. "I'll help you forget your troubles."

"I'm sure you could." Tom offered a ghost of a smile, then arched his brow toward Terry. "Let's move on for now."

They sauntered a little distance from the girls before turning into the narrow way's entrance, framed at the top by a curtain of wooden beads. Ducking under them, Tom scanned the gravel path. Only four people were in sight.

Terry's steps faltered. "We're gonna look like turkeys among chickens. Turkeys that don't belong."

"Can't be helped. But where'd they go?"

The yelp of a kicked dog drew Tom's attention to the path's far end, where a man smoked in front of a storage-type building.

"Is that one of them down there? I didn't get a good look at their faces."

Terry leaned forward, staring. "Think so. He's got the same leather jacket. But we gotta find a policeman. Doesn't matter how tough you are if you're looking down a gun barrel."

"No police around. I looked, and we're out of time. We can't desert her."

"I know. I know," Terry huffed. "But we can't just trot up to that guy and hope to live."

A pigtailed Chinese man ogled them as they walked closer. Having a wild thought, Tom leaned in toward Terry. "Go along with me." He bowed, then spoke to the elderly man, using the few Japanese words he'd picked up from Sara and her brother.

As expected, the man shook his head and muttered a reply in Chinese.

Tom nodded, then proffered one of his two packages to the man.

The man waved it away as if it would explode. "You make mistake."

"You aren't Mr. Mar?" Tom brandished his free arm at the shacks along the path. "Which place belongs to Mr. Ah Mar?"

"No Ah Mar here." The man executed a stiff bow and turned to enter the nearest doorway.

To keep up the charade, Tom took several hesitant steps, crisscrossing the path. A moment later, he stopped. "Loan me your package, Terry, and stay back, at least a few feet. All right?"

"Whatever you say, but I don't like this." He dropped his parcel on top of Tom's.

"Just stay back." Eyeing the lookout at the end of the path, Tom walked forward.

The apparent guard snuffed out his cigarillo with his heel. His hand slid inside his jacket.

4

Tom kept going, heart pounding. Hopefully his sweaty appearance would be attributed to frustration, not raw nerves. "Think you could help two fellow Americans make a delivery?" he asked at last, drawing as close as he dared.

"Out o' luck, buddy. Not helpin' nobody today." The man thrust out his other hand for them to halt.

Tom obeyed abruptly enough to make the packages fly from his arms. Swearing, he moved forward as if to retrieve them, stooped, then leapt at the man like a ravenous beast. Using a joint lock, he got hold of the pistol and kneed the man's legs sideways.

The lookout landed facedown. When he didn't move, Tom checked him for breath and gave a relieved sigh. The fellow had knocked himself out.

Looking around, he saw the Chinese man had changed his initial intention and was watching them from nearby shadows. He cupped his hands to his mouth. "Get the police!" he called softly. He held out a one-dollar gold piece. "I'll pay you." He pointed at the lookout. "This man's a thief!"

The elderly man didn't move, eyeing Tom as if he were a lunatic.

Tom pivoted to Terry. "Looks like you're the one to track down the police." He gathered their packages and held them out. "Take these with you. Once you're back on Dupont, ask everybody you see where an officer is. Can you do that?"

"Guess so. I got two feet." Hugging the packages, Terry headed toward the path's entrance.

Tom shuddered as he studied the surroundings. Sara had been inside the building for less than ten minutes, but her kidnapper could be slapping her around, even preparing to do the unthinkable. A gun still had to be trained on her, or she would have freed herself.

One look told him the entrance's metal door would be hard

to dislodge, and the effort would alert the abductor inside. The left side of the building mashed up against its neighbor, but the right side had a two-foot clearance between it and a high retaining wall. After making sure the guard was still out, he edged along the narrow space, counting on a rear door.

There was a back door, all right, but his tugs on the knob showed it was barred. A dirt-encrusted rear window offered the only alternative. With just a nick on his finger, he managed to slide his hand through a missing part of the pane and up to the lock. He gritted his teeth at the scraping noise while he pushed the window up.

He should wait a minute and listen. If riddled with bullets, he couldn't very well help Sara. But he'd already lost too much time.

After checking that the lookout's pistol was loaded, he climbed through the opening and crouched on the dirt floor behind tall piles of crates. Inching over to a crack where two piles met, he viewed the room, lit by one flickering lantern.

Sara was perched on a waist-high barrel with another barrel in front of her. Her kidnapper stood with his gun pointed at her, unfortunately with his side, and not his back, toward Tom.

"Please repeat about place to send money." Sara's voice was firm. She held a quill poised above a sheet of paper. "My English and your English are little different."

"Listen hard then." The villain rocked his gun. "You speak good enough. Don't be tryin' my patience none."

Tom sucked air between his teeth. If he shot the kidnapper point blank, the man might shoot Sara reflexively. If he drew the man's fire toward himself instead, the man might grab Sara first to use as a shield.

But Sara was smart and quick—quick enough to get out of reach despite her voluminous skirts.

He stretched up with his left hand and shoved the top crate in the neighboring stack. It crashed and splintered. The next second, the hoodlum's bullet penetrated the crates, missing Tom's head by a foot.

Tom shoved another crate, then leapt to the far side and poked his head out to aim.

He didn't have to fire. The kidnapper lay on the ground, and Sara held the man's pistol.

She breathed out a *thank you* to Tom as he strode forward.

"On your knees! With hands behind you," Tom ordered. Another step let him get a better look at the abductor's bearded face. He stopped and gaped. "Zeke? It's you!"

"Don't shoot yer ole shipmate, Tom," he whined.

"Mate, you say? The rat who marooned me? Hah! Hands behind you. Now!" Tom clamped his mouth closed to keep from spewing his revulsion. God would have to do a mighty work before he could possibly obey the *love-thy-enemies* command. He was as far from even tolerating Zeke as the north pole lay from the Antarctic.

"If you kill me, havin' busted in here, it'll look like murder." Zeke's face was ashen.

"I'm not killing you. Neither is my friend, though it'd do the world a favor."

Tom bound Zeke's wrists with a rope he pulled from under an empty pallet, then used three loops of it to lash Zeke's arms tight to his body.

The building's front door rattled once and then a second time. Before Tom could reach the door, it banged open. A burly policeman filled the entrance. A second officer, grasping a billy club, stood behind him. And sitting on the ground was the lookout, rubbing his jaw.

The first policeman pointed his pistol at Tom. "Drop the

gun!" he ordered. "Hands up!"

"Sir, you're making a mistake." Tom obeyed so he'd live to explain. He took a quick look at Sara. The gun she'd held had vanished.

He scuffed his boot toward Zeke. "This fellow and the man out there are the criminals. This lady was waiting for me to join her at Ah Lam's tailor shop on Dupont. You can see her two packages there." While keeping his hands in the air, Tom pointed to the parcels on the floor behind the barrel. "These two men abducted her and forced her inside here at gunpoint."

The officer's eyes flicked toward the packages while keeping his pistol steady.

"Sure," Zeke said. "I kidnapped someone while I knelt here, tied up. Who had the guns? And watch out fer the innocent-lookin' girl, officer. She's as guilty of thievin' as the fellow and knows how to fight. If you search her, you'll find her gun."

"I *am* innocent!" Sara looked straight into the policeman's eyes before modestly dropping her gaze. "While I waited for my companions"—she motioned toward Tom—"to bring me to Occidental Hotel for the lunch, this man and his companion snatched me and brought me here. He ordered me write for a ransom." She tapped the paper lying on the barrel.

The officer glanced at it. "Ransom note? It's blank." He turned toward his skinny partner behind him. "Right-smart puzzle we have. One fellow tied up. The other knocked out by the dandy here, according to a pigtailed elder. And then a doll of a Chinese girl, alleged to be some kind of wildcat, claims she and the one with the pistol were the victims."

His partner shrugged. "I don't know how much credit I'd give a Celestial, Sergeant Mason, especially a female. Looks clear to me who the robbers and victims were."

"The lady is Japanese, not a Celestial, or whatever you

Californians call the fine Chinese people," Tom interjected indignantly. "An American vice consul, traveling from Japan, is with us as her guardian. This thief, whose name is Zeke Bonner, must have been a stowaway on our ship, the *SS Retriever*. There's a warrant in Nagasaki, Japan, for his arrest on a charge of attempted murder, and our ship's captain as well as the vice consul can testify to that."

"Don't pay no attention to the liar," Zeke snarled. "He and his China doll are real good at weavin' spiels, waylaying lonely sailors. My friend wouldn't 'a' stayed here fer the police if we was the robbers, would he now?" Zeke looked toward the door.

The first officer—Sergeant Mason—looked too. The accomplice was nowhere to be seen.

"Innocent men don't run away," Tom said. "And I sent my brother to bring the law."

"An old Celestial alerted us, not an American, so that dog won't hunt." Mason beckoned for his partner to come farther inside. "But I can see it's one man's—and one female's—word against the other. We'll find the truth. Don't you doubt that." He glared at both Zeke and Tom while ignoring Sara. "One of you is already nicely tied up." He faced toward Tom. "Now then, let's complete this job. No funny business, or you'll be meeting your Maker, not the judge."

Sara's shake of her head was so forceful a strand of dark hair came loose from her Western-style chignon, despite her bonnet. "*Please* believe me! Zeke is the thief. Tom—"

"We're just following procedures, miss," Mason cut in, keeping his pistol aimed at Tom.

"But—"

"Pro ... ce ... dures. The rules. That's how we do things in this town."

The skinny officer handcuffed Tom, then picked up the

pistol. Tom guessed Sara had hidden Zeke's pistol deep within her gown.

Mason walked over to see Sara's packages better. "Miss, I need to check inside one of your parcels. Maybe that'll help me decide what to do with you."

Sara lifted the top package by its strings and laid it on the barrel. "Here, sir." She took out a kimono and held it up to herself. "This is what ladies wear in Japan."

"All right. Guess we can eliminate you as a main suspect. Armed robbers don't tote their specialty goods. You can pick up your other parcel."

"If she's not a suspect, can't you eliminate me as one too?" Tom asked. Surely the men couldn't miss the logic no matter how dense they were. "We're together, you remember."

"Yes, and remember who had the gun," Zeke rejoined.

"Enough guff from you two." Mason picked up the lantern. "The sheriff's the one who'll do any more eliminating. Both of you come out and follow me. The jailhouse is close to this crime area—conveniently close."

When Tom stepped outside, he looked in every direction for Terry, but he wasn't there. Was he still hunting for help? Surely something bad hadn't happened to him too. The whole situation reeked beyond belief.

Tom faced the skinny officer guarding him from the rear. "Uh, sir. I really did send my brother to get a policeman. He's only seventeen. Doesn't know San Francisco at all. Did you meet a fellow asking for help on your way here?"

The policeman snorted. "You can drop that line, buddy. We'da helped a lost stranger."

Tom fisted his hands, feeling the handcuffs gouge his wrists.

Sergeant Mason joined Sara on the path. "To be safe, miss,"

he said, "you must also come with us. This neighborhood's o'erflowing with wickedness. Should be safe enough to go alone from the jailhouse. Just a short distance to Montgomery Street. From there, you can ride the Omnibus Railway to the hotel if that's really your destination."

Sara shook her head. "I can't go to the hotel without my companion's brother."

"That's up to you. But you'd be safer leavin' this part of town straightaway."

She stepped back next to Tom. "We will all pray for you, and I *will* find Terry." Tears, forbidden to the daughter of a samurai, glistened in her eyes.

"I must ask you not to speak with either suspect." Mason wiggled his gun.

She scowled at him, but drew away.

At the steps leading up to the two-story, brick fortress of a jailhouse, Terry rushed toward them. "I told a policeman inside about the abduction, but he ordered me to wait out here until someone could go with me."

The skinny partner held his palm up. "We've already dismissed that story, son."

"What?" Terry gawked at Tom's handcuffs, then glared at Zeke and the two policemen. "What are you doing to my brother?" Terry sounded like a general reprimanding subordinates.

"Your brother's in deep trouble." The skinny partner smirked. "If you don't want to join him in the lock-up as an accomplice, you'd better quit the sham and learn from your brother's mistakes."

Tom shook his head at Terry, whose face looked like a boiler ready to explode. "Leave it alone for now. Won't do any good."

Sergeant Mason ignored Terry and beckoned Sara over. "Sheriff Tinsley is out of town until tomorrow. He'll be the one detailing the crime's evidence, so your captain and that vice consul—if they give a red penny—needn't show up today. Tell anyone aimin' to testify to be at City Hall tomorrow by ten. There's some backlog, but the judge gets caught up fast."

"Yes, sir. Captain Whitson, Vice Consul Pendleton, and I *will* come." Her voice shook with anger. "We will *prove* this friend of mine is innocent. Completely *innocent*!"

"Mind your manners, miss." The skinny numbskull leered at her. "The truth will out."

Tom seethed inside. The man was a complete jackass, and his sergeant didn't have the fortitude to correct him. As he mounted the stairs, he turned for his last view of Terry and Sara.

"Caught you now, huh," a gaudily-clothed bystander taunted. The fierce look Tom sent the loiterer only made the man laugh. He shouldn't have let the fellow get under his skin, but hadn't he already had enough trouble for a lifetime? Marooned on an island with earthquakes, a cavern full of bats, and to cap it off—cruel pirates. Didn't he deserve a break?

Inside the jailhouse's *reception* room, Tom frowned at the worker booking him into the jail. While the clerk recorded him as a nineteen-year-old male with blond hair, blue eyes, and a height of five-feet, eleven-inches, Tom's eyes fell on a plaque tacked to the dingy-gray wall behind the man. Contributed by the St. Mary's Cathedral, it warned, "Son, Observe the Time and Fly from Evil." Tom grunted. He'd be happy to do just that. His New York home beckoned, and all he desired was for him and Terry to see their parents again and maybe even introduce Sara to them. But avoiding evil that chased you down like a hound on a rabbit wasn't one bit easy.

Of course, he'd been able to rescue Sara, and Terry had made it to the jailhouse safely. Thank goodness neither had been harmed. And he couldn't forget that God spectacularly answered his plea for help when marooned. But did that mean he'd be rescued this time? Or rescued quickly? In the biblical account he'd read of the Israelites' bondage in Egypt, long *years* crawled by before God saved them.

An armed guard led Tom and Zeke through the heavy door separating the jail cells from the front room. A rank smell of body waste and mold struck Tom full force. When the door clanged shut, an uproar erupted of prisoners' curses and pleas. Tom took in the dim corridor lined with metal doors. A cold bleakness stretched out before him.

Until yesterday, Terry and he had been making great progress across the miles separating them from their Albany home—a beacon growing brighter each day. If he were found guilty somehow, what would happen? Fear, which he hated, gnawed at the corners of his mind.

CHAPTER 2

Arriving at the corner nearest the Occidental Hotel, Sara gave her two packages to Terry to hold while she stepped down from the horse-drawn railcar. If the morning hadn't turned out so awful, her first-ever travel on rails would have been a treat. But she could hardly keep herself together.

What a mistake she'd made in joining the group's shopping plans! She should never have left their ship's refuge. But she hadn't wanted to miss even one day of exploring America and its famous city, "the gateway to the hills of gold." And now Tom was in jail—on her account.

Brushing the sand off her cheeks from a gust of cold wind, she joined Terry at the four-story hotel's ornate door. Ironically, her guardian waited inside to provide the group with lunch in the "sumptuous" dining room, celebrating their arrival in the United States. The meal would be anything but celebratory.

Once the hotel's surly doorman half-heartedly stepped aside so they could enter, Sara rushed toward Vice Consul Pendleton, who was tapping his way across the lobby, his cane in one hand, his other hand outstretched.

He grasped her shaking arm. "Is something the matter?" He

looked behind her at Terry crossing the lobby alone. "Is our Thomas all right?"

"Something terrible has happened to him!" Despite her efforts, her voice trembled.

"She's right," Terry said as he came up beside them. "Tom needs your help."

"Oh my!" Mr. Pendleton pointed to a small room adjoining the lobby. "You claim that parlor for us, Terrence, and gather the other two while we deposit all these packages."

Once they were settled in the side room with her brother Daisuke and their youngest companion, Jim Mankin, Sara told what had happened, with Terry inserting the parts he'd witnessed. The others frowned and groaned all through the account.

"The two policemen wouldn't listen at all," she said at the end, her voice cracking.

Daisuke muttered '*yabanjin*" in Japanese, then "barbarians" in English.

"Oh Golly. Golly!" Jim burst out, looking at Mr. Pendleton and then Terry. "I thought the arrest warrant for Zeke in Japan would be the end of him. He's like an octopus—growing back lost tentacles."

"A monster," Terry hissed.

Mr. Pendleton nodded. "Unfortunately, those are apt descriptions. Yet we've all faced odds far worse than the present ones. Almighty God brought us through, and he will this time too, won't he?" He turned expectantly to Terry.

"Yes, sir ... uh, *you* could say that." Terry's sheepish expression didn't give much of a confirmation.

Mr. Pendleton patted Sara's arm next to him. "We must thank God, though, that you're unhurt, dear one." He suddenly frowned. "You don't still have the pistol, do you?"

"I do not." She struggled to smile. "Before we reached the

rail track, I loosened my sash. So the gun fell on the sidewalk. Terry kicked it into a hole by a lamppost."

"A clever disposal. Well done." Mr. Pendleton stroked his gray beard, then looked over his spectacles at the group. "I hate like the dickens to say this, but we still should dine while we're here even though our appetites have taken a thrashing."

Terry shook his head fiercely. "Sir—"

"Keep in mind," Mr. Pendleton cut in, "there's nothing we can do for Thomas this instant, no matter how much we want to take action. I've already turned in a reservation and have taken the liberty of ordering for us. But the main reason to follow through is due to my request for the hotel's manager to meet with me when we finish eating. The doorman was downright rude when the three of us arrived. The manager needs to be apprised of this. And you never know—a lot of people flow through this hotel. He might be able to help us locate Jim's long-missing uncle. I'd hate to give up that chance."

"Thank you, sir," Jim said, his face turning red at Terry's sigh.

Sara bit her lip. Jim didn't complain about his lot in life although the pox had made him an orphan. The boy had even taken over Terry's responsibilities in Japan so Terry could go on the *Retriever* steamship to rescue his brother—and as it turned out, rescue her and her brother too. No question, Jim deserved their help. But should they have a feast while Tom was jailed?

"We can go back to the *Retriever* and plan our strategy after my interview with the manager," Mr. Pendleton added. "Would everyone be amenable to that?"

Sara voiced her agreement after Terry gave a reluctant *yes*.

The iced-shrimp appetizer, garden-fresh-vegetable soup, lamb chops with mint jelly, hot-house asparagus, and crème brûlée were no doubt fabulous, matching the hotel's well-designed dining room in excellence, but no one at their table ate more than a few bites.

When the waiter came to fill their coffee cups, he brought a message that the manager was ready for a strictly-limited, seven-minute meeting with the vice consul alone in his office. Ten minutes later, the maître d' himself brought a message that the manager, Mr. Abernathy, had invited all of them "to be so kind as to join the meeting."

Mr. Abernathy, a chunky man with a thick neck and bushy eyebrows over gray eyes, stood when Sara and the others came to his office door. "Come in. Come in," he gushed. "Please have a seat." He motioned to several chairs. "First, I wish to assure you that from today, *all* our guests will be shown proper respect, including the hard-working Chinese immigrants with whom this honorable brother and sister were confused." He smiled at Sara. Then turning, he cast a questioning look at Terry and Jim. "I understand one of you is named Jim Mankin and hails from Newburgh in New York."

Jim's eyes widened. "Yes, sir, that's my name and my hometown."

"Vice Consul Pendleton here says you have an uncle by the name of Theodore Mankin."

"That's right. My father's older brother." Jim clasped his visibly shaking hands.

"I'm acquainted with a man by that name, originally from that same town. An argonaut—that's what we call the gold hunters—who invested his considerable treasure of nuggets wisely. Now don't get your hopes up too high, but it seems not a common name or hometown."

"No indeed," Mr. Pendleton said.

"I have sent Mr. Mankin a message by courier. His rather large residence is close by on California Street. While we wait for his response, I've reserved one of our parlors for us."

The group followed the manager back to the room where they had gathered before their meal. Sara tried to quiet her heart. No telling how long it would take for Mr. Mankin to appear.

"I wonder, Mr. Abernathy," Mr. Pendleton began, "if you could share a little about Theodore Mankin. Just whatever might be common knowledge."

"Well, I wouldn't want him to accuse me of gossip." The man hesitated for all of an eye blink. "But I can tell you he's currently in the lumber business. He married late—a severe shortage of women afflicting California at the time. But the gentleman has a fine family now, made up of his wife and two sons. A third son was killed as a toddler in a carriage accident."

The manager and her guardian went on to discuss San Francisco's amazing growth, the Cliff House, known for its "highfalutin" gatherings, and California's confusing politics. Sara tried not to squirm. She would have been eager to learn as much as possible about the state at other times, but not when her world was unraveling at its seams.

At last, a stocky man with a mustache curled at the ends, a full crown of brown hair, and a short beard hurried in. "I've come to see my nephew," he announced, "and I spy him now."

He headed toward Jim, whose face was a younger version of his but without the facial hair. Jim jumped up, and Theodore Mankin shook the boy's hand so hard, he grimaced. Within minutes, Jim and his welcoming uncle delved deep into their personal histories. The uncle shared he'd sent a letter to Jim's aunt, offering to adopt the then fourteen-year-old, but Jim had already been assigned to the cook on the *William Parton* merchant ship and had sailed away.

Sara peered at Terry, who had been Jim's closest friend on the *William Parton*. He was leaning forward in his armchair, clearly interested in Jim's situation. However, the wait to aid his brother had to be at least as excruciating for him as it was for herself.

The next minute, Mr. Pendleton caught everyone's full attention.

"We met with a great injustice this morning," he was saying. "One of our members has been arrested for a good deed. His brother here and Miss Sara Ogawa, our traveling companion, can share their accounts of her kidnapping and the outrageous outcome."

When Terry and she finished their retelling, Mr. Mankin spoke up. "I can help in this travesty. I don't expect any of you will be pleased with the so-called trial's result. Our Sheriff Tinsley is an overzealous law-and-order man, notorious for assuming anyone brought to the jailhouse has to be guilty of something."

Sara voiced her dismay along with everyone else.

"If need be, however, I can solve the dilemma." Mr. Mankin's smile exuded a sly confidence. "The city used to have a Vigilante Committee. I wouldn't want my actions confused with how that sorry lot behaved. My solution is a nonviolent, honorable one, but it would be outside of the law's directives. Therefore, it must be the last resort." He fixed his gaze on Mr. Pendleton. "But to prepare for this contingency, Vice Consul, a step must be taken today."

"I'm all ears," Mr. Pendleton said.

"Our last resort in quickly freeing the young man would require that you and your companions set out from San Francisco the day after tomorrow. Is this feasible?"

Mr. Pendleton reared back as Sara and the others gasped. "The day after tomorrow?" His brow creased, absorbing other wrinkles accumulated during his more than seventy years. "We thought it could take weeks to locate you—having no address other than 'near San Francisco.' Why, I thought we might be scouring gold mines even after the *Retriever*, the steamship that brought us, left for the Far East. But to answer your question, departing that soon does appear *feasible*, since we found you."

Sara's mind whirled. Daisuke and she would have only one full day left together. But if Tom were sentenced to prison for helping her and if leaving San Francisco would lead to his release, a quick departure had to be the right thing to do. The day could hardly have gotten worse, but it just did.

Mr. Mankin nodded his approval. "Well then, this brings the next consideration. I understand you as a group are headed to the Northeast. Have you decided your route?"

Mr. Pendleton glanced at the ceiling, then said, "Yes, I believe so. The least taxing route appears for us to take the Pacific Mail steamer south to Panama, cross the isthmus by the new railroad, and travel up the east coast on the Atlantic Mail steamer. The pioneer trails across the high mountains and wild prairies strike me as too risky and time consuming. Of course, either way, we'll be forced to skirt the war, but perhaps more easily with the mail steamships' help."

"Yes, best to avoid the Mississippi River. The papers report much bloody fighting there." Mr. Mankin adjusted his cravat and gave a slight smile. "Here's one piece of good news since you're choosing the isthmus route. The *SS Orizaba*, a Pacific Mail ship, is scheduled to depart for Panama City the day after tomorrow—auspicious timing, since they depart every ten days. Also, the steamship can carry more than eight hundred passengers, providing good cover for a fugitive. The line uses the Brannon Street docks."

"Fugitive?" Terry asked, his blue eyes narrowing. "My brother didn't break *any* law."

"Like I said, I'm not divulging details unless my radical plan proves necessary. You'll have to take my word that reservations for staterooms need to be made today in case we do have to help the young man avoid an unjust sentence."

"I see." Mr. Pendleton ran his eyes over the group. "Any objections if I make the reservations for such an immediate departure?"

"No objection, sir, so long as Tom's included," Terry said.

Mr. Mankin gave him a sympathetic smile. "That's the idea." He jotted a note on a business card, rose, and handed it to Mr. Pendleton. "Agent J. R. Ruby can find space for you on the steamer and will use discretion."

Taking his seat again, Mr. Mankin turned to his nephew. "Now, how about it, Jim? Can you see yourself living with me and my good wife and our two sons?"

Jim's face clouded for a second, but then cleared. "Yes, sir. I'd be very pleased to live in a family with my own people ... if Mr. Pendleton approves. He's been a good employer and like a father to me."

Mr. Pendleton clicked his tongue. "Of course, I approve, Jim. Your duty as my travel companion has been carried out perfectly."

"Well then, that's settled." Mr. Mankin clapped his hands together. "Our family has had a hole for many years. Seems the good Lord is filling that empty place."

"Jim's new home is a monumental ray of sunshine in what's been a very dark day," Mr. Pendleton said, standing. "Handshakes all around."

Sara couldn't help smiling at Jim's grin as his hand was thoroughly shaken and his back thumped by the four men. But as more details were arranged for Jim, Sara noticed a pensive expression slip through her brother's usual samurai mask.

Her guardian apparently caught the look too, for he focused on them as the men retook their seats. "Miss Sara and Daisuke-*san*," he said, using the Japanese honorific, "this sudden turn of events must be an added shock for you. But surely your abrupt parting is temporary."

"My, my! Are you two separating?" Mr. Mankin asked.

"It is necessary." Daisuke's voice was tight. "I must bring news to our parents in Japan of our escape from pirates and also our rescue off the Pacific island, which these two companions helped carry out." He nodded to Terry and Mr. Pendleton. "But because of Japan law, I have to use disguise. If a person, except foreigner, leaves my country, cannot return."

"The penalty is prison or death for a Japanese citizen who does so," Mr. Pendleton explained.

"I have hope for myself," Daisuke continued, "but Sara-*san* cannot use disguise of a *ronin*, a samurai with no master. She will stay with Mr. Pendleton. He is a good Christian, and he agreed to take charge her future."

"It's my privilege," Mr. Pendleton said. "It was hard for me to leave my adopted country of Japan, even temporarily, especially as it was the place of my dear wife's passing. But I shall have one of its finest young ladies with me during my sojourn."

"I'm thankful for your care." Unable to speak further, Sara offered a bow.

As the meeting with Mr. Mankin drew to a close, arrangements were made for Jim to join his uncle's family at the time all of them, except Daisuke, disembarked from the *Retriever*. Mr. Pendleton instructed the group to return directly to the ship while he took a horse-drawn cab to the Pacific Mail's offices.

Following the hotel staff's directions, Sara and the others set out for Stockton Street, where they would take the Omnibus

Railway to the area of Meiggs Pier. From there, the *Retriever*'s cutter would transport them through the harbor. As they walked, Sara drew close to Daisuke, unable to keep silent. "I thought we had more time." She used Japanese for ease and privacy. "My heart is torn in two."

Daisuke frowned, but his eyes reflected compassion. "A daughter of a samurai must be strong," he said, using Japanese also. "Go explore like you've always wanted. I hear there are mountains in this country taller than Fuji-*san* and rivers so wide you can barely see across. But watch out for danger." He looked her in the eye. "Tamo deserves our highest regard for defending you this morning, and he is like an American brother to me. But in the eyes of our countrymen, he's a barbarian. And although he is now a Christian, he knows very little about the faith—less than I do."

She gave a small bow while staying a half-step behind him. She tried to speak the promise he sought—to never care for Tom more than as a friend or brother—but the words wouldn't come.

When she didn't confirm her bow with words, Daisuke fell in step beside her. "Do not forsake your family or your country, Sa-*chan*."

"If only you could come with us," she risked answering. "You could return to our home later when you wouldn't need to become a *ronin*."

"What are you saying?" His frown deepened into a scowl. "How could you suggest I so greatly dishonor our parents—to allow them to continue fearing we have perished?"

His rebuke felt as bad as a slap. "Then please allow me to ask why you didn't return on the gunship immediately after our rescue from the island?" She shouldn't be so impertinent. But why should he scold her when he himself had already delayed his return?

He abruptly stopped walking. "I saw the value of learning the ways of a sea-going ship. I hadn't known how far our country lagged behind Western nations in that area. A samurai must put service for his country before his family. You know this."

"*Ah so.*" Sara bowed low. "Please forgive my thoughtless question." How terrible if they parted at odds with each other.

"You know I cannot stay angry with you. To be honest, I'll miss your prodding, especially your not-so-subtle hints to obey our Master Jesus."

The renewed lump in her throat made it hard to speak. "I must ask you to forgive me again—for tears." Her sobs escaped as she stumbled forward.

Daisuke squeezed her shoulders affectionately. "I wish I could stay with you. Believe me. I'm sad to leave you. Very sad." He dropped his arms. "Now, as your elder brother, I direct you not to return to our country until the foreigners open it further. If I live to see our parents, I can tell them of your wellbeing ... and of your faithfulness to your heritage."

"You coming?" Terry called back to them. "The railcar's almost at our stop."

"Sorry!" Daisuke wheeled and walked at a fast clip.

Sara followed close behind, her heart warming at her brother's affirmation of their Master Jesus. Furthermore, he had not *expressly* forbidden her to care for Tom more than as a brother. She fully intended to be "faithful to her heritage." She would not be swept into Western thinking haphazardly—*willy-nilly*, as she'd heard—or be misled into caring too much for Tom.

Hard as it was sometimes to remember, Tom and she were likely mismatched deep inside, as her brother alluded and others in her country would state unequivocally. But neither would she cling to a custom or belief just because of tradition. Daisuke and she would never have become Christians if they hadn't looked for truth regardless of their ruler's prohibition.

The four of them found seats on one of the two long benches in the railcar. Sara's packages almost slid off her lap as some of her worry dissipated. What an unexpected help Mr. Mankin had turned out to be for Tom. And Terry's faithful shipmate had found himself welcomed into his uncle's family. Moreover, Daisuke was on a path to success. As her spirits rose, she gazed at the passing scenes.

Between the buggies, wagons, and animals clogging the street, she caught glimpses of the tall brick buildings of the city's up-and-coming firms and the small shops lining the sidewalks. If only the dreadful Zeke Bonner hadn't shown up, they might have had a pleasant stay in San Francisco. The fiend must have hidden like a demon in the depths of the ship.

Hidden like a demon? How had that been possible? Zeke seemed to be in perfectly good health when he seized her. If he'd scrounged for food while hiding in the ship's bowels, he'd be emaciated, weak. The remnants of her cheer crumbled. Zeke's survival for six weeks as a healthy stowaway had to mean someone helped him hide. It hadn't been the morning's second kidnapper. Neither Tom nor she had seen him before.

Then who was it? And why?

CHAPTER 3

After finishing breakfast, Terry found a seat by his companions at the long table in the *Retriever*'s Great Cabin. The others were in the middle of telling Captain Whitson about Sara's abduction and rescue.

Upon hearing the news of Tom's arrest, the captain turned toward Terry with a shake of his head. "After your brother gets out o' this dilemma, I'll not be helpin' with any more rescuin'. Better warn the fellow he could run out o' luck one o' these days."

"Yes, sir, I will." Terry was torn between defending his brother and saluting. Captain Whitson brooked no disrespect, yet he watched out for his crew, not at all like the *William Parton*'s captain, who had shown no concern for Tom and him during their first experience as sailors.

"There is a fact, though, that affects this ship's future." Captain Whitson shed his jacket. "One o' my crew must've helped Zeke Bonner stow away. Anyone got an idea who the schemer was?"

Terry jerked as though Mate Talbot had materialized right in the cabin. After pirates had sunk the *William Parton*, First Mate

Talbot had managed a ride on the *Retriever* by hiring on as a lowly assistant bosun.

"I'd guess Assistant Bosun Talbot, sir," Terry offered. "When he was first mate on the *William Parton,* he favored Zeke—didn't force him to take his turn in the crow's nest, or reef the top sails in rotten weather. He was a master at handing out extra work to the rest of us, though."

The captain waved the steward away when he poked his head in with a coffee pot. "Anyone else care to add his observations?"

"I have an idea, sir." Jim squared his shoulders. "While I was assistant to the *William Parton*'s cook, I overheard Zeke and Captain Madison talk about treasure. They thought pirates hid a pile of it on the island where Tom and the Ogawas was marooned. I feared for my life 'cause the captain hadn't wanted anyone else to know about that treasure and its whereabouts. In fact, he had First Mate Talbot change the log for the day our ship visited the island, so maybe Mr. Talbot was in on the secret. And Zeke threw his dirk at me, trying to kill me, probably because I'd learned of the treasure."

"Navigator Stargazer informed me of the doctored log." The captain rubbed his chin, as if pondering things. "When Consul Cardiff showed me the warrant for Zeke Bonner's arrest, I learned about his crimes. Didn't hear about anyone's interest in treasure, though." He turned toward the Ogawas. "From your time on the island, do you know any more of how this all fits together?"

Sara spoke to her brother in Japanese.

"Please speak up, Miss Ogawa, if you have something to say," the captain ordered.

She dipped her head. "Zeke ordered me to write a ransom note to my brother because he said we had many riches from the island."

"Thank you, Miss Ogawa." The captain eyed the group. "We're filling in gaps about Zeke, but Talbot's only *clear* connection to the villain so far is that he was soft on him."

"One more thing," Terry said. "I saw Talbot going down the forward companionway to the ship's storage room a number of times. But since one of his duties was to replenish supplies, I thought nothing of it … until now."

"Well, at last we're primin' the pump. Better late than never." Captain Whitson directed a cool stare at Terry. "Shouldn't have listened to Talbot when he begged to hire on." The captain's gruff voice had come close to a growl. "May not be able to prove the son-of-a-gun's guilt good enough for a judge, but I can, sure as the tides run, not renew his contract."

The ship's bell clanged the half hour. Captain Whitson stood. "Better see what we can do for Ballard. Hearing the whys and wherefores makes me more eager to help him. But before we scatter, I have another word. We're losing Terrence as assistant navigator. The boy's done a good job."

Terry straightened. "Thank you, sir." He forgave the captain's earlier lack of tact.

Whitson turned toward Daisuke. "Mr. Ogawa, you've shown interest in how ships are run. If you're willing, I'll order Stargazer to give you the basics of navigation. Then as part of your training, you can help guide us back to Nagasaki. Would that suit you?"

"Yes, very much, Captain." Daisuke shot a look at Sara, who smiled.

Terry felt a twinge in his spirit. Did it bother him to be replaced? It shouldn't. He was on his way home. And one of Tom's so-called "excellent friends" wouldn't be claiming Tom's time and attention as they journeyed on. Daisuke, and his sister too, had been inseparable from Tom on the journey from the island. It wasn't his own fault he hadn't been marooned with his brother, but instead had slaved to rescue him. And now it was because of Sara that Tom got arrested.

Terry paused to check his reflection in the mirror by the Great Cabin's door before following the others out. He'd grown a good three inches since he'd sailed away from home, now as tall as Tom. He was wearing his good-fitting Sunday trousers, waistcoat, and the ankle boots that Mr. Pendleton had bought him in Nagasaki—an unasked-for gift out of pure kindness.

The vice consul was a saint. The elderly Christian genuinely cared for him and Tom, though they'd done nothing for him. The man doubtless felt great affection for the Japanese pair, and might even be praying for Zeke and Talbot to *believe in Jesus.* Mr. Pendleton set the bar for goodness so high it made him dizzy to think about it.

But he had better try to like Sara more, or he'd drive his brother further away than he already was. Tom had changed, but they were brothers. He couldn't bear to lose him.

Following Captain Whitson up the steps to City Hall, Terry prepared himself for a farce. Even if Mr. Pendleton and the captain did a great job testifying, Sara's shy hesitancy to speak and the loony sheriff and judge didn't bode well.

A broad staircase led to a second-story courtroom, where trials were already in session. Terry filed into the audience section after Sara. They were twenty minutes early, so he'd get a chance to see whether the "hanging sheriff and judge" deserved their horrid reputations.

Sure enough, Sheriff Tinsley explained the charges against two other suspects, and Judge Walker affirmed their guilt and handed out sentences lickety-split, each one in less time than it took to shave a beard. Then right on the dot of ten o'clock, the bailiff led his manacled brother and Zeke to a table on the other side of the railing. Putting the two opposing suspects together into one trial had to be a breach of justice in itself. But what happened in San Francisco appeared to be up to the sheriff, judge, and perhaps the city councilmen, not to the citizens.

Sheriff Tinsley gave a brief account of what the police had reported from the crime's location and summarized Miss Sara Ogawa's "interpretation" of the offense. "In conclusion," he said with a swagger as he approached the judge, "a painstaking investigation found that the rear of the building had been broken into by Thomas Ballard, *allegedly* to rescue Miss Ogawa, and a single shot had been fired by the pistol found in *Mr. Ballard's* hand. However, since Miss Ogawa's claims differ from the circumstantial evidence, both suspects are charged with the abduction and attempted ransom demands. Mr. Ballard is accused additionally of breaking and entering."

The judge raised his gavel as though to give out sentences.

Tom's hand shot up.

The judge glowered at him. "You have something to add?"

Tom rose. "Yes, Your Honor. I'd like to call three witnesses for my defense."

"Then do so, and be quick about it." The judge plunked his gavel onto the desk.

"Mr. Richard Pendleton, Vice Consul of the American consulate in Nagasaki, Japan," Tom called out.

As Mr. Pendleton strode to the front, Terry imagined himself confronting the judge after the trial, surrounded by a pack of newspaper reporters. *Is it correct that you couldn't care less if innocent people are jailed so long as you get to the track in time to bet on the horses?* He pictured the shamefaced judge's hemming-and-hawing response.

Terry refocused on the courtroom as Mr. Pendleton finished taking the oath to tell the truth and began his testimony.

"As Miss Sara Ogawa's guardian, I have accompanied her across the Pacific Ocean, having been charged by her elder brother to care for her. I—"

"Get to the point, Vice Consul." The judge moved his gavel.

"Duly noted." Mr. Pendleton stood straighter if that were possible. "The defendant, Thomas Ballard, has been a fellow companion. We arrived two days ago on the *SS Retriever*. I carry with me the warrant by the American consul in Nagasaki for the arrest of Ezekiel Bonner, the other defendant here, on the charges of assault and attempted murder." He held up the warrant. "It should be obvious—"

"All right. All right. I've got it. However, we're not trying anybody here for a warrant from the Japans." The judge waved his hand in dismissal. "Next witness."

Mr. Pendleton stalked from the bench with the most obvious sign of anger Terry had ever seen in the man.

Captain Whitson, impressive in his dark-blue captain's attire, advanced toward the judge, after taking the oath. He had the look of one who'd faced nature's wrath and won, which, of course, he had. "With all due respect, Judge Walker, there's only one man here who should be on trial." His commanding voice suffered no opposition. "That man is Ezekiel Bonner, who I have confirmed was an illegal stowaway on my Cardiff and Associates' ship. I can also testify that the honorary Nagasaki consul told me directly to be on the lookout for Mr. Bonner because of the arrest warrant. Finally, I am personally aware that Mr. Thomas Ballard and Miss Sara Ogawa are fellow travelers with Vice Consul Pendleton and possess good character. It is beyond belief that Mr. Ballard would attempt to kidnap and rob his *companion*, Miss Ogawa."

A general murmur of appreciative comments came from the audience.

"Order in the court," the judge demanded with a rap of his gavel. "All right, Captain. Your opinion is understood. Final witness."

Terry yearned to stand and give a victory sign to Captain Whitson, but gave a nod of agreement instead.

Sara walked forward. She still wore a Western-style gown, short cloak, and bonnet, probably trying to avoid the Celestial designation given to the hapless Chinese immigrants.

The judge held up his hand. "Chinese in this state cannot testify in court. Your testimony would have been a useless repetition at any rate, unless you planned to contradict Sheriff Tinsley's account of your *interpretation*."

Apparently unfazed by the judge's attempt of curtailment, Sara raised her chin. "Your Honor, I am not Chinese. I am a citizen of Japan, and my words were not an *interpretation*. I *know* who kidnapped *me* at gunpoint." She pointed at Zeke. "It was Ezekiel Bonner and his companion, who escaped." The judge raised his gavel, but she ignored him. "I also *know* with absolute certainty that Thomas Ballard *rescued* me from their grasp. I am—"

"Enough said, Miss Ogawa." The judge banged his gavel. "You may retake your seat."

The audience, most of whom were obviously not related to the accused, gave a collective gasp, causing the judge to cast a sour look at those watching him, as though aware of their attentiveness for the first time. When chatter erupted, he banged his gavel again.

Sara bowed, then pivoted, head still high.

In the midst of his anger at the judge, Terry had to admit Sara had stunned him. Shy? Weak? The girl was more like a steel girder for one of those tall high-rises.

The judge raised his gavel. "Ezekiel Bonner, you are found guilty of abducting Miss Ogawa without inflicting harm. Eighteen months in the county jail." The judge glanced at the audience, who once again seemed unified, this time holding their breath. "Thomas Ballard, you are found innocent of the abduction, but guilty of damaging private property by breaking and entering. The court points out that two officers were able to enter properly through the building's front door. Four weeks in the county jail." He pounded down his gavel. "Next case."

Terry and his companions shouted their objections.

The judge rapped his gavel. "Order in the court! Bailiff, clear the courtroom of malcontents."

"Let's go, people." The bailiff pointed Terry and the other three toward the door.

The group filed out in icy silence. Terry jammed his hands in his pockets to stop himself from pounding on the nearest wall.

Mr. Mankin met them on the sidewalk in front of City Hall. "I assume, from your expressions, justice was not served." He nodded at Terry and patted Jim on the shoulder.

"Far from it." Mr. Pendleton gave a shake of his head.

"Then let's find a spot to talk in Portsmouth Square over there." He pointed his silver-tipped walking stick across the street. "Prepare yourselves for a radical solution."

"Afraid I must beg to be excused." Captain Whitson adjusted his snug jacket. "But I'll be on hand to see you off my ship tomorrow and to give Mr. Talbot the old heave-ho."

When the rest of them had found a deserted area in the park, Mr. Mankin insisted on standing while the others sat on the two benches. "First off," the man began, "I hope, Vice Consul, that you succeeded in reserving staterooms on the *Orizaba* for tomorrow's departure."

"Yes, the agent was most helpful." Mr. Pendleton leaned forward. "But it's hard to imagine any way to have Tom with us."

"That's what we're about to solve." Mr. Mankin turned toward Sara. "All but Miss Ogawa have probably heard of crimps. A crimp, young lady, is someone who uses trickery or a drug like laudanum to get an unsuspecting man onto a ship. By the time he realizes he's been shanghaied, the ship is out to sea and he's trapped."

A fire sprang up within Terry. "You're proposing to have my innocent brother shanghaied? To make him toil for a pittance for another two or three years?"

"Hold your horses, son. I'd never suggest such a thing. You'll see where this is going soon enough." Mr. Mankin waved off a horsefly as though waving off Terry.

"Now, here's the thing," Mankin continued. "An employee in my lumber business is a former crimp who has turned over a new leaf. Yet he owes me a favor for hiring him, a former convict. The man still has useful contacts at the jail, who, by the way, are not the dirty scoundrels that crimps typically work with. As you can guess, Judge Walker's judgments cause the jail to often overflow with prisoners. The authorities turn a blind eye if a jailbird finds himself in the crow's nest of a ship, finishing out an extended term. 'Course, they wouldn't want a drugged prisoner to end up in a steamer's stateroom, but what they don't know, won't hurt them."

Mr. Mankin turned toward Terry. "That sound better? Your name's Terry, right?"

"Yes, sir. I spoke too fast." When would he ever learn to wait before diving off a cliff?

"You have an important role in our scheme. As closest relative, you must persuade the sheriff's men to give you five minutes today to visit your brother. You simply need to tell Tom to drink all the slop ... er, soup, he'll get for supper. Because of eavesdroppers, just advise him—with a wink only he can see—that he needs to keep his health up even if his appetite is gone. Then rant a little about the undeserved sentence if you have any time left. Are you game?"

"Yes, I'll do anything." At least, Tom was easier to get to than when he'd been marooned on the island.

"All right." Mr. Mankin stared at Terry like he was evaluating his abilities. "While drugged, Tom will be brought to my warehouse, and my man and I will see that he ends up in the stateroom along with some of our goods supposedly ordered—a gift from me for bringin' my nephew to me safe and sound."

"I'd gladly pay for the goods." The frown on Mr. Pendleton's brow threatened to become a canyon. "But is this plan foolproof? We don't want Sheriff Tinsley to charge Thomas with an attempted jailbreak. Nor do we want to bring trouble down on your own head."

"No money is changing hands." Mr. Mankin displayed his empty palms. "I have enough friends that no one's in danger if discovered. However, if Tom's awake and prevents the transport, or if the guards think he's aware enough to escape the crimp, that would throw a wrench into the works. He'd be stuck in jail for the full sentence."

Terry winced. Why was his brother's well-being once again falling on *his* shoulders? Someday his shoulders would collapse.

"We'll wait for you here, Terrence, and be lifting up our prayers." Mr. Pendleton nodded to the others.

Mr. Mankin tipped his hat. "I'll bid you farewell so I can tend to my part in this maneuver. I'll see you tomorrow when the storm clouds have cleared." He smiled at Jim, then with a twirl of his walking stick, he headed to the street and his waiting carriage.

Terry chose the square's sidewalk taking him toward Kearny Street, and from there, toward Broadway Street and the jailhouse. He rehearsed every conceivable reason to be allowed to see Tom. *Just five minutes!*

Thirty minutes later, he walked through the heavy door opening to the row of cells, remembering he could have been incarcerated in a similar place on a charge of insubordination if the Nagasaki tribunal hadn't been so merciful. He could make it through five minutes on the free side of the bars.

As Tom came up to the door's open slot, Terry swallowed a clawing acid. "Everyone's disgusted with your sentence, Tom." The sight of his brother crammed into the small space with three dirty cots and a stinky pot in the corner stole all else he'd planned to say. The stares of Tom's two morose prison-mates made it worse. But at least, Zeke wasn't in the same cell. Someone had exercised a lick of sense there.

"You can be sure I'm revolted." Tom's mouth twisted on one side. "The best-laid schemes of mice and men—especially us men—don't work too well, do they?"

A handy thought danced into Terry's vacant mind. "You're the Christian. You're taught to trust, right?"

"Yes, but this sentence is a hard lesson. Four weeks for doing the right thing? I might not pass." Tom closed his eyes as though warding off a vision of dreary days and nights.

"Well, listen … and think. *Trust* is the *key*, you hear? Now pay attention. You *got* to eat or drink whatever passes as food here. *Trust* me. You got to do that." Terry got his face right at the opening so Tom could see him wink in the dim light.

The two sharing the cell with Tom chortled. "You got your momma visitin' you?" one jibed.

Terry kept his focus glued to Tom. "Eat and drink *whatever* these no-goods bring." Another wink. "It's important."

"I'm hearing you, little brother. What's got into you?"

Terry gulped. The minutes were zipping by. Another thought popped into his mind. This had to work. "Remember when Tuffy got sick. If the mutt hadn't eaten his morning-and-night meatballs, he wouldn't have recovered, right?"

"Yeah. And?" Tom scrunched his mouth.

"Well, you gotta eat and drink too, so you get good results like Tuffy. So take it to heart. Trust me."

"Man! This situation is bad, but don't talk hogwash about our dog." He cocked his head. "Oh, say. I *do* remember Tuffy and the meatballs."

Terry winked again, wishing he could get his mouth close enough to Tom's ear to whisper, but the door barred him.

Tom, looking none too certain, returned the wink.

"Time's up." A guard pointed toward the exit.

"Have to go before they throw me in with you. But Tom, *trust* is the *key* for tonight, and you got to eat and drink *everything*." Terry took a breath. He turned away and was joined in the corridor by another visitor being ushered out.

"Hey, bring me a Bible and a blanket next time you come. Will you?" Tom called as Terry reached the door. "Don't forget. And send our folks a telegram, but not about jail."

Won't be a next time, you blockhead, was on the tip of Terry's tongue, but he shot back over his shoulder, "Sure, I won't forget. And I won't mention jail."

All the way to Portsmouth Square, he picked over their conversation. Had Tom really understood? Had he recalled the medicine mixed into their dog's meatballs? Or had he been humoring Terry because he judged him to be falling apart?

When he reported their words to his waiting companions, they claimed the wink proved Tom got it.

"But then, why did he ask me to bring things during the next visit? He sounded like he really meant it." Terry choked back a sob.

"So people wouldn't suspect a plot." Jim's cheerful look proclaimed his simple belief in answered prayers, a belief Terry had often observed in his good friend … and always questioned.

As the four of them took off toward the road, first to stop at the telegraph office and then to catch a cab, Terry muttered to no one in particular, "Anyway, I gave it my best."

But had that been enough?

CHAPTER 4

Tom cracked open one eye. He was dog tired, like he'd been drugged in addition to spending a night on the jail's hard cot. If only he could lie still another hour or so, but daylight streamed in from somewhere. His two fellow prisoners must have assumed he was deathly ill. Otherwise, they'd be arguing with each other like they had hour after hour the previous day.

He opened his other eye and turned his head. The source of the sunshine was a porthole. A porthole with a thin curtain.

Good night! He must have really been drugged. He sure hadn't walked onto a ship with his own two feet. Had he been shanghaied? But he wasn't in a hammock in a smelly forecastle. He was on a soft, clean mattress.

A door clicked shut.

"Hey, you're awake!" Terry's voice greeted him.

Tom raised up on his elbow. His brother, standing at the edge of the mattress, grinned like it was Christmas morning. Terry wouldn't have been shanghaied too. Nothing made sense.

"Man! I'm glad you're all right. I was worried the fellow in the jail added too much laudanum seasoning."

"Laudanum, was it? Feels like he added enough to put an elephant under." Tom rubbed his forehead, trying to clear his thinking. "Where are we? And why the opiate?" He swiveled off the bed and looked in amazement at the carpeted floor under his feet. They were in a first-class, oak-paneled stateroom. That was clear enough.

"We're on a Pacific Mail steamship, headed for Panama City, and you're safe now, out of the harbor and the city's clutches."

"You broke me out of jail?"

"With help—mainly from Jim's San Francisco uncle, Theodore Mankin, who had connections with a former crimp, who also had connections."

"Well, I'll be. What about the others? Sara, Dice, Mr. Pendleton, Jim himself?"

"Jim's uncle is adopting him. Daisuke—or Dice, like you say—is going back to Japan on the *Retriever*. The other two are on board. Mr. Pendleton's two doors down in number six. Sara's in number ten by the ladies' salon, glum as all get out 'cause of leaving her brother."

A surge of energy propelled Tom across the room to the wardrobe, where he found his clothes hung next to Terry's.

"You can't go in her room."

"I know, little brother. But I can knock on the door and invite her to the … what? Library, I guess. Try to cheer her up."

"You might let me catch you up on a few things before you go tearing after *her*."

Tom blinked at his brother's cross tone. "Right. You're absolutely right. There's no rush. Sara's strong."

"Like a steel girder."

"I wasn't picturing that exactly, but close enough. So, catch me up."

As Terry bounced into a chair and started relating the hotel feast that no one enjoyed, Tom sat cross-legged in the middle of his bed. He did need to get caught up, and not just with the news. In the last month, Terry and he had hardly spent any time by themselves except when asleep. Naturally, they disagreed from time to time, but when it mattered, they stood together, like when Terry risked life and limb to rescue him from the island.

The last thing he wanted was for Terry to think Sara and Dice had taken his place. Brothers would be around each other more or less the rest of their lives. Dice was already gone. In a matter of weeks, Sara would continue on with Mr. Pendleton to visit his Massachusetts family. Then if Japan eased its strict laws, she'd reunite with her own family and be happy—according to her anyway—to enter into an arranged marriage. He grimaced at the repugnant idea.

An hour later, when he and Terry had covered every minute of the previous day, Tom's stomach announced with a growl that it demanded food. The clanging of the ship's eighth bell spurred him into changing his clothes. "Wish that bell were for us. I'm starved."

"Why wouldn't it be? We're first class. Heard the main course this evening is duck."

"This evening? What about now? I could eat ten ducks, maybe twenty."

"This evening starts about now. You slept close to all day. You didn't know?" Terry took his breeches and frock coat out of the wardrobe.

"No, I didn't know." Tom started unbuttoning his shirt. "From the looks of your evening attire, guess I'll have to wear my best. Wouldn't want to upset society."

After Tom finished getting dressed, Terry led the way at a fast pace. Tom had to push himself to keep up, still not entirely himself. As they turned from the passageway to enter the aft saloon's dining area, he stopped dead in his tracks at the glimpse of an all-too-familiar face. Mate Talbot? On the same ship? He tried to get a second look, but the man had leaned over to clean up someone's spill. Before he could call Terry's attention to Zeke's likely conspirator, the sailor had whipped around and disappeared down a staircase.

Tom's stomach churned. He had as much desire to meet Talbot in the ship's confines as an ox to meet a butcher in its stall. Maybe the drug still muddled his mind, dredging up fiends. Even though Talbot had been kicked off the *Retriever* yesterday, according to Terry, he wouldn't just land on their ship when hundreds lay in the harbor, would he? And besides, the conceited toad would never work as an ordinary sailor. But the resemblance had been striking, more than striking. Identical.

Mr. Pendleton pushed back his chair and stood to greet Tom. "How good to see you looking so well!" He shook Tom's hand as though he'd been imprisoned for years.

"Thank you, sir. It's good to be here. I'm grateful for everything each of you did." He swept his gaze around and paused on Sara.

She gave a tremulous smile. "We met Jim's uncle just in time. That judge was dreadful."

After Mr. Pendleton thanked God for the meal, Sara gave Tom a bigger smile. "I will always thank you, too. You maybe saved my life. Daisuke reminded me of the samurai code to 'show you great regard' for the rest of our lives."

Tom's heart warmed. "A big step up from being a barbarian," he teased. "But you and I overcame those hoodlums together."

"You two are an outstanding team," Terry stated, his voice flat. "Maybe I could have done more if I'd known those fancy jiu-jitsu moves too."

"Hey, hey." Tom held up his hand. "You helped me out of that dirty jail—got the message through my thick skull. I'll teach you the moves I know anytime you want, and I won't lay you flat like Dice did me." He chuckled, then sobered. "Preparing to defend yourself could be important—maybe for all of us. On the way here, I saw one of the crew who I'd swear was Talbot if it's possible. Think there's a chance he followed us?"

"Couldn't be him," Mr. Pendleton said. "He wouldn't have guessed we were disembarking to board another ship within hours."

Terry plunked down his water glass. "I remember Talbot frowning by the gangplank while we collected our valises, including Tom's, and your trunk, sir. We left the *Retriever* much sooner than planned. He could have had a wild hunch and tracked us."

"Could a sailor get on a crew that fast?" Sara glanced from Terry to Tom.

Tom nodded. "If the ship's short of men. In fact, Terry and I did just that when we signed on to the *William Parton* our first time at sea. But with Talbot's experience, he could have searched the harbor for a day or two and got on as a first or second mate. A much smarter thing to do—roast pork at the captain's table versus hardtack in the fo'c'sle.

"*If* he's on board and maybe following us," Sara said, "why would he do that?"

"I can give a couple of reasons." Tom stopped talking until the waiter finished serving the pea soup *de jour*. "He could be after our rumored treasure—since he appears to have been in cahoots with Zeke, at least on the *Retriever*. Or maybe he's mad about our good fortune in escaping the island while the *William Parton* was sunk, along with his seaman's chest and the pay due him. Maybe he resented how Terry became the *Retriever*'s assistant navigator while he ran errands for the bosun." Tom picked up his soup spoon, but set it back down with a sigh. "He might be blaming us for getting kicked off the *Retriever*. The reasons just keep coming."

"There's also your participation in the Nagasaki tribunal, sir," Terry added, inclining his head toward Mr. Pendleton. "Allowing me to go free when Captain Madison and Talbot tried to put me away for years. And there's the whipping on the ship. Both Zeke and Talbot were plenty angry George got in trouble when they thought it should've been Tom."

Tom grimaced. "Seems like whoever shared their wine with George was more responsible for that whipping than my unrelated theft of a different person's bottle."

Terry shrugged. "Talbot thought I should have told on you before the captain tested everyone's breath. He spewed curses at me one time about how George might never recover."

"May I remind you young people that Thomas merely said a sailor resembled Talbot." Mr. Pendleton wiped his spectacles, then ran his gaze over them. "If he truly is Mate Talbot, consider a more benign explanation. No longer under contract to the *Retriever,* he could have decided to take the quickest route to New England without having to pay for this leg of the trip. Otherwise, the fare from here to the Northeast would cost him two hundred dollars at a minimum. Since most people in California do hail from the East, his motives may be innocuous."

For the sake of politeness, no one showed signs of disagreeing with their elder. But Tom was sure he wasn't alone in his thinking. Mr. Pendleton's supposition had no more credibility than assuming Talbot took the low crew position as penance for sin.

If the sailor was Talbot, they had a treacherous enemy on board. Yet there were four of them, and just one of him. Besides that, God had taken care of them in San Francisco. He shook off the chill running up his spine. He needed to get a hold on his new life as a believer.

At the delicious smell of the two smoked ducks the waiter placed on the table, Tom's appetite leapt to attention. He pushed away his last concerns about Talbot.

"Ah, look at this promise of succulence." Mr. Pendleton waved away the waiter's offer to carve and picked up the long knife to do the honors himself.

Sara turned to Tom. "Does this remind you of the island?"

"It reminds me of your and Dice's archery skills, compared to how I aimed at treetops."

"Daisuke told me you were a quick learner." Sara's lips turned up at the corners, but then her body sagged. "I miss him."

"I do too, and I'm sorry I didn't get to say goodbye." Tom looked away, fighting the ache at his loss of a true friend.

"We may all meet again." Sara blinked several times. "At least, I hope so."

"Yes," Mr. Pendleton said after an awkward minute, "although we cannot imagine how this will take place in the near future, we have a trustworthy Shepherd." He gave a gentle smile.

"Now, I have a piece of news to share from the captain," Mr. Pendleton continued, nodding to the attentive waiter to serve their plates. "After our meal, the first-class passengers are invited to promenade on the upper deck. And I understand that eight crew members will give a demonstration of the Virginia reel, four of the sailors taking the ladies' role—a refresher for those among us who might have forgotten the sequence. Then the crew will open up the deck to any who wish to do the steps."

"Now's your chance to prepare for what's coming at home, Terry," Tom ribbed. "You used to act like holding a girl's hand would be the next thing to being on a chain gang. Guess you're a bit more enlightened now at seventeen."

"Yep, you could say that." Terry quirked a half-smile. "Still, holding a girl's hand in order to do-si-do, can't come close to riding Admiral across the pasture or maybe a game of horseshoes."

"Depends on who the reel is with."

A glint lit his brother's eyes. "Like Peg Stevenson?"

"My old girlfriend," Tom said for Mr. Pendleton's sake. Sara had heard about her. "Of course, she might not be my special friend now. I wasn't courting her. We were both too young."

"Well, you'll know soon enough if she's still moonstruck over you and if her father still objects to stolen kisses." Terry smirked.

Tom chuckled, while wishing he'd kept his mouth shut. To his relief, the topic changed when Mr. Pendleton brought up what he'd learned about the Panama Railroad—how it reduced the journey across the isthmus to four hours, but had done so at a great cost of lives. A rehash of the trial took up the rest of the time until they finished eating.

Along with about fifty other first-class passengers, the four of them headed for the uppermost deck. Tom's pulse sped up when Sara slipped her hand under his elbow at the stairs.

"Do you mind?" she asked, her cheeks turning pink.

"Not at all." Tom gave her hand a pat. "You're doing great at adapting to our customs. And I hope you'll participate in the dancing tonight when the crew offers the chance."

"I'd like that." Her eyes shone.

Volunteering to be her partner for the whole evening was on the tip of his tongue, but he quenched the words. He had to keep their friendship on an even keel. That required his restraint.

He glanced at her from the corner of his eye. Actually, he needn't carry his concerns to an extreme. Partnering with her in one or two country reels would be harmless enough. And it was the courteous thing to do. Now if only his pulse would cooperate.

He led Sara, Mr. Pendleton, and Terry to a good spot at the quarterdeck's starboard railing, where they could enjoy the breeze and have a clear view of the Virginia reel's exhibition. The starry sky, the congenial crowd, and his fine companions promised an enjoyable time—the exact opposite of the jail's bleakness. How quickly life could change.

A sailor broke out his button accordion. He squeezed and expanded the bellows, letting loose a note that ended with a squeak.

Sara, eyes wide, turned to Tom. "That instrument is like a living animal."

Tom laughed. "It's an accordion. Once the player starts moving the air inside the instrument and pressing its keys, the accordion's *breath* flows over reeds to make the music."

A fiddler stepped up to join the accordionist, and the crew of eight took their center places for the reel. Tom tapped his foot as the tune began. But then, a sailor interrupted the dance and grabbed the reel instructor's bullhorn. "I'm sorry, ladies and gentlemen," he called. "One of our performers is needed in the engine room. We'll have to delay the demonstration unless someone here volunteers to take his place."

The moment his three companions turned toward him, Tom wagged his head *no*.

The sailor noted the looks and pointed to Tom. "Sir, would you do us the favor?"

Four or five persons called for him to show off his stuff.

Seeing no way out and having the reel down pat, he agreed to take the missing position.

The musicians struck up "Three Men Went a Hunting." All went well until the instructor called out, "Peel the banana." Tom circled to the end of the line as required. Halfway back to the head of the line, he looked to his right. He was alone. Then he remembered the arch he didn't make with his partner. "Great Scott!" he moaned.

The instructor motioned for Tom to back up. The accordion wheezed to a dying stop. The fiddler dangled an eighth note, mid-measure. The crowd tittered, and Tom saluted, determined to be a good sport. Of course, Terry would never let him hear the end of it.

Sure enough, Terry piped up when he rejoined the others. "Hey, when you peel the banana, you're not supposed to gallop off with it."

"Do tell. And thanks for staring at me, so I had to *volunteer*."

The instructor shouted through the bullhorn for attention. "While our sailors hang the lanterns from the rail poles to further illuminate our ballroom under the stars, those of you who wish to do the reel, please form two lines with eight pairs of partners."

Tom seized his chance to even the score. "Terry, how about you show us your smooth steps?" He turned to Sara. "Would you be willing to try the reel with my brother?"

She blushed and looked at Terry, who had the grace to offer his arm.

The fiddler and accordionist struck up the tune, "Wait for the Wagon."

Tom leaned back against the rail, relishing the sight. Sara, clad in a sky-blue kimono, outshone the other ladies in their fussy, beribboned gowns. Although Terry had seen the reel performed at barn dances, Sara had only seen the one demonstration, culminating in the misstep. Yet she was performing perfectly.

Then, all at once, the ship careened to its starboard side under a rogue wave. The dancers and spectators from the lee side came slipping and sliding full blast toward the starboard rail, shouting and laughing. Sara bumped into Tom's chest, and his arms folded around her before he knew what he was doing. The next minute, the deck tilted to the leeward side. Tom grasped the rail with one hand, and Sara's arm with the other.

"Oh, I couldn't stop. I'm very sorry." She took hold of the rail too. When the ship righted itself, she pulled a fan from her sash. Instead of fanning, she hid her blushing face behind it.

"Well, we could say I was in your way." Tom grinned. "You and Terry were doing fine. I think you would enjoy the waltz. I can help you learn the steps." Holding her in his arms probably wouldn't be overly wise, but it would be less intimate than their momentary embrace.

However, the moon and stars that had shown so well early in the evening had disappeared. Lightning forked in the distance. While the interrupted dancers were still milling around, the ship's captain, who had taken a position next to the musicians, raised his own bullhorn. "Ladies and gentlemen, we must end the festivities," he announced. "To avoid being drenched, you should return to your rooms without delay."

Mr. Pendleton offered to conduct Sara to her room, so Tom followed Terry to theirs.

"I gotta say, Sara caught on fast to the reel." Tom plopped down on his berth.

The expression on Terry's face was closer to a frown than a smile. "After that embrace, looks like you wouldn't have minded taking turns around the deck to the 'Allegheny Waltz.'"

"Don't give me a hard time. If I'd stepped aside, she'd have had a hard bump."

"So, if I'd been the one who ran into you, you'd have hugged me? Stretches belief."

"Believe what you want, but here's the truth. Sara's a good

friend, like a sister, and it's going to stay that way." He ignored Terry's snicker.

"You know what?" Tom waited until he had his brother's full attention. "There's a much more important item to talk about than my imaginary romance. If Talbot *is* on this ship, it'd be best to stay clear of the rigging. I thought coconuts tossed at me by the island monkey were plenty dangerous, but they don't compare to a wrench dropped from thirty feet up."

"I'll tell *you* what." Terry slammed himself down on his bed. "I'm sick to death of the garbage from *William Parton*. Maybe it's Talbot who better watch *his* step. Accidents can happen any number of ways." Terry yanked up a sheet. "I'm turning in. Spent last night making sure you were alive."

"You're the best! Guess I don't say that enough."

"Sorry. I wasn't hinting for accolades. Stay up as long as you want, seeing as you were a Rip van Winkle most of the day. Won't bother me. And by the way, there's a pistol in the bottom of your valise. The jailer sent it to Jim's uncle to dispose of. Said it was the gun the policemen found on you. Mr. Mankin thought you might need it. And I reckon you just might."

"I doubt having Talbot on board will come to a shoot-out as if we're cowboys out West. But good to know the gun's there anyway. Guess I'll read awhile."

Tom got out his Bible and the book, *Two Years Before the Mast.* He'd read and liked his grandfather's copy of the sailor's true account, so he'd bought a copy for himself in Honolulu. He half-closed the lantern bracketed to the wall and settled in the nearby chair. Now that he, too, had lived as a sailor, it was fascinating to read about the similar experiences. But a lot had changed since the author had described San Francisco. The small village had grown up, and so had his brother—in a much shorter time.

He glanced at Terry, who had turned away from the dim glow. Could he have actually meant his threat toward Talbot? Maybe tiredness had overwhelmed him. Or even the shock of being trailed. After all, he had never been aggressive back home. As far as he knew, Terry had never even swung a fist.

He puffed out a breath. Most likely, if his brother hadn't followed him out to sea, he'd still be that quiet boy who loved his stallion and fishing and tried to please people.

He set aside the Harvard student's description of a sailor's life and picked up the Bible. As he expected, the never-changing truths took hold of him, calming him.

He'd led Terry into a sea of trouble. Now if only his brother would also find the lifeboat.

CHAPTER 5

"It seems we will safely disembark tomorrow." Sara took a bite of her fruit salad and looked at the two brothers, who had finally gotten over their reserve in talking with each other—as if they'd been walking on tightropes for the last six days. Even the charming town of Acapulco they'd visited during the ship's coaling hadn't brought the brothers fully back to their cheerful bantering.

Tom nodded at her comment. "Your abduction and Talbot's slinking about got under my skin—maybe all of our skins. Got us imagining the worst."

"Have to agree." Terry narrowed his eyes. "Still, I can't get away from this ship and that villain fast enough."

"Panama City should be a nice change," Sara ventured, steering toward a better topic. "I am eager to ride on a true railroad."

"We're in for a treat." Mr. Pendleton blew on his tea and took a sip. "After I rode the train six years ago, the forty-niners I met in San Francisco, who struggled across the isthmus by dugout and mule only a few years earlier, could hardly believe my account of the train's speed."

"I'm looking forward to the ease too," Tom said, "and seeing first-hand what the press extols as an exotic country. In the meantime, I suggest we make the best of our situation here." Setting aside his half-eaten dessert, he looked at Terry and her. "The weather's good. Since it's our last evening aboard, shall we try out our waltz steps in public? I think you're both ready."

Before either of them could reply, Mr. Pendleton arched an eyebrow and asked, "In public? So, there were private waltz steps?"

"Semi-private," Terry said. "We got to know a family in the library a couple of days ago. Turned out their two sons and two daughters wanted to learn the dance. We were the only ones in the room, so Tom taught everyone."

Sara's cheeks grew warm at the memory. Tom had spent most of his efforts on the other family, practically ignoring Terry and her. But when he finally took her for a spin around the room, his touch delighted her. And perhaps he'd felt that way too. His brief look of longing when she'd tried the curtsy at the end would say *yes*. But on the other hand, he could have been thinking of that girlfriend of his named Peg. She'd better stick to her goal of guarding her heart.

"Ah. Very thoughtful of you, Thomas." Mr. Pendleton smiled, yet looked a little sad.

Terry set his napkin by his plate. "I'll try out the steps, I guess. I'd like to finish a book from the ship's library—Dickens' *Great Expectations*—but I'm sure I can get it elsewhere."

Tom wrinkled his brow. "Do you have plans, Sara?"

"I would like to try the dance tonight too. One of your proverbs says, 'Nothing ventured. Nothing gained.'" After all, the waltz was important in the Western cultures, wasn't it? And she couldn't help it if Tom and Terry were the only partners available, could she? That is, unless Mr. Pendleton, whose agility sometimes surprised her, was capable of doing the steps. She turned to him. "Do you enjoy the waltz, sir?"

He gave another sad smile. "I did at one time, but my dear partner is too far away, perhaps dancing in the heavenly kingdom. You three go ahead without me. There'll be plenty of people to watch over you at the party."

"Shall we?" Tom said, half-rising.

They all pushed back from the table. She took Tom's proffered arm, trying to imagine as part of her *cultural analysis* how an American would feel so close to a good-looking male. Her concentration faltered due to the disconcerting twinkle in his blue eyes.

The Virginia reel was half-finished when they arrived on the quarterdeck. The next dance was an even livelier one, the polka, which started out looking easy until some of the couples added quick steps and fancy kicks. Then at last, a waltz was announced.

Sara concentrated on *step, together, step* for as long as she could, ignoring the sensation of being held close by Tom again. On the island, Daisuke hadn't allowed Tom to touch her or even talk with her alone. Now she understood her brother's wariness about the touching part. How easy it would be to lose control of her heart if Tom's breath mingled with hers for long.

From somewhere, a hand tapped on Tom's shoulder, startling her.

"May I?" Terry asked.

Tom nodded and stepped aside. After an awkward moment, Sara placed her hand on Terry's shoulder, her arm barely crooked due to the gap he kept between them. He took her other hand in his.

"Are you looking forward to seeing Panama as well as getting off the ship?" she asked, happy to have thought of something to say.

"I suppose so … and here we go." He touched her waist and guided her backwards into the circling couples. He maintained the gap between them while still managing to waltz.

She peeked at his face. His expression said he would carry on no matter the cost. Did he resent her presence? Fortunately, the piece ended after a few more measures.

The next dance, called the galopade quadrille, was performed in groups. Neither Tom nor Terry suggested participating, and she soon saw why. Dancers had to repeatedly gallop sideways.

Terry folded his arms. "If I'm going to gallop, I want it to be on my horse."

"I agree," Sara said. Terry's edginess would not keep her from being agreeable. "I miss the pony I had in my country." Then an ache for her home and family slid into her chest. How pleasant it had been to step into her home's garden with her mother or father to watch the fish-pond glimmer under the same moon shining above. To walk along the moss-covered stones with Daisuke while fireflies flitted above the dark bushes.

"What about the Virginia reel and the waltz? Would riding your pony be better than those dances too?" Tom's serious voice drew her back to their conversation.

As her eyes met Tom's concerned ones, she summoned up a smile. "No, just better than the galloping, galloping one." Pining for the past was foolish. No matter what the future held, the life she'd known as a girl could never be resumed. And one thing for sure, she could not have danced in her garden's moonlight, especially not with one of these American friends.

"In that case, let's hope for more waltzes and reels." Tom had perked up.

When another waltz was announced, Sara lowered her eyes, waiting for Tom to act. But one of the boys from the library family asked her for the dance before Tom stopped talking with Terry. Then the library boy's brother moved in for the waltz following another polka. Yet another quadrille was called, and then Terry asked her for the interspersed waltz, a strange glint in his eyes.

Tom was frowning every time Sara glimpsed him over Terry's shoulder. When they returned to the sidelines, he all but leapt next to her. "May I have the final waltz of the night, Sara?" he practically pleaded. "You've certainly charmed other admirers this evening."

"Yes, please." She started to protest humbly that obligation rather than charm had to be the explanation for her popularity, but instead murmured, "You're too kind," the response she'd overheard from a few American ladies.

Tom rolled his eyes at her. He knew her well.

Once again in Tom's arms, she longed for the music to never end. Admiration for his strength, his thoughtfulness, even his *foibles* swept through her. How would it feel to marry *him*? To sleep, eat, live with him? She jerked herself to attention. The music had stopped, and her far-fetched dreams had better stop too.

After they trouped down the stairs with the other passengers, Tom accompanied her to her stateroom door. She bowed and slipped into her room, while her pulse insisted on acting like a runaway colt. If she wanted to keep a calm, neutral outlook, she was going to have to be careful about waltzing.

CHAPTER 6

Terry ran his hand along the gangplank railing and casually dropped the iron-pipe joint into Panama Bay. He could always pick up another weapon if a later situation demanded it. He sure wouldn't have wanted to be caught if he'd been brave enough to carry out what Talbot deserved.

Leaving the dock, Terry strode down the narrow, stony road, keeping to the edge, out of the way of donkey carts and a rare carriage. Behind him, Tom and Sara talked about the Panamanians' tall houses and their ornate balconies, apparently enjoying the sights even though Panama City had the look of a town struggling to survive. According to Mr. Pendleton, a mix of squatters, peddlers, and a few wealthy merchants had taken over the place.

Terry dropped back and jabbed Tom's elbow. "Not the safest appearing road in the world, is it? If Sara could get kidnapped in San Francisco, imagine what could take place in dark corners here, where we can't even speak the language."

"You're right there." Tom peered around at the surroundings. "I suspect no-goods would happily rob travelers who might have struck it rich in California. But they'd be sorry if they picked on us, wouldn't they? We're experienced victims." He actually chuckled.

Terry failed to see the humor.

Tom pointed to a steeple rising in the distance. "Too bad we won't have time to tour that old cathedral before the train leaves."

Mr. Pendleton, who was leading the way, turned toward them. "Sorry about the sightseeing. We'll have just enough time to eat lunch before boarding. Our tickets are for the first train they've scheduled for steamer passengers."

A commotion down one of the alleys drew Terry's attention. "Speaking of robberies, look there!" He moved toward the alley's entrance, and the others followed.

"Those guys are beating up Talbot." Tom drew out his gun.

"Leave it alone!" Terry's voice rose an octave. "He's getting what he deserves."

Tom fired his gun into the air.

Terry groaned as the robbers took off. An instantaneous crowd gathered along with an approaching policeman, who was shouting in Spanish. "Oh man! Look what you've done." Terry glanced from the policeman to Talbot, who hadn't risen. "If Talbot's alive, you've rescued a rotten rat and gotten us all in trouble while doing it."

After waving away the crowd, the policeman spoke a stream of Spanish to Tom and made obvious gestures for him to stay put. Then he walked over to Talbot, still sprawled on the ground.

"I speak English," a heavily accented voice said from behind Terry. "I saw robbers. I help if you want."

"Thank you." Mr. Pendleton gave a small bow. "We'd appreciate your help."

The plump, middle-aged woman held out her palm.

"We can't pay," Mr. Pendleton said to Terry's horror. "It could look like a bribe. That would be illegal."

What about firing a gun? Terry wanted to ask. *That appears to be strongly prohibited here.* His stomach knotted as the woman took a step away.

"But after you translate for us," Mr. Pendleton added, "we can buy some produce if that's your stall behind you."

"Yes. Very fresh fruit." The lady gave a nearly toothless grin. "Good price for bananas, mangoes, guava, pineapple spears. I translate for you. I am honest."

Out of the corner of his eye, Terry saw Tom slip his gun under his jacket while the others watched the policeman help Talbot stand.

"What're you looking at?" Talbot muttered when brought to where they stood. "Suppose you're happy to see an innocent person beat up and robbed."

Before anyone in their group could speak, their translator held up her hand and faced Talbot. "I tell what happen." She turned to the side and translated for the policeman, who lowered his gun. "Three men attack. Right?" She didn't wait for an answer, but immediately translated again. "This man shoot gun into air." She pointed at Tom. "Scare robbers. He save your life. Better you thank him." This time she waited.

When Talbot stayed quiet, the lady poked his chest with her finger. "Better you thank him," she repeated.

Talbot frowned. "All right, all right. Here's my thanks."

For a second, Terry thought Talbot was going to spit, but after a glance at Mr. Pendleton and the policeman, he held his hand out to Tom.

"Don't take it, Tom." Terry wanted to spit himself.

"Of course, they'll shake hands and demonstrate to the law what civilized men they are," Mr. Pendleton said, voice tense, innuendo clear.

Tom and Talbot shook hands and faked smiles.

After holstering his gun, the policeman spoke to their translator.

"Officer say no one shoot gun in town, but this one time he allow." The woman pointed from the policeman to Tom. "If shoot again, you must go to station. To jail."

"Please tell him I understand." Tom gave a slight nod to the officer.

As Terry and the others picked out fruit to eat in place of their lost hotel meal, Talbot stood with his hands in his pockets, staring into the distance until Mr. Pendleton approached him.

"Here you are." Their elder held out two bananas. "I bought a little extra. I hope those thieves didn't get all your money."

"They missed a little in my boot." After hesitating, Talbot took one of the bananas with no word of thanks.

Terry had a sinking feeling Mr. Pendleton would be compelled to show the mercy he loved to praise.

"If they hadn't picked on you," the saint was saying, "they could have easily set upon one of us. Let me buy your rail ticket. I don't imagine you can get on that rail crew like you could on a ship."

Talbot jerked back. "I ... I don't ... well, all right."

Curses threatened to erupt from Terry's mouth. He didn't care what Mr. Pendleton or Sara or Tom believed their God wanted from them. He despised Talbot with every ounce of his being. Memories seared his mind of being thrown into the *William Parton*'s brig, the punishing assignments, and Talbot's eagerness to prosecute him in his Nagasaki trial. Moreover, the brute had been more than happy to leave Tom marooned, and everything pointed to his having aided Zeke stow away.

Terry swallowed the acid boiling up his throat when he joined the others in overseeing the porters transfer their luggage to the train. While boarding, he assumed a nonchalant expression, continuing his charade. He couldn't let visible anger bring about a lesson on forgiveness by Mr. Pendleton or alert Talbot to his hatred.

The shrill steam whistle blew, and the train jerked into motion. Tom had managed to squeeze ahead and get seats at a small, round table for three people in the first passenger car. Mr. Pendleton insisted it was for the "young" and joined Talbot at a table for two right behind them.

While Tom and Sara watched the last of the town's buildings slide by their window, Terry's gaze was drawn to Talbot. The man's cold eyes met his, then flitted away as he replied to something Mr. Pendleton had said. For his own sanity, Terry turned his full attention to the scenery as the train chugged along tracks laid through a jungle of vine-covered trees.

Tom pointed out the window. "Viewing nature's wilds while sitting on padded seats sure beats gathering bat guano in our island's forest."

"Beats swabbing decks too." Terry sighed. This was going to be a tiresome trip if Tom and Sara kept reminiscing about every little thing that happened while marooned.

"I hope we get a peek at the wildlife here." Sara tapped the closed window next to her.

Tom peered out the window too. "We'll probably see alligators after we pass the continental divide. That's when we'll reach the river, according to the pamphlet in the ship's library. It also said jaguars, pumas, and anteaters roam the forest, but they won't come near this roaring monster."

"We have another monster not ten feet from us the animals know nothing about." Terry rubbed his forehead, trying to ease the start of a headache.

"Duly noted, my brother." Tom peeled one of his bananas

and took a bite. "Reckon Mr. Pendleton is talking to Talbot about God?"

"I hope he is." Sara opened a paper pouch of cashews she'd bought on the train platform, then laid it in the center of the table. "Please take some."

Terry took several nuts, then ate a little of his banana, liking the fresh-picked flavor. He also liked the idea of Talbot having to hear Mr. Pendleton's "axioms" about faith. "Isn't there a famous saying—maybe from the Bible—about a leopard not changing its spots?"

Sara nodded. "Yes, it is in the Old Testament."

"I guess the Creator of a leopard has the ability to change his work when he wants to," Tom said, "like an artist can. He's working on me." He raised an eyebrow at Terry.

"But you never were two-faced like that rat."

"No, I didn't bother hiding my real charming self. Dice called me a barbarian."

"As you once called us, I remember." Sara snickered.

Terry held back a groan. The island again. As the two talked on and on about their experiences, his mind returned to what Mr. Pendleton could be telling Talbot about Jesus. Talbot might hide his rejection better than Terry had when cornered by the vice consul on their trip to rescue Tom. But no matter how agreeable Talbot pretended to be, he'd never change.

Tom's interference with the robbery and Mr. Pendleton's payment of twenty-five dollars for Talbot's ticket defied logic. Now they'd be stuck with the parasite—feeding off them and threatening them—all the way to New England since he was sure to get on the Atlantic Mail steamer too.

As drowsiness overtook Terry, one question came to him: Where did Tom keep his pistol at night now that he carried it with him in the daytime?

CHAPTER 7

Tom held his breath, then sighed. His shuffleboard disc had taken a detour off the hopscotch-type diagram, chalked onto the planks of the Atlantic Mail steamship's deck. The crazy game, known as *horse billiards,* had been tied before his wayward thrust.

"Too bad, Ballard. You know what people call those who don't win." Talbot followed up his fake camaraderie with a sneer. "Should've calculated the rogue wave's impact. Guess your brother listens better to the sea—all that navigatin' he did. And how about the lovely lady? She knows how to aim a disk. Never off course."

Tom wouldn't have cared anything about losing the game if Talbot hadn't joined the small audience watching him compete with Terry and Sara. Unfortunately, the leech was freer to roam the ship on this northeastern leg of their journey. Talbot had replaced an ill second-mate when the steamer connected with their train at Aspinwall's port.

"So, you're a qualified judge of horse billiards these days. Must have taken hours of observation." Tom chuckled at Talbot's confused look. "At any rate, you're right about one thing: Lovely Miss Ogawa's aim is terrific."

During the game, Talbot had paid Sara a ton of compliments—how attractive her kimono was, how well she spoke English—enough to make Tom gag. If the man's attention to Sara had been genuine, he would have halfway accepted the interference. But contempt for their group had flickered several times across Talbot's face. Apparently, Terry was right—Talbot wouldn't change his spots, and his rescue in Panama had been a colossal blunder.

The rogue wave turned out to be a forerunner of a brewing squall. The first mate called 'all hands on deck' as Tom accompanied Terry and Sara down the corridor to their staterooms. It looked like nature was providing Tom with the last laugh. Talbot would be soaking wet within the hour.

By the evening meal, the squall had picked up energy from the warm Caribbean water. It was their group's turn to sit at the captain's table, but due to the intensifying storm, Captain Franklin and the first mate stayed on the quarterdeck to issue orders. Thus, they were saddled with Talbot at the head of the table.

"What is your prediction about this gale, Mate Talbot?" Mr. Pendleton tilted his head toward the man to hear above the wind and wave's roar.

"Don't rightly know. Gathering strength for sure." Talbot shot a look at Tom, who suppressed a jab about needing more sensitivity to the sea.

"We've turned away from our due north heading." Terry pointedly addressed Mr. Pendleton rather than Talbot. "I'd guess we're making for the Gulf of Mexico. Since the ship's owned by a New Englander, it's not neutral other than on paper. And there's no nearby, deep-water port controlled by the Union, far as I know. Captain Franklin's got a big problem ahead."

"Plenty of Southerners on board," Talbot muttered. "A refuge at Mobile could be welcomed."

"Surely you yourself don't actually side with the Confederates, do you?" Mr. Pendleton peered at him over his spectacles.

"I'm from Kentucky. We haven't left the Union up to now."

"But Kentucky's a slave state. How do you feel about that?" Tom sensed a debate in the making and enlightenment for Sara in case the snake had hoodwinked her.

Talbot glared at Tom. "I'm not a crazy abolitionist. Nothing wrong with having slaves. If they behave and work hard, no whippin' post's needed. They get housing, food. Should count themselves lucky."

Tom hadn't expected such an easy win. "They're to be treated no better than animals in your opinion, then? It's okay to sell off spouses, children, like we do mares and colts?"

"People pay good money for both horses and slaves, don't they?" Talbot didn't wait for an answer. "No one could raise and sell cotton or tobacco or sugarcane without either one. What do no cotton sales mean? No houses or food, that's what. If people don't agree, let 'em move up north and see what takes the place of plantations—millwork, ironworks, fighting Indians on the prairies, for both Blacks and Whites."

Before Tom could list the North's good occupations, Mr. Pendleton spoke in the calmest of tones. "We must remember how our forebears fought for freedom. Freedom to have our beliefs, family, education. Those are worth more than the so-called comforts of shelter and two or three meals a day. 'Give me liberty, or give me death' were not idle words."

Talbot lifted his chin. "Freedom for folks to choose how they live is *exactly* what Southerners want."

"*All* people, Mate Talbot, not just pale-skin folks, are created in God's image and deserve the same freedoms." Mr. Pendleton's tone had lost much of its calmness.

"The Bible says something different—the curse on Ham." Talbot glanced around the table.

"That curse fell on the forefather of the ancient Canaanite tribe, who were Semitic, not Africans, and were assimilated into other nations thousands of years ago." Mr. Pendleton used his better-listen-to-me teacher's tone. "There's no effect from it now."

"Obviously, a Bible passage that's misused by ignorant persons," Tom interjected. He hadn't heard anything about a curse himself, but his elder was bound to be right in explaining it.

Mr. Pendleton gave a quick nod to Tom. "Understanding some parts of the Bible requires a knowledge of long-ago times. However, the Almighty clearly spelled out two rules in the Old Testament that shed light on our subject. If Israelites owned Israelite slaves, they had to give them their freedom without any charge after six years—blocking a lifetime of forced slavery. Further, God gave the order to *not* return any runaway slave to his master."

"So much for bounty hunters." Tom didn't bother to disguise his smug tone.

"Now the New Testament says," Mr. Pendleton persisted, "that slave traders are among the wicked who forfeit a heavenly inheritance. Without the heinous trade, slavery would end, which is exactly what occurred in the British Empire, as I'm certain you're aware."

"Many Christians in Kentucky own slaves." Talbot puffed up like the toad Tom imagined when not seeing him as a snake. "Confederate generals think God's on ... uh, their side."

"All too often," Mr. Pendleton responded, "Christians are

known to ignore Scripture when they don't wish to obey its teaching—not only concerning slavery but also ones against hatred, adultery, greed, lying, stealing. Ignoring God's standards doesn't make any of that right."

Tom suddenly lost his desire for debate.

"Stealing and deceiving should be first on that list." Fury flared in Talbot's eyes as he honed in on Tom.

Tom flinched. How on earth could Talbot still be indignant about the wine bottle's theft? His small offence hadn't hurt Talbot himself. Yes, their crewman George had been whipped when the captain smelled wine on the man during the investigation the theft caused. But even a child would grasp that abandonment on an isle in the middle of the ocean more than paid for his theft's unforeseen consequences.

Terry shot Tom a told-you-so look.

"All sins lead to death," Mr. Pendleton said, breaking the tense silence. "How thankful I am for the Savior's payment for my own."

"Of course. Of course," Talbot huffed, his words barely audible over the storm's blasts.

"The ship seems to be having a hard time," Sara said, looking green after the ship twice tilted, then righted itself.

"Indeed." Mr. Pendleton clutched the edge of the table as the ship lurched again. "If you'll excuse us, Mate Talbot, I for one wish to skip dessert and take to my room. If we're going off course, as Terrence postulated, this probably isn't a passing squall." He unfolded a rain poncho he'd purchased at the Acapulco port. Tom regretted not having done the same.

"As you wish." Talbot rose and gave the hint of a bow.

The group followed Mr. Pendleton out. Dry under his poncho, he refused their aid, but then accepted the escort of a passing waiter who insisted on helping him.

Sara stepped across the covered gap to the ladies' salon.

Tom, with Terry, made a dash to the shelter of awnings and then to their room.

"Thank God we're not climbing the rigging or stoking the boilers in this storm," Tom remarked as they changed out of their damp clothes.

"Or thank our lucky stars," Terry answered.

Tom studied his brother. "Then, do you attribute the slaves' rights to the action of stars?"

"I wouldn't base it on the Bible like Mr. Pendleton does."

"But, Terry—"

"Hold on before dishing out the lecture. All right?"

"Sure. Whatever you want." He didn't hanker to debate Terry, anyway.

"I guess slavery *is* bad," Terry said after a minute. "I just haven't thought it through. You've been the debater, quick on the trigger with your answers. I don't work that way."

The ship bucked toward the bow, then rode smaller swells.

"Whoa! You smell smoke?" Tom sniffed the air twice. The air always had a smokey smell on deck from the two smokestacks, but not in their room and not in a rainstorm. He joined Terry as he pulled their door open.

"Something wrong?" Tom shouted above the howling wind to two bent-over sailors hurrying past.

One fellow spun halfway and yelled back, "Number two boiler overheated while trying to outrun the storm. Fire's out."

"Number one stopped working earlier," the second fellow yelled over his shoulder.

Tom, with Terry's help, shoved their door shut. "Lucky the canvas is already furled. Be ripped to shreds, otherwise."

"That's lucky too." Terry slapped him on the back. "But losing steam in a storm is devilish."

Helpless against the storm's westward drive, the ship shuddered and groaned, cresting the waves and plunging into troughs. Tom extinguished the lantern, then crawled to his berth. The flickering light from their deck's promenade passage caused eerie shadows as fellow passengers raced to their own rooms.

"Guess Mr. Pendleton will keep an eye on Sara." Tom clambered over the berth's low rail. "If this storm continues to worsen, her steel girders might not be enough."

"Yep, Mr. Pendleton's the guardian, not you," Terry answered from his own berth.

"As if I didn't know." Tom leaned back on the pillow propped against the wall and held onto both of the berth's side rails. He refrained from saying more. Instead of resenting his brother's taunts, he should appreciate Terry's determination to save him from himself. Although he didn't want that kind of saving, he absolutely should.

The wind's shrieking reminded Tom of a tornado's ferocity as it passed close to their home when he was fifteen. While the family hunkered down in the root cellar, his father had quoted Scripture in his lawyer voice, which, sounding artificial to Tom, ground on his nerves.

Digging into his memory, he whispered the quote to himself the best he could remember: *Neither death, nor life ... nor things to come, nor height* [of the waves, he added], *nor depth* [of the sea] *... can separate us from God's love, which is in Jesus.* He repeated the words in his mind twice. Not only did they no longer irritate him, they comforted him.

He looked over at Terry. Facing away, his brother had both hands on his bed's far rail. "You all right?" he called above the storm's noise.

Terry rolled over enough to answer. "Sure, so long as I'm not tossed off the mattress. You needn't worry about me. My steel girders are fine." Then he faced the wall again.

Tom's words of encouragement died on his lips. An effort to buck up Terry would simply vex him. Anyway, the ship was a good one with an experienced captain. The real peril wasn't the storm. It was their unknown destination.

Tom stretched as morning light penetrated the room. Although he'd fallen asleep sometime during the night, he couldn't have slept more than four or five hours. He pulled his sheet over his head, but when the smell of coffee reached him, he forced himself up.

"Do you know where we're headed?" he asked the cabin boy, who was about to leave the room. Then he did a double take. The youth was fairly light-skinned, but undoubtedly not the previous boy.

"New Orlean', suh. Use to be my hometown."

"Oh? We're a lot farther west than I expected. Guess I should be glad since the city's under Union control."

"Yes, suh. I'm thankful o' that."

"I hope you get a chance to see your family. Been about eighteen months since my brother and I have seen ours." He gestured at Terry, who still snored.

"My family's scattered to kingdom come, suh. I'll be staying on this ship. Slavers don't care if you're a freedman if they get their hands on you."

"Such evildoing! I have to admit I don't know enough about the South, but it seems that'll change in my near future." He ran his eyes over the youth's wiry figure. "I'm happy you're all right, at least. But where's our regular boy? Hope he's not sick." *Especially not sick with yellow fever or pox.*

"He hurt his ankle durin' the storm. I'm the cook's helper,

but the captain sent me on Charlie's rounds, seein' as I come close to fitting the part. Speakin' of, I'll be on my way, with your leave."

"Go ahead. Didn't mean to hold you up." Tom nodded to the young man as he backed out the door.

Picking up the cup of coffee, he sighed. Home had been tantalizingly close, only about ten days away. And now they would be stuck in New Orleans with both boilers broken. Caught in a city known as a cauldron of diseases while a war raged close by. A lengthy, uncomfortable delay. Hopefully not an unsafe one.

CHAPTER 8

The omnibus rattled to a stop at the Mexican Gulf Railroad depot. Sara looked around, ready to take in more curious sights. When Mr. Pendleton decided to check out the cabin his brother had deeded him years earlier, he opened up the opportunity for their omnibus ride through New Orleans, followed by a short train trip into the countryside.

The excursion had already provided plenty of unusual scenes, such as the hundreds of blue-coated Union soldiers patrolling the city as well as a market area full of turbaned, dark-skinned shoppers in apparel very different from the clothing worn in San Francisco. From there, the omnibus had passed a little park where an old man was drumming on a large cask while a group of adults and children swayed in a new form of dance—at least, new to her. Dancing in public, for every passing stranger to see. Remarkable!

After Terry assisted her off the omnibus, she accompanied the two men into the depot's dusty waiting room. Mr. Pendleton took charge of paying their fare and soon had the paper tickets in hand. "We can be thankful for the Union passports Captain Franklin wrangled for us," he said as he handed her a ticket. "The station master issued these without a moment's hesitation."

"I am thankful to both the captain and you for our outing." She inclined her head to him as they walked outside. "I hope you find your property has good value." She belatedly took his extended arm at the steps to the station's brick platform. The Westerners' chivalry still caught her unawares at times.

"There's no telling the cabin's condition. My brother says he left it in decent shape after the nearby malarial swamps proved too much for him, but it may have become an eyesore after all this time." The elderly man used his cane to steady himself.

"I hope you get a good sale price too, sir," Terry said, having followed them onto the platform. "I do have a question, though, about our trip's safety. When Captain Franklin approved our travel outside the city, he based it on reliable information, didn't he—as far as you know? I didn't see any Union patrols during our ride's last mile or so. Makes me wonder how well the outskirts are guarded."

"The captain said going only five miles out of New Orleans should be fine since the area consists mostly of marsh, bayou, and sugarcane plantations. Not ideal as hideouts for troublemakers."

Terry gave a halfhearted nod. "Our substitute cabin boy couldn't believe we were going one step outside the city. Said there were Confederate bushwhackers everywhere. 'Course Jacob hadn't met any himself, so I don't see how he could really know. But ... well, I can't stop thinkin' about his qualms anyway."

"That cabin boy's skin color makes every place in the South dangerous for him. I suggest we not borrow trouble. But it's not too late if you want to change your mind about the train ride and meet us back at the inn."

While Terry appeared to debate his options, Sara patted her glistening face with the requisite lace handkerchief. The sticky, warm air promised an uncomfortable day. Yet comfort didn't matter much when you were able to sightsee. On the other hand, safety mattered a great deal, as her kidnapping had proved. Was going outside the city risky?

Terry cleared his throat. "Guess I'm just on edge, sir, after the trouble in San Francisco. I don't want to pass up getting a look at plantations, hanging moss, bayous, all those southern things we don't have in New York."

That was exactly what she felt. After a week on the anchored steamer and only one night at a French Quarter inn, where they'd finally relocated, she'd jumped at the chance to observe more than coastal birds, fishing boats, and military craft. Tom's absence on the trip was her one secret disappointment. Because of rumors that war shortages could delay repairs to their steamship indefinitely, Tom had stayed behind to secure their passage on a civilian merchant ship headed for New York.

"How about the station master?" Terry looked back at the depot, apparently still unsettled. "Did he have any word of caution?" He gave Mr. Pendleton an apologetic look. "I'm sorry, sir. It's just that the cabin boy spoke as if we were going to our *doom*."

"The station master assured me we'd be safe, Terrence. He said civilians operated both a sawmill and a brick factory that lay along the train's route and that the Fort Proctor garrison at the end of the line oversaw the railway's safety. The man confided that the fort's Union soldiers belong to the Black Home Guard. I imagine they'd know what's what in their home territory."

"Still, I'd feel better if Tom had loaned me his pistol." Terry curled his lips. "Guess he's not going to trust ..." His voice was lost in the shriek of the locomotive's whistle as plumes of smoke shot from the engine's smokestack and the clanking cars rolled into place.

Before she climbed aboard the one passenger car, Sara looked up and down the track. Terry's doubts were disconcerting, especially since she knew so little herself about anything in America. However, the railway and station appeared to be functioning normally. Her guardian didn't seem worried, and Terry wasn't going back to the inn. Everything should be fine.

She sat next to Mr. Pendleton and faced Terry. Her morning gown with its bothersome hoop brushed his trousers, but it couldn't be helped in their tight quarters. To avoid the stares of every man, woman, child, and even the dogs she met, she'd reverted to dressing in the Western-style gown, like she had in Honolulu and San Francisco. Her bonnet kept her face in a convenient shadow. So far, she hadn't attracted any curious attention.

The train chugged by the factory, whose chimneys puffed white smoke, and then by several men on horseback who had moved over on the track's raised ground, their horses dancing nervously. Right before the train pulled into the first station, she glimpsed a white-columned mansion set back on a ridge. If this was a plantation owner's magnificent home, he had to be far richer than even Theodore Mankin. How astonishing that Southern landowners could gather so much profit, evidently from forcing slaves to do the work. Of course, in Japan, the domains' warlords, living in castles, gathered wealth from hard-working peasants. But the warlords and governing samurai provided safety and order in return. Did the landowners only provide their slaves shelters and the plainest of food? Or did they provide more, such as schools?

Sara set aside her musings as the train arrived at their destination. Following the directions the terminal's station master had given when Mr. Pendleton paid for the tickets, they walked a quarter-mile along the track and through a field of weeds before they came to the log cabin.

"The building itself doesn't look too bad." Mr. Pendleton gave the front door a shove. It swayed open on one hinge.

Putting her hand over her nose at the rank odor, Sara peeked inside. The next second, she jumped backwards, yelping, as a rat scurried out. The cabin had concealed its bad shape.

"Squatters for certain." Mr. Pendleton entered and moved an empty tin can out of the way. "Been here recently. I apologize for the smell as well as for the rat. You both may want to wait outside while I measure the two rooms. Then we'll be off." He unwound a wire tape measure.

"I'll help," Terry volunteered.

"I will too," Sara added. After all, daughters of samurai couldn't be put off by a rat or a smell.

Bending over, Terry inspected the fireplace. "Still some live embers on top of the ash pile, sir," he said in a low voice, straightening. He crept toward the second room's door, which was slightly ajar. "Let's make sure there're no surprises inside there," he whispered.

Sara moved up behind him. Tom would have been able to handle any hidden enemy. Terry probably couldn't although he had learned a few jiu-jitsu moves from Tom on the steamers.

After maneuvering the front door shut, Mr. Pendleton, raising his cane, took a position next to it.

Terry pushed the bedroom door open with a bang.

A blur rushed out and sprawled on the floor. Sara stared at the gangly, dark-skinned youth whom she had just thrown face down, accidentally tripping him instead of using her intended move. His shirt was in shreds, revealing long ribbons of scabs on his back.

The boy, with eyes full of terror, rose onto his knees. "Mercy!" he pled.

"Easy, son." Mr. Pendleton offered his hand to help him up while leaning on his cane. "Looks like you're in need of mercy, all right. We won't hurt you."

"Thought you was slave catchers, suh," the fellow mumbled, managing to rise by himself. "If the hunters find us, they'll hang me."

Us? Sara looked into the second room and gasped. A girl, also in rags, huddled in a corner's shadows.

The boy turned toward Sara. "If they find her, they'll brand her and maybe they cripple her."

"We can't let that happen." Mr. Pendleton struck the floor with his cane. "We can't and we won't."

"But, sir, we can't take the two with us, can we?" Terry looked at Sara, as if for support. "We'd be breaking the law if we helped runaways."

"Some laws are meant to be broken when they contradict God's ..." Mr. Pendleton broke off at the sound of a distant whistle—not a train whistle—and then a horse's whinny.

"Run!" the boy yelled, motioning to the girl. He tore out the back door.

The girl, tears running down her face, stood but didn't move, as if she'd been turned to stone.

Sara dashed into the room. Grasping the girl's arms, she dragged her into the main room and then to the cabin's one rickety chair. She sat in the chair and lifted her skirt's crinoline cage. "Quick! Get under here!" She pointed to her legs as the two men turned their faces away.

The girl shook her head, sniveling.

"Save yourself! Do it." Sara pointed a second time.

The girl obeyed, scrunching her body as tightly as possible, and Sara lowered her skirt.

Terry spun around and frowned at Sara. "Now you really are aiding a runaway."

The front door grated open. Three men stood against the outside light, guns drawn. One was Talbot.

Sara started to rise in her relief, then drew out her fan instead. Mate Talbot, she cautioned herself, was not only pro-slavery, but still a suspect in Zeke's survival as a stowaway.

"Throw down your weapons!" Talbot ordered.

Shocked at the gruff command, Sara stiffened. Were the men planning to rob them? Did Talbot think she had the pirate's treasure hidden within her gown? Didn't he value the aid both Tom and Mr. Pendleton had given him in Panama?

"We're unarmed," Mr. Pendleton said, his voice steady, "and among friends, are we not?"

"*You* may be, sir," Talbot sneered. "The turd here is not." He stepped into the room.

"Frisk them," Talbot commanded the two men who entered behind him. The open jacket of one of them revealed the brown shirt of the Confederacy.

Sensing the slave stir under her puffed skirt, Sara ran her trembling fingers over the lavender gown in the pretense of calming herself. She struggled to clear her thinking. What could she do in this unfolding nightmare? Using jiu-jitsu to overcome three armed men would be impossible. She'd be a sparrow torn apart by falcons. But might there be a chance Talbot, who had paid her compliment after compliment, would listen to reason … or be moved to pity?

"Don't worry, Miss Ogawa." Talbot gave a slight bow. "We're Southern gentlemen."

"Is this how you return kindness in the South?" Mr.

Pendleton asked as one of the men ran a hand under his coat.

"This is how we return eye for eye," Talbot snarled. "The turd here let my cousin George take a whipping 'cause of his brother's thievin'. George never was the same. Saw things not there before he drowned himself. So maybe the good Lord you worship opened the way for a payback. Landed us in New Orleans. Let me fight for our state rights and lower the Almighty's whip on this Ballard's deserving back."

Terry's face turned white. "I ... I didn't know Tom—"

"See, Mr. Pendleton. He's a liar too. All the sailors 'fore the mast knew his brother stole the bottle."

"Surely you remember how Tom scared away the bandits in Panama City." Sara's voice shook, to her shame. "Maybe he saved *your* life."

"That didn't bring George back, did it? And Tom Ballard's not here, is he? But the turd is."

Mr. Pendleton stepped forward. "Take me instead, Mr. Talbot. Terrence is like a son to me. Surely you can extend mercy to an old man. Break my body, but not my heart."

"Nah," the taller of the other two men cut in. "Lieutenant wants spies brought in, not decrepit grandfathers with one foot in the grave."

"Spies!" Sara turned her eyes to Talbot. "You wouldn't lie yourself, would you? You know our past. Marooned. Then crossing the Pacific Ocean. And on the mail ships." Spies, she'd heard, were always executed.

"The lady's a charmer," Talbot said to the other men. "We have a little history, her and me." He raised an eyebrow.

Sara tightened her churning stomach, refusing to show her revulsion. She couldn't keep her cheeks from burning, however.

"So, Miss Ogawa, as a favor, you have my word on this. My men and I will turn in Terrence here, not as a spy, but as a captured Union man. After all, he's a New Yorker and a Yank at heart. You'll get him back, Mr. Pendleton, if he survives our Jackson prison. Unfortunately, the accommodations aren't so grand as a first-class stateroom."

Mr. Pendleton drew up straight. "Obviously, your captain was the most at fault, ordering a whipping for a minor offense. Why—"

"Discussion's over." Talbot turned to the shorter, Spanish-looking man and tossed him a leather strip. "Tie the prisoner's hands behind his back, Raphael. Tight."

Terry, still pale, stood stiff as a board while his hands were bound.

"Oh, Jesus! Help us!" Sara cried, startled a second later that she'd voiced such obvious desperation. Her gaze lit on Mr. Pendleton. He was leaning heavily on his cane, undoubtedly praying too.

Talbot gave a malicious smile. "Only a plea to Jesus, is it? No fond farewells? No thanks for our gallantry? Soldiers are not always so thoughtful of a pretty wench, Miss Ogawa." He grasped Terry's arm. "Walk out ahead of us. One false move, and you're full of lead."

When the men's voices faded, Sara's words burst out like water from a broken dam. "What will we do, Mr. Pendleton?" she sobbed. "Oh! Oh! Oh, what can we do?" She half rose, but dropped back onto the chair, the slave's tight grip on her legs crippling her.

"The fiends are gone. Come out." She couldn't help her sharp voice. Her whole body was aflame. She reached under her skirt and pulled on the girl's arms.

"Please, ma'am, take us with you," the girl begged, scooting a few feet from her. "We'll be your slaves. Serve you right good."

Sara stared at her, reaching for an answer. She was thin as a rail with drooping shoulders, obviously malnourished, ill-used. The slave wasn't a child, but how old was she? Sixteen or seventeen perhaps? If so, the girl was younger than Sara herself, yet fleeing what had to be brutes. But how could she and her guardian possibly take on more trouble?

Mr. Pendleton balanced on his cane while helping to pull the girl to her feet, then faced Sara. "We've got to help them. It's the right thing to do. I can claim the pair came with the house until we get them to a safer place—that is, if we see the boy again." He turned to the shaking girl. "We can't delay another minute. We have to reach the New Orleans terminal and report the abduction."

"I fetch Elijah now. He prob'ly be in the outhouse. Don't leave us! Please, suh."

"I'm slower than you. You can catch us at the train's right-of-way south of here."

The girl took off through the back door, her bare feet stirring up puffs of dust.

While plodding next to Mr. Pendleton as they crossed the field, Sara set aside her distress. She had to think, not fall apart. Clearly an entanglement with fugitives was not something they needed.

"Couldn't the two runaways stay in your cabin, sir, since Mate Talbot was looking for us, not for them?" It seemed a solution that made sense without being hard-hearted.

"I'm afraid not. The house—unprotected and now associated with Yanks—will get burned to the ground within the week. And the slave catchers could still show up."

"But what can we do about their clothes if they go with us? And shoes? The way they look, everyone will know they're escaped slaves."

"Yes, another difficulty. We have to talk to God about all

these dilemmas." He picked up his pace. "Let's get on that right-of-way and down on our knees."

Sara bit back any further objections. How could she argue with Mr. Pendleton's trust in the Almighty? And his concern for the pitiable escapees?

The two slaves ran up to them at the incline to the tracks. "You help the lady climb up, Jessy," the one called Elijah instructed. "I kin help the master. Now his boy can't help, we got to watch out for 'em."

Once they had made it onto the right-of-way, Mr. Pendleton knelt on the gravel. Sara, still standing, bowed her head, and the two slaves copied her. Before Mr. Pendleton breathed a word, a donkey pulling a farmer's cart rounded a distant curve.

"Look at that!" Mr. Pendleton stood with the boy's help. "Before we called, the Almighty answered. He's with us, Miss Sara. Don't you fear. The waters are troubled—deeply troubled, but he'll bring all of us and Terrence safely through."

The farmer stopped his donkey when he came close and looked them over. "Your slaves not appearin' none too good."

"We've been set upon," Mr. Pendleton said. "These two were on my land. I assure you, we are innocent of their mistreatment. If you'll let us pay for a ride to the train's terminal, I'll explain our situation."

"Northerners, are ye?"

"Yes, part of the reason we were attacked although we're no one's enemies."

"I'm leanin' toward the Union myself although mah neighbors give good arguments for the other side too. At any rate, you or the young lady can ride on the bench by me. The remaining three of you will have to make do with the cart."

Mr. Pendleton shot his hand out to stop Sara from speaking.

"I'm not so far gone I can't be a gentleman." He walked around to the back of the cart and climbed in with the two slaves' energetic assistance.

After hearing Sara's account, the farmer refused payment. While Mr. Pendleton sent a wire from the terminal's depot to Fort Portersville, asking that sentries search for the bushwhackers, the Good Samaritan helped Sara find the community's general store. When she had finished purchasing decent clothes for the slaves and walked back to the station, the farmer and his cart had already left.

"About as close to an angel as you can get," Mr. Pendleton said after sending Elijah and Jessy, whose names he'd confirmed, into the grove behind the station to change. "I imagine the donkey and farmer were really flesh and blood, but God blessed us, didn't he?"

"Yes, he did." Sara held back the questions grinding in her mind. Couldn't God have blessed them sooner, with an escape from the Rebels? Couldn't he have blessed Terry, and Tom as well, with a safe passage to the New York home the two so greatly yearned to reach? But she'd entertained similar thoughts while marooned week after week on the Pacific island. That trouble had brought Tom into her life, and he had become a Christian in that dark place. Light had shone, brighter than she'd believed possible.

Still, reports she'd heard about the war pointed to an outcome for Terry that could bury him in a grave. According to the ship's newspapers, thousands of young men, devoted to either side, had already died on the battlefields and in appalling prisons.

If only she had faith like Mr. Pendleton's.

CHAPTER 9

Tom climbed the Creole inn's steps, sorry to have to report to the others that the one available steamer bound for New England had already filled up with soldiers—ones that were either wounded or had completed their tour of duty. A few civilians, mostly families of officers, had squeezed into the last spaces.

He halted in the doorway of the inn's parlor. Sara's tear-streaked face and Mr. Pendleton's pacing announced all too clearly that something had gone terribly wrong.

"Hello there." At their startled, ghostly looks, he cleared the lump clogging his throat. "Where's Terry?"

"Tom, Tom!" Sara called out. "He's been captured! Taken!"

"No!" Tom sucked in breaths as if getting the last of the room's air.

"Sit down, Thomas. We'll fill you in." Mr. Pendleton sat in one of the armchairs and motioned for Tom to take its twin.

Tom's fists tightened. "Connected to Talbot, isn't it? When I checked on the mail ship's status, Captain Franklin asked me to tell Mate Talbot, if I saw him, he was overdue from his shore leave."

"Yes, Thomas." Mr. Pendleton scooted his chair closer. "The turncoat joined up with the Confederates. Followed our train on horseback with other irregular soldiers—two bushwhackers that we saw. Burst in on us. Nothing we could do."

"Unarmed, of course you couldn't take them on. Curses! Curses on the lot of 'em! Should've let Terry take my gun."

Mr. Pendleton shook his head. "Would have gotten us killed. Talbot and two gunslingers against your brother? Impossible odds. And not only those three. From the sound of the whoops after they left us, more men waited on the edge of the marsh behind my land. I telegraphed the fort. Asked them to contact us here if they apprehended the villains."

"I can't stay here and do nothing!"

"It's been more than seven hours. You can't go after them. There's a morass of bayous and cypress swamps surrounding the area. You'd be swallowed up before you got close to Terrence."

"Please don't try to follow them, Tom." Tears clung on Sara's eyelashes.

"I can't just sit here, like a bumpkin on a log! Of course, I have to go after them."

"I'm telling you, *no!*" Mr. Pendleton struck the elbow table next to him with his fist, his voice taut. "If they had barges to cross Lake Borgne, they could be far beyond Union territory. And that's most likely."

"But, sir, if they're in a nearby swamp or on the lakeshore, now is the time to act." Unable to sit still a minute longer, Tom jumped up.

"Now listen. And get this straight!" Mr. Pendleton stood also. "Talbot said they were taking Terrence to a prison at Jackson. Jackson is way, way up the Pearl River in Mississippi, jealously guarded by the Rebels because of the town's two rail lines. Why did they tell their destination—if it even is their real destination? To lay a trap for you! That's why."

Tom started to shake his head, but leaned his forehead into his hands instead, unwilling to express more disagreement with an elder he respected so much.

"We have an appointment tomorrow at nine o'clock with a colonel in the Army of the Gulf," Mr. Pendleton continued, his voice calmer. "His assistant came here to set it up. Not a pleasant fellow, practically treated us as the enemy. But if the army can help us, that'll be much more effective than striking out on our own."

"Terry's my brother. The two of you have no obligation to help. I came in to tell you I didn't succeed with reservations. No spaces left, but if anything opens up, then take them. You have to *take* them."

"No, Thomas." Mr. Pendleton looked at Sara, who nodded in agreement. "My heart's broken, and I led Terrence into danger. I can't leave. I should have advertised the fifteen acres in *The Picayune* and taken whatever offer came. Curiosity got the better of me. Wanted to see where my brother had stayed."

"It wasn't your fault. Not at all, sir."

"I believe it was." Mr. Pendleton's lips formed a firm line.

"The truth, sir, is that Terry had been talking about hiring a horse and riding out to see the plantations and such on his own. With the delay we're now facing, he'd have gone sooner or later, especially with Captain Franklin's reassurances. And if it weren't for Talbot, I guess it would have been safe enough. So, look out for Sara and yourself. Please."

"Sara and I are staying. That's final." Mr. Pendleton shook his finger with the last two words. "I offered to escort her to New England, thinking you'd probably gotten the reservations, but she insisted on remaining unless that would hinder me."

Sara raised her chin in the determined look Tom admired. "I cannot leave my best friends."

"The truth is we're a team." Mr. Pendleton stepped back to the side of his chair and gripped his cane. "We belong with you, and we can't leave Terrence any more than you can. There's strength in numbers."

Words deserted Tom. What would he do without these two? Anyway, his elder was right about the obstacles to trailing Terry, especially with the night coming on. Before taking off, he should at least see what the army would do.

A gong sounded, announcing the evening meal.

Mr. Pendleton pointed toward the hallway. "Let's take some sustenance. This city is famous for disease, especially yellow fever, but also cholera, measles, dysentery, and the list goes on. We need to guard our health, or we won't be any use to Terrence."

"Shouldn't we tell Tom about Elijah and Jessy?" After patting her face with her handkerchief, Sara stood to join them.

"Elijah? Jessy?" Tom looked from Sara to Mr. Pendleton.

"Oh yes. They slipped my old mind." He lowered his voice to just above a whisper. "We have two runaway slaves who have latched onto us. We'll tell you the details after supper. We're claiming they're my brother's former household slaves, not fugitives. The Emancipation Proclamation holds less authority among the townsfolk than a beggar's plea for whiskey. Plenty of people would turn the two over to the bounty hunters without an ounce of compunction."

"Where are they?" Tom glanced around.

"They're in our rooms right now, but the innkeeper's wife says they are to eat with the other people of color on the back verandah. Under guard from the inn, I might add. She ordered them to sleep in the 'holding pen' by the stable—no separation of the women from the men—but we've modified that putrid requirement."

"Ugh!" Tom slapped the frame of his chair. "Can any more

wickedness show its face? We can't let them be treated like chattel, can we?"

"Only Elijah and only tonight." Mr. Pendleton leaned toward Tom and spoke in a true whisper. "It's dangerous for them to draw too much attention. Jessy has already gotten glares for not wearing the required headdress. We said the *tignon* got lost in the attack at the cabin. She's allowed to tend Sara tonight because of a fabricated breathing problem her 'mistress' has while sleeping. I've drawn up manumission papers and will accompany the two so they can register as freedmen tomorrow after our appointment. Then we'll move to another inn if Elijah can't be allowed to share my room here."

"So we have to find a way to rescue three people. Right? Three who are in life-and-death situations." Tom sighed. Their troubles were unending.

Sara nodded. "I guess we must believe that something good will result. But I feel like I am aiming at a target I cannot see." Her voice quivered.

"For me—it's a whiteout blizzard." Tom thought back to the one time he'd gotten lost in a snowstorm. Their dog Tuffy had led his father to him. No dog or posse would help him track Terry through swamps and bayous. But he could not—would not—let his brother rot in prison, no matter what the team or army told him.

CHAPTER 10

Terry rowed with all his strength, careful to keep the rhythm with the other eight men on his side of the keelboat. One flick of a lash on his back had cured his refusal to work with his fellow captives in loading the torn-up train rails onto the boat. His arms felt like lead, worse than when he'd had to holystone the decks during his first time as a sailor. Sharp pain rode between his shoulders. The keelboat had been slogging through the lake's waves for hours and hours. Dawn and the shore had to come soon, or he'd collapse.

Mist rose off the lake, shrouding his view of everything except the water beneath his oar. Surrounded by darkness and mist, the boat and its crew could be all that was left in the world. Wearily lifting the oar, he blinked to clear his eyes. The waves were breaking as though in the shallows. He squinted, peering past the other rowers' heads in front of him. To his unbounded relief, the watery moonlight showed phantom-like branches of trees—trees that had to be lining land.

The boat made a sharp turn into the mouth of a river. The tidal tug and strong current made it nearly impossible to row.

A guard shouted orders the next minute. "Release your oar!

Pick up the pole next to you! Stand!" Everyone obeyed. "Angle your pole in front of you and plunge it down to the river bottom!" Terry slid his hand to the middle of the twenty-foot pole and plunged it. A whip cracked against his neighbor. "Hold the pole against your shoulder! Keep the pole steady! Push and move your feet toward the stern!"

When Terry had "walked" the narrow deck and stood at the stern, the whip's stinging lash forced him to take up his pole, carry it along the side plank to the bow, and plant his pole again.

The heavy boat slowly moved up the snaking river, overcoming its downstream tow. Terry and the others made the trips from bow to stern, over and over and over. A few rays of the rising sun filtered through the gloomy overhang. The dragons of exhaustion and hunger and more blisters dogged Terry, but he struggled on. Talbot wouldn't hesitate to shoot him if he fell.

At last, after rounding bend after bend, the boat was brought to a standstill close to the river bank. The three front prisoners and the three at the back were commanded to use ropes to secure the boat to oaks. Terry and the rest kept their poles anchored in the mud.

"This is your one chance to sleep in the next twenty-four hours," another of their captors growled once the ropes held the boat in place. "Relieve yourselves in the water next to you. Don't drink the water. At dusk tonight, we'll pass out less dirty water along with hardtack. It's the last meal you'll get handed to you. Your berth is where you're standing. Enjoy the luxury."

As the men turned to each other with curses, Talbot picked up the bullhorn. "If I can hear your voice, I'll give you a better reason to curse."

The volume dropped to a hum. Terry kept his eyes down as they all dropped their trousers. Suddenly, the prisoner next to him flailed his arms, trying to keep his balance. Terry grabbed his waist, noticing the faded blue shirt. "I've got you. Can't lose a Union man."

The soldier, shivering, managed to finish and sit back down. "Thanks. I owe you one," he muttered with a New England accent.

After Terry finished his own turn, he leaned close to the New Englander's ear. "I'm Terry, and from Albany. Are we neighbors?"

The fellow scrunched around as much as the space permitted. "Joshua. From Schenectady. About as close as towns can get, I reckon. Three of us were captured from the 128th New York Regiment, Company C."

"All from Upstate?"

"Yes, but the other two were shot trying to get away."

While Terry was explaining how he'd ended up as a prisoner, Joshua slumped over into sleep. Terry laid his head down in the remaining space, aware of the swarm of mosquitoes now that the other miseries had paused. Soon even the ferocious, whining pests faded into his oblivion.

CHAPTER 11

Sara clasped her hands, losing patience. Seated with Tom and her guardian in a line of straight chairs fronting their interviewer's desk, she felt as if they were on trial. Colonel Irwin, assistant adjutant general to the Union's Army of the Gulf, was decidedly unfriendly. His assistant, standing by the colonel's office door, acted more like a guard. No doubt the colonel's rank caused soldiers to submit without objections—to treat him like a *daimyo* warlord—but Tom, Mr. Pendleton, and she were not Union soldiers. She wasn't even an American.

When Mr. Pendleton finished his brief report of Terry's abduction, the colonel scowled at Tom. "Before your brother's abduction occurred, I received an anonymous tip that a Thomas Ballard, who had broken out of a San Francisco jail, arrived in New Orleans on the disabled Atlantic Mail steamer. You were described as a rabble rouser, known to stir crowds up against authorities. I need an explanation before proceeding further with the abduction's investigation."

"*I* can explain, sir. I was the victim in San Francisco." Sara spoke before either man had a chance. She'd faced a hanging judge. She could stand up to another uncouth official.

"If you insist, lady." The colonel crossed his arms. "Let's hear it."

"Thomas Ballard"—she tipped her head toward Tom—"rescued *me* from two armed thieves, but broke into a building to do that. The San Francisco sheriff accused him of 'breaking and entering' and unjustly sentenced him to one month in jail. The *real* criminal, Ezekiel Bonner, was sentenced to only eighteen months. A guard in the jail drugged Mr. Ballard and allowed him to be, uh—*shanghaied*. But God in mercy got the shanghaier to put Mr. Ballard on our ship."

"Well, now. Wasn't that convenient to have God intervene." The colonel's tone was not quite sarcastic. "And I've been told you're from Japan, not China?"

"Yes, I am from Japan."

Mr. Pendleton drew out the letter from the American Consul General of Japan appointing him as a vice consul and slid it across the desk to the colonel. "I can testify to the good characters of Miss Sara Ogawa and the two Ballard brothers and to the criminal character of Ezekiel Bonner, wanted also for attempted murder in Japan. I would guess that anonymous tip came from his fellow conspirator, Second Mate Talbot, whom we now know to be a traitorous Rebel."

The colonel drew air through his teeth. "All right. We have sent telegrams to the San Francisco sheriff's office and the 6th California Infantry Regiment, asking for information. The sheriff's office may not bother to reply, but the military will. If your claims about the trial are substantiated, we will consider that matter closed. However, a different situation suggesting duplicity also must be examined."

He glared at Mr. Pendleton. "As a vice consul, you are expected to act as an honorable appointee of our federal government." He tapped the document. "However, after interviewing you and Miss Ogawa about the abduction, my assistant came across severely mistreated slaves. The two claimed to belong to you, but were so fearful, they refused to answer innocuous questions."

Mr. Pendleton's jaw tightened. "We found the two slaves hiding in what had been my brother's cabin. Since they were on my property and desperate for help, I have claimed them as part of my brother's deed and have letters of their manumission right here." He drew the pages out of his satchel. "Elijah and Jessy will register as freedmen immediately after this meeting."

The colonel ran his eyes over the pages. "Although these appear genuine, I shall send for the two fugitives and interview them myself to remove all suspicions. I hope for your sakes that your accounts of the San Francisco trial and these slaves prove true. Confederate spies are not prisoners of war, you know. They are shot, even women." He raked his eyes over Sara. "In the meantime, you will wait in the reception room."

After Sara seated herself next to Mr. Pendleton on a bench across the room from the receptionist's desk, Tom plopped down next to her. "I should have let those ruffians in Panama finish Talbot off," he grumbled. "Terry would be with us—alive and well—and we'd be on our way home as soon as the steamship got fixed."

Mr. Pendleton peered over his spectacles at Tom. "We're in the middle of a valley of dark shadows. Let's walk on with our Shepherd. It wouldn't be at all wise to tackle the lurking wolves on our own. And God values mercy. You did the right thing."

Sara yearned to tell Tom she agreed with him. How could she not desire the death of the betrayer who had trapped Terry and sneered at their distress in the cabin? Yet Mr. Pendleton spoke undeniable truth. "I despise Talbot," she admitted after a moment. "But I will try to be a better sheep."

When Jessy and Elijah followed the colonel's assistant into the room a half hour later, Mr. Pendleton smiled at them. "Just tell the truth in your interview. Colonel Irwin wants to help. Then we'll register you as free persons and do all we can to keep you safe."

Elijah nodded stiffly. Jessy trembled like a tree branch in an oncoming storm.

Fifteen minutes later, Colonel Irwin invited the three of them to join him and the two fugitives. The colonel waved for all of them to take their seats on the divan and soft chairs, which, no doubt, had been taken from one of the luxurious building's parlors. The occupying Union army had taken over the St. Charles Hotel, considering it contraband. Elijah and Jessy moved behind the divan and remained standing, evidently uncomfortable about sitting like equals with White folks.

The colonel took his seat behind his desk. "Our pair here have verified your well-meaning assistance, Vice Consul." He tilted his head toward Mr. Pendleton. "They have a legitimate fear of the bounty hunters and must find a refuge. You and your party are eager to reunite with your captured member, who will soon be enduring a Rebel prison, most likely at Jackson on the Pearl River. Jackson is east of Vicksburg, deep in Confederate territory."

The colonel directed his attention to Tom. "Is it correct, Mr. Ballard, that you want to be as close to your imprisoned brother as possible?"

"Yes, sir. In fact, I *will* help my brother escape." Tom gave the officer a steady stare.

"That, young man, is beyond the realm of possibility for incontrovertible reasons. First, if you didn't fall prey to swamp fever, typhoid, dysentery, or yellow fever, the bushwhackers would either capture or kill you. The bayous and swamps are riddled with native Rebels. The three men abducted your brother despite his being only a few miles from our *thousands* of troops stationed here.

"The second is that every prison is set up with high walls, hostile obstacles of nature itself, and, of course, sufficient guards. The prisoners are fed only enough to sustain life. Attempting to dash away with you through swamps crawling with snakes, alligators, unhealthy vapors, and the enemy would—to put it bluntly—kill your brother."

Tom swore under his breath. "Even if I die, I have to hunt for him."

The colonel studied Tom's face. "How old are you?"

Tom's head jerked. "I turned nineteen last summer."

The colonel narrowed his eyes. "You just miss the conscription order by our federal Congress."

"I hadn't heard of the order."

"Some news makes it faster in military channels. From the first of this month, all males who are age twenty through forty-five must register for military service. I trust you'll do that when you reach your hometown. But for now, I have a proposal that can help your private cause, the Union cause, a deserving family of loyalists, and these two slaves. So, a third reason for you not to conduct a solo rescue mission concerns the opportunity for the three of you to be of voluntary service to this nation."

Mr. Pendleton put a restraining hand on Tom's arm. "We are most anxious to hear this possibility."

The colonel pulled a Louisiana map from a set of files. "Although no place is safe during a war, my introduction would open a *relatively* secure place for you to stay and contribute. The army can provide temporary passports for your movements within Union territory. I'll arrange your transportation to the designated spot. As you've no doubt heard by now, we Federals control the Mississippi River from the Gulf to a few miles north of Baton Rouge." He held up the map and ran his finger up the river to a point just past Baton Rouge. "This area north of the city is the closest you can get to the Jackson prison, and that's the sensitive area where I'm proposing to send you."

Tom opened his mouth to speak, but the colonel forged on.

"Perhaps you've also heard that Admiral Farragut, after being fired upon by Baton Rouge townsmen, burned one-third of the town to the ground. In addition, once elegant mansions on the town's periphery are now chimney stacks. Mansions that weren't destroyed, as well as a number of farms, were unfortunately looted by out-of-control Union troops. But a few farms were left intact. What does that tell you about those untouched farms?"

"Their owners were most likely Union sympathizers," Mr. Pendleton answered while Sara tried to order her thoughts.

"Exactly." The colonel looked at Tom. "What does that make such a farmhouse and family?"

Tom grimaced. "A Confederate target."

"If posted at such a farm, we would expect you to protect the place. I assume you can shoot, Mr. Ballard? You also, Vice Consul? We would provide arms."

"We both have experience," Mr. Pendleton answered.

Tom glanced at Sara. "Miss Ogawa is a marksman, too. With a bow and arrow. She's far better than I. Brings down pigeons on the wing. I saw her expertise when marooned with her and her brother."

"Is that so?" Colonel Irwin screwed up his mouth.

"I will add my small ability if provided the bows and arrows." She couldn't bring herself to brag like an American.

"I'll have my assistant check the armory. May have bows and arrows leftover from the Indian wars." The colonel nodded at her, then turned toward Tom. "Obviously, both our side and the secessionists want control of the Mississippi River. When the Union succeeds, the Rebels' prisoners will be released, and before that, a few prisoner exchanges may continue to take place. If we can count on you, Mr. Ballard, not to go on a one-man crusade to free your brother, his name will be placed near the top of the list for an exchange."

"How long will you wait for the California telegram?" A frown had replaced the glimmer of hope crossing Tom's face at the mention of an exchange, like a breeze's ripple on a pond.

"One more day." Colonel Irwin rose, causing Sara and the other two to stand also. "Do you have plans for your brother's property?" the colonel asked Mr. Pendleton, coming around his desk.

"I plan to sell it. Since the bushwhackers now know the place belongs to a Union sympathizer, the unprotected cabin won't last a week, but someone might want the fifteen acres."

"The St. Louis Hotel has daily auctions. Used to be slave auctions, but we put a stop to that villainy. I imagine you could find a buyer there. At any rate, before the end of tomorrow, if no problem is reported at San Francisco, you can expect to receive instructions at the inn. I require an immediate reply regarding your acceptance or refusal of the proposal."

"We will certainly give it our most careful consideration." Mr. Pendleton turned, beckoned to the two fugitives, and motioned for Sara to exit first.

None of them spoke while they could be overheard in the corridor. At the elevator, Elijah was the first to break the silence. "We best not ride with White folks. We kin use them stairs o'er yonder."

"Sadly, that's probably wise for the time being." Mr. Pendleton glanced at the elevator operator holding the door open. "But change is coming, Elijah."

While locked in the metal cage rattling down the shaft, Sara closed her eyes. She should have taken the stairs too. The ride down was worse than the ride up. Finally, she arrived safely on the main floor, and the five of them made it out of the hotel.

"If this place had a moat, it could act like a castle." She summoned a smile, relieved her stomach had settled down.

Mr. Pendleton looked back at the ornate building. "Yes, a place built for lavish comfort has morphed into a citadel. We can take heart that the *domain ruler* we met seems to have a soft spot for abolitionists and fugitive slaves. Otherwise, after determining Thomas wasn't an escaped felon and you and I weren't spies, I doubt he'd have given us the time of day."

Tom kicked a pebble down the walkway, still damp from a recent shower. "Guess I'd be mustered into the army here if the colonel had his way. He reminded me of a hawk eyeing a mouse. But Terry and I have to get home. We owe that to our parents. I know this war is being fought for a really great cause. But to me, it's practically like two foreign countries decking it out. San Francisco and New Orleans are nothing like New York, at least not how I remember it."

"I feel the same." Mr. Pendleton steadied himself with his cane after skirting a puddle. "When an ocean separates you from any significant event, you can't help feeling like an outsider. And yet, I imagine nearly every American feels the war has turned his world upside down." He took Sara's arm. "Let's get across to the far side. I'll call a cab for you and Thomas." He cocked his head at Elijah. "You and Jessy need to stay with me. We'll get those manumission papers notarized."

The five of them dodged men on horseback, several ox-drawn carts, and a dozen pedestrians before reaching the other side. The shower had muddied the street, rife with manure, which in turn, soiled the hem of Sara's gown and splattered the men's trousers.

Sara puzzled over the English phrase, *misery loves company*, as she and Tom rode in the foul-smelling cab to the inn. Why would a miserable person want to be with other miserable people? She'd rather avoid the Americans whose world had fallen into chaos. While marooned on the island, she'd imagined traveling to *Christian* America as an incredible dream. Instead, on top of the attack in San Francisco, she was in agony over Terry's fate, distressed for Elijah and Jessy, and trapped in the middle of a cruel war.

After changing into a fresh gown, Sara entered the small inn's billiards room, which was empty except for her guardian, Elijah, Jessy, and Tom. They had taken over a round table in the far corner, normally utilized by card players. Tom stood and pulled out a cushioned chair for her.

Mr. Pendleton raised his cane in a greeting. "Welcome, Miss Sara. Thomas and I have been getting to know our companions, whom we persuaded to sit with us. They are actually a married couple and are now legally recorded as such after having married one year ago."

Sara smiled at the two former slaves. "Legally recorded today? I am happy to hear it although is not the recording overdue?"

Mr. Pendleton nodded. "Overdue, indeed. Slaves aren't allowed to have any records, even of marriage or childbirth. Elijah and Jessy's wedding was carried out in a secret 'jumping over the broom' ceremony with an elder's blessing. They've entrusted us with their secret, and I'm honored they took Richard as their family name at the Registrar's."

"May they be as lion-hearted as you, sir." Tom's tone gave a brief hint of his usual good humor. "Richard the Lion-hearted was a brave king," he explained, addressing Elijah and Jessy, "who lived seven hundred years ago."

"Sadly, they will need that great courage." Mr. Pendleton pulled a torn paper from his vest's inner pocket. "Their wicked master's plantation is in this state, just west of the Mississippi River. He's posted this notice of an award for their capture all along the river. The night the two ran away, Jessy darkened her skin with dye from walnut husks and changed her hairstyle. Elijah has grown a beard, as you can see, but their disguises are not sufficient." He pointed to the handbill. "The master had their likenesses sketched on the page and added two renderings to show possible disguises, coming close to the real ones."

Jessy began to shake.

Elijah took her hand. "We gon' trust the good Lord, remember."

"We'll try to trust him with you," Tom said. "Right now, I'm having a bloody hard time with my brother's abduction."

"Their situation appears as dire as Terrence's." Mr. Pendleton stuffed the handbill back in his pocket. "We already knew Elijah would be hung if caught. He has told me more about Jessy's situation. If she were returned to the plantation, the overseer would not only use a branding iron to deface her forehead, but most likely violate her, having almost done so once before. Her mistress would whip her within an inch of her life. After that, she would become a field slave, no longer working in the 'big house' even if crippled."

Sara grasped the edge of the table. "I hate all these awful people!" She couldn't hold back a second longer.

Mr. Pendleton whispered a *shhh,* glancing around the room.

"I'm sorry. I'll be more careful. But the cruel slave owners are not the only wicked ones. People who excuse the suffering are wicked too—like our innkeeper. And these hypocrites attend churches. How can they say they are Christians? They are barbarians!"

"We live in a fallen world." Mr. Pendleton leaned forward. "People who justify greed and selfishness may do 'acts of piety' because their conscience functions in other areas. There is a great blindness here in Louisiana. But people misuse other people the world over. Many factory owners in the North get rich by grossly underpaying and overworking their employees, yet their fellow townsmen often consider those owners successful. Even in Japan, my dear, there seem to be blind spots."

"Are there?" Sara felt her face flush. "I have not seen this."

"Have you thought about the peasants who produce all the food? Can they become an artist, warrior, or shop owner if they don't want to toil long hours in the rice paddies and fields? Aren't the occasional rice riots due to their desperation to keep more of their crops and allay their hunger during lean years?"

Sara started to proclaim her ignorance about the peasants, but Mr. Pendleton continued.

"Furthermore, would you want the burdens of an Untouchable's life?"

"No, but I was not born an Untouchable or forced to become one for a shameful action." She wanted to escape, run to her room. Her guardian was always so kind. So thoughtful. How could he attack her like this?

"I am not saying *you* misuse people. You are a loving, genuine Christian woman."

She sniffed, unable to come up with a response.

"The important fact is that the world as a whole is wrapped up in a reign of spiritual darkness, which can foster evil, like the enslavement of Africans. As rescued citizens in God's kingdom of light, we must ask him to open our eyes to blind spots we may have, and then cooperate with his transforming work."

"Is it wrong to hate slave owners like Jessy and Elijah's?" She glanced at the couple, both of whom were wide-eyed. "Is that a blind spot? Because I hate those owners with all my heart."

"I know that answer," Tom interposed. "'Love your enemies.' That's one of the first things I came across in the Bible. But who can do that? I've heard there are kind, caring slave owners, but—like Mr. Pendleton said on the ship—liberty is priceless. And the brutal owners and overseers? They are fiends from hell! I hate them too."

Mr. Pendleton squinted up at the ceiling, then ran his eyes over the group. "I'm also struggling. I'm no angel—far from it. Of course, we should loathe the unjust, wicked system. But not the slave owners themselves. It's hard to separate the two. Maybe we can't unless God overrules our hearts."

He cleared his throat. "Let's lay this topic aside for now and consider the decision of the hour. Is everyone in favor of accepting Colonel Irwin's proposal—for us to help the farm family on the edge of Confederate territory?"

Tom frowned. "The army's help in rescuing Terry could take a long time coming."

"Yes, but do we have better options?" Mr. Pendleton tapped his fingers on the table in the lengthening silence.

"I guess not." Tom finally answered.

"Then I have one requirement. I will turn down the proposal unless you swear, Thomas, that you will not light out across the swamps to try to reach your brother. The army will be counting on your presence at the farm, and I agree that your attempt to go alone would not only be futile, but suicidal."

Tom's face turned red. "I don't … think I can swear that."

Sara gasped. "You can't throw your life away, can you, Tom?"

He didn't answer.

"Then I won't go along with the colonel's proposal, and we will *not* have passes or transportation out of New Orleans." Mr. Pendleton stared at Tom.

"All right, sir. I swear." He folded his arms and looked away.

Mr. Pendleton turned to Jessy and Elijah. "Mr. and Mrs. Richard, do you agree with the plan? You are free to do whatever you wish although your manumission papers will not protect you from the hunters."

"We gon' with you, and mighty grateful. Mighty grateful," Elijah said. The two gave several bows of their heads.

"Then we'll see what the good Lord lays in front of us." Mr. Pendleton raised both hands in a type of blessing. "May he lead us—all of us—to our old homes or to new, welcoming ones."

"Glory!" Elijah cried.

Sara scanned Tom's face. His shameful accounts on the island of having broken deals with his father had been before he became a Christian. But was he truly committed to keeping agreements now? How awful for him if he fell prey to any of the horrendous perils the colonel described. And she'd be left with a gaping hole—her heart breaking the whole rest of the fearsome journey through America. She could hardly stand to think about it.

CHAPTER 12

Terry woke with a start. How many days had passed since they'd entered the river? He'd lost track of the route the boat had taken. The river's tributaries were impossible to distinguish from the snaking river itself unless you had grown up in the wilderness. But knowing how many days they had traveled upstream helped him judge their distance from Lake Borgne, somehow providing a thread to his former life.

Joshua straightened from his slouched position next to Terry and groaned.

"This is our eighth day in this boat, isn't it?" Terry swatted the closest mosquito he could reach without yanking the chain. He guessed the chains were used at night so prisoners wouldn't attack sleeping guards. It certainly wasn't to prevent escape attempts. You'd have to be insane to go even a short distance through swamps at night.

"Don't know. I'm dizzy. Can't think."

A guard shouted for the starboard-front group of three men to walk forward. After getting unchained, they were to pick up buckets and tend to the crawdads that had been netted overnight. Starboard middle, which included Terry, Joshua, and a prisoner named Jake, were to find dry kindling and start the fire. The starboard-back group of three were to gather larger firewood and maintain the fire. Groups from the other side were to catch and clean fish and any critters they came across, such as racoons, possums, rodents, turkeys, or other fowl. After their captors helped themselves to the food first, the prisoners would get the leftovers, so the more food they caught and prepared, the more chance to fill their empty bellies, cramping with hunger.

Terry offered his hand to Joshua and flinched at the heat radiating off his skin. "You're red hot. Is your throat sore?" He sure hoped the fellow didn't have typhoid.

"No, I'm cold." His body quivered. "Head hurts. Ache everywhere."

"Malaria, then?"

"Yes. They call it 'swamp fever' or 'shaking fever' down here." He took Terry's arm and struggled to stand, finally pulling himself up against the rail.

Stragglers for any reason felt the whip although the guards had eased up somewhat after breaking the spirit of the only two men who had offered continued resistance. One sick man, after not responding to the whip, had been left by the riverside to die. The man's pleas still echoed in Terry's mind.

Not offering any assistance, Jake had stood at the same time and now scowled at Joshua. Terry turned his face away. The fellow could stew in his own rotten juice. Keeping Joshua upright and finding enough dry kindling in the dawn's dampness needed his full attention. When the port-front group fell short of enough firewood after a soaking rain, the guards had pitched in, but punished all the captives by withholding food until the next day.

Keeping a sharp lookout for alligators, which liked to feed between dusk and dawn, Terry sloshed through the river's edge with the others and helped Joshua clamber up the bank. No prisoners could use the narrow gangplank because the guards claimed it wasted time.

"Look over there." Terry pointed to a log. "Let's check under that one." He forged ahead, thankful the other two stayed close behind him.

Jake kicked the log and scooped up the dry sticks and twigs underneath before Terry could grab them. "I've got my load," he sneered.

"I was here first, but I was gonna share," Terry grumbled.

"Ever hear *he who gives much has little*?" Jake guffawed.

"Quit yappin' over there and get moving," a guard shouted.

Joshua pointed to a huge fan-like branch with auxiliary smaller branches, half broken off from an oak. When they reached the spot, they found a pile of smaller branches and lots of twigs lying under the branch's protection.

"You have a sharp eye, Joshua," Terry rasped out when the guard wasn't looking. He very carefully moved one of the small branches with his boot. Tarantulas jumped every which way from the exposed nest. He stumbled out of the way, shoving Joshua away too.

"Hate these things," Terry mumbled. "But to blazes with them. We gotta get the wood." He pulled Joshua to the other side of the half-broken branch. After brushing off a couple of spiders that had landed on him, he helped Joshua fill his arms and then filled his own with the limbs and twigs farthest from the nest.

"If that weaklin' don't pull himself together, get his own load, he's gonna get us all killed," Jake snarled on the way to the cook fire. "Might not be so lucky next time."

Terry gritted his teeth, wanting to bash the brute over the head with the largest bough he could find. But he didn't dare, and Jake knew it. The three reached the cook fire just as Talbot struck a prisoner who had sat down, or else fallen, next to it. Hatred for

Talbot boiled up far hotter than his revulsion for Jake. Someday he would pay Talbot back, not only for himself and Tom, but for Joshua and the man writhing on the ground.

The seventeen prisoners ended up with more breakfast than usual. They each had the equivalent of a small fish, doled out from a cauldron of crappie, two catfish, and sunfish that had been sliced up together with their scales, bones, and all. The guards filled up on the crawdads, a stew of possum and raccoon, and genuine coffee. And then the routine of silent poling for the next twelve hours began again. Before they collapsed at the end of the day, the supper that inevitably waited for them would be hardtack and leaves of the old cabbages the Confederates had taken from a farmer's garden—just enough nourishment to keep their bodies functioning well enough to trap the food and pole the boat.

Terry kept his head turned away from Joshua whenever his friend didn't need his support. Who knew what caused swamp fever? The doctor on his old ship said it was swamp vapors, but the doc hadn't known for sure. If he was fated not to reach home, he at least had to outlive Talbot. One thing for sure—the rat deserved to die. As for Jake, he wouldn't outright finish off the lout, but he wouldn't grieve if a water moccasin or alligator did the job.

CHAPTER 13

Mid-March 1863, near Baton Rouge at the Evans' farm

"I don't wanna study fractions," ten-year-old Robert Evans whined. "You're not my pa. You can't make me."

Tom put down the knife he was about to use in quartering two apples for the lesson. "Do you want to grow up and be ignorant then? Not know how to order seed or lumber for fences?"

"I'm not gonna be a farmer. I'm gonna be a soldier, like every patiot."

Tom tensed at the jab. "You mean *patriot*. Let me tell you something. I love my country even though I'm not fighting right now. And here's why I'm not. I made a big mistake almost two years ago. I have to make that right with my parents before I sign up. And you know I have to find my brother."

"Soldiers don't need fractions."

"Grunts might get by without knowing fractions, but every officer uses them to calculate rations, ammunition, the strength of their troops and enemies, on and on."

Robert slid down in his chair. "Still not learnin' them things."

"Robert!" His mother, Agatha Evans, stood in the parlor's doorway, her blue eyes blazing in her plump face.

Robert jerked up straight.

Tom stood.

"I know how to use your father's strap. You apologize to Mr. Ballard."

"Sorry, Mr. Ballard." His tone didn't sound repentant.

"You will not ride Silver this afternoon, or any afternoon, until you can show me that you can add, subtract, multiply, and reduce them fractions to the rule of three. Before you're out somewhere soldiering, you'll be back in school. My boy isn't going to be the class dunce."

Robert couldn't have looked more crestfallen.

While listening to Mrs. Evans scold Robert about past truancy, a little sympathy sprouted in Tom's heart. He, too, had hated the classroom at Robert's age, and to be honest, all through school except for the subjects of geology, physics, astronomy, and botany. Science resembled gigantic brainteasers. Algebra and calculus held interesting puzzles, too, but solving routine math problems had bored him to death. How ironic he had become an arithmetic tutor.

When Mrs. Evans took a break to let her latest salvo sink in, Tom saw his chance to offer an incentive to the boy. "Excuse me for interrupting," he said to the lady. "Since our study of fractions will take a couple of weeks, I wonder if you would permit Miss Ogawa to show Robert how to use a bow and arrow in his afternoons' free time? This might prove to be a useful skill."

"Miss Ogawa hunts?" Mrs. Evans wrinkled her nose as if she smelled a skunk. "I'd have expected a lady from *any* country to master domestic skills instead of ones better left to men."

Tom resisted asking Mrs. Evans how she could judge Sara since she knew less than nothing about her culture. Instead, he said, "I've learned that daughters of samurai train with weapons chiefly for defense. From what I could tell while marooned with her, she's mastered weaving and culinary skills too—preparing bread, soups, puddings, and the like." He didn't tell her that Sara's materials for weaving had been bamboo, palm fronds, coconut fibers, and fish guts. Their hostess also didn't need to know the cooking had consisted mainly of boiling gourds and fish, simulating "bread" with ground cattail roots, grilling pigeons and their hearts, fermenting duck eggs, and smoking jerky.

"Well, one never knows what to expect from our boarders."

"Guns are what soldiers need." The boy crossed his arms as if he'd settled the matter. "Never heard tell of other weapons, like bows and arrows. Maybe they're for cowards."

Tom's former crotchety teachers would have given the boy a piece of their mind, but Tom held onto his patient tone—as if the sky had opened and drenched him with a dose of remarkable restraint. "American soldiers don't use arrows in the fighting going on now, but the skill is great for hunting. Archery skill lets you take down fowls and even doves without a noisy musket attracting too much attention. American Indians are experts in hunting that way, and so is Miss Ogawa. She learned from her brother, a top-notch *samurai* warrior."

Robert's mouth formed a large *O*.

Mrs. Evans' forehead puckered in thought. "Is Robert old enough?"

"Sure, Ma." He flexed his skinny arm, suddenly changing into a pro-archery enthusiast. "Look at my muscle."

"Hunting takes brains too." Tom raised an eyebrow at the boy, then looked at his mother. "If he's old enough to learn fractions, then he's *probably* old enough for the bow and arrow."

"Then we'll see how he does with fractions." The lady

crossed the room and patted her son's shoulder. "Do your best," she admonished him, then flicked her hand behind the boy's back in a kind of salute to Tom before she walked out.

Tom guessed Mrs. Evans was in her early forties, but a little gray already streaked her reddish-brown hair. She and her husband, Thaddeus, whose bald head made him look close to fifty, were dedicated abolitionists, endangering themselves by harboring fugitive slaves as a *station* on the underground railroad. This, of course, was a closely kept secret. Mr. Pendleton, Sara, and Tom had been told the first day in the plainest of words that discovery would result in their two freedmen being strung up or tortured. Mr. Evans had added that no one on the farm would escape. The rest of them would be burned alive in the house.

Robert looked up as Tom took his seat. "It's a good thing you got Ma to agree to Miss Ogawa's lessons. I can help defend us."

"You'll probably need a lot of practice before using the bow for defense. But hunting birds, like a turkey? That's a real possibility."

Robert thrust out his bottom lip. "Then I gotta get good fast 'cause we got some bad neighbors—real bad, like the one who torched our barn."

Tom stared at Robert. "When was that?" Why the deuce hadn't anyone spoken of it?

"Two months ago. Pa doesn't like to talk about it since Joseph's pa helped raise our new barn. Joseph's who did it."

"What got into Joseph?"

"Well, when the Yanks took all the animals from his family's farm and none of our pigs, mules, chickens—not even our two horses—he started carrying on about us bein' disloyal to the South's cause. He said the bluebellies must like us 'cause they was always talking to Pa."

"Did Joseph get in trouble?"

"No, he joined up with some regiment. Went east with the Rebs."

"Oh, one less troublemaker around here then."

"Bet there's plenty left. Wish Pa hadn't gone to Baton Rouge this morning."

"He's selling the produce to buy the things needed here. Mr. Pendleton, Miss Ogawa, and I are keeping a lookout for trouble, and that's something *you* can do too. You can let us adults know if you spot anything out of the ordinary."

"Like a torch in the barn at midnight." Robert gave a self-satisfied sniff.

"Yes, like a torch." Tom picked up the knife. While slicing the apples, he mulled over the barn fire. No wonder Robert talked of weapons. An attack coming from an acquaintance didn't lend itself to peace of mind. Undeniably, the family needed an extra level of support, like he and the other two had been charged to give.

But thus far, all he'd been doing was helping with chores and tutoring—practically twiddling his thumbs—while his brother suffered. If he hadn't sworn to remain at the farm, he'd scour the swamps by himself if he had to. The nearly impossible task was staying put.

When he finished cutting the two apples into fourths, he picked up one of the pieces. "What fraction of all these pieces am I holding?" He looked steadily at the boy.

"One-eighth," Robert answered in the meekest of tones, as if he sensed the exasperation fermenting within his tutor.

"Dust the board with more flour, Sara," Agatha instructed. After their first week in the home, their hostess had suggested Sara and she go by first names. "I heard from Mr. Ballard that you're a fine cook, but I guess you haven't had much opportunity to bake, other than bread."

Sara smothered a giggle. Tom must have referred to the round patties she'd made on the island for the Moon Festival. He was kind to brag on her since those patties had been like eating sand. "That is right. This is the first time to bake a pie. Thank you for teaching me."

The Evanses' fifteen-year-old daughter, Marylou, pranced into the kitchen, hugged the family's border collie, Shep, and then put her hands on her hips. "Mother's had *me* baking pies since I was ten. I could do it in my sleep. But Robert says you can shoot arrows like a man, and he's going to learn." She faced her mother. "Can I learn too, Mama?"

Agatha threw up her hands. "Certainly not, child! My goodness! Can you imagine what our friends would say?"

Sara looked from Marylou, who was pouting, to her mother. "Is there something wrong with using a bow and arrow?"

"Not for you, perhaps. You're a foreigner. People may excuse your peculiar customs." Agatha floured her hands and scooped the dough from the bowl. "At any rate, you'll be moving on before long, and no one around here needs be the wiser."

"I see." Sara dusted more flour onto her hands. The lady hadn't answered her question, but apparently Americans didn't think archery was *ladylike*. That wasn't so different from Japan, actually. A woman shouldn't openly display a samurai's combat skill and certainly not out-perform the men. If she hadn't been marooned, she wouldn't have become proficient herself. Secretly, her mastery of the skill delighted her, especially since Tom admired it and Mr. Pendleton approved.

Sara rolled out the dough and got it situated in the pie pan on the second try amid Marylou's snickers. After the filling was added and the lattice strips of dough had been crisscrossed over the top, she copied Agatha's example in pinching the edges into scallops.

"At least, you did the edges good enough," Marylou opined.

"Yes, she did." Agatha carried the mixing bowl to the stone sink, then looked at Sara. "I'm excusing you from any more work in the kitchen today to allow you to prepare for Robert's archery lesson. Marylou can stay and regulate the fire lest our good efforts turn to ashes."

Sara bowed to show appreciation, humility, whatever was required, and hurried out while Marylou was still objecting.

Tom, with Robert trailing behind, met her in front of the barn. "Robert and I will roll hay bales against the fence over there." Tom pointed to an open spot between the edge of the vegetable gardens and the pigpen. "I think it's far enough from the pen in case of a stray shot, and we won't have as many arrows banging against the fence." He looked at her for approval.

"I like the distance from the pen's smell too." She pinched her nose. "Mrs. Evans gave me part of an old sheet and a piece of charcoal to make our target."

"I'll help you draw one with expanding circles. I'm looking forward to seeing you hit the bull's eye—the center of the target—every time."

"I might not be as good with the American bows." She turned to Robert. "This bow is about half the size of our Japan ones and a little shorter than the bamboo ones we made on the island."

Robert wagged his head. "My pa would say don't make excuses. American bows are just as good as yours. No, I think they're better than a Japan bow."

115

She begged to differ, but determined to keep the peace. "A child must listen to his father. It is wise to listen to elders."

"And wise to be polite to elders too," Tom added. "Miss Ogawa, would you like to cancel the lesson? I can make sure Robert has enough assignments to fill his time."

Robert's mouth drooped. "I didn't mean nothing."

"I will not cancel the lesson this time." Sara assumed a stern face to match Tom's. "Let's prepare so we still have good light when we shoot."

Sara's heart warmed at Tom's defense. For some reason, waltzing together on the mail steamer came to mind. How she had loved being held in his arms. But she'd better not confuse friendship with something more. Not only were their customs different, but his country had terrible problems. She'd better focus on teaching Robert, not on Tom.

After the target was drawn and draped over one of the hay bales, Sara demonstrated the right stance, perpendicular to the target. Then, slipping on the glove she'd made from an old one, she showed Robert how to attach the arrow's notch to the bowstring and set the arrow. Finally, taking a big breath, she drew back the arrow and released it.

She couldn't help grinning as Tom pulled the arrow from the dead center of the target and held it up like a torch.

"I didn't know it'd be so easy," Robert crowed, notching in the arrow she handed him. He drew back and let the arrow fly. It flew into the far side of the hay bale.

Robert's face turned red, and he slung down the bow.

"Hold it, Robert," Tom ordered. "It's not as easy as Miss Ogawa made it look. A big reason she's so good, better than I, is the time she took to practice for hours and hours."

"And had a better teacher," Robert muttered.

"You didn't let her teach you anything, nincompoop," Marylou called from behind them.

All three of them whipped around to see the girl, who smiled coyly at Tom.

"It is all right, Robert," Sara cut in before the initial volleys could escalate to an all-out sibling battle. "You did well for the first time. The arrow flew far and in the right direction. You have much potential … if you listen and practice much."

"How good are you? Can you hit an apple on Mr. Ballard's head?" Robert looked like he'd thrown down a challenge she couldn't refuse.

"An apple? On my friend's head? Why should I do that?"

"William Tell shot an apple off his son's head. *Everyone* who's anyone knows that's the test of a really good shot."

"This is a great big world, Robert." Tom spread his arms apart. "Just because Americans hear the tale doesn't mean that people in all the other countries are familiar with it."

"I can bring an apple. We can set it on the top of the hay bale," Marylou said, a tad smugly. "Mr. Ballard doesn't have to risk his life so that Miss Ogawa can prove something a little boy suggests."

Tom shook his head. "Miss Ogawa doesn't have to prove anything."

"I can try." Sara reached for an arrow. After all, the apple wouldn't even be a moving target.

With the apple in place, Sara moved back a good twenty-five yards, close to the house. As she set the arrow, murmurs caught her attention, and she looked behind her. Agatha, Jessy, who had come down from the second floor, and Elijah, who had been shelling butter beans in the pantry, were watching from the kitchen window. Mr. Pendleton stood in the doorway, next to Marylou.

117

Her muscles tensed. Although there weren't many people watching, they'd be judging her. But, what would it matter if she failed? The people who counted already liked her, and the family could think whatever they wanted. She inhaled while forcing her shoulders to relax. Then she drew back the bowstring and released the arrow.

It zinged straight into the apple.

Other than the collie's whines from inside the kitchen, dead silence met her ears. Then her audience erupted in exclamations.

She gave a bow, surprised at how pleased she was with their reactions after all.

When she straightened, she spied a flash of something yellow in the woods' shadows beyond the fence. A yellow animal? More likely a two-footed observer. But maybe she didn't know all the Louisiana creatures.

Robert nearly fell over himself to reach her. "Teach me! Teach me!" he begged.

She set aside her uneasiness about the shadows for the task at hand.

The ten-year-old's enthusiasm knew no bounds. "Wait till my friends at school see me shoot," he bragged after finally hitting the target itself. "They'll be so green with envy, their hair'll look like moss!"

Tom and she laughed, then worked with Robert until summoned for supper.

Sara relaxed in the more openhearted atmosphere around the dining table as the peppery jambalaya, which even contained a form of rice, was passed from hand to hand, followed by boiled cabbage and yellow cornbread. Perhaps demonstrating her archery skill had served as a type of qualifying test. Marylou and Robert plied Tom and her with questions about their experiences while marooned. They were especially fascinated by the monkey's antics.

As Sara lit a candle to take up to her room, Jessy stopped her in the hallway. The girl looked around, then said, "Miz Ogawa, I'm sorry."

"Why is that? I can't imagine how you could have anything to be sorry for."

"I been hatin' you. I thought you never had no trouble. But you had a load of it. So I don't hate you anymore. I'm sorry."

Sara blinked at the surprising admission. "It's all right. I understand," she offered after gathering her thoughts. "You and I have had a hard life, yours far harder than mine." She gave a weak smile at Jessy's nod. "I'm thankful we are friends now because we are still in a hard place. We need each other ... and God. Sometimes I forget God is here."

"Yes'um. I know how that is, and I see the good Lord shelterin' us now. And your arrows got to be some of his supplies."

"I hope those supplies will not be needed." The flash of yellow pricked her mind.

"Yes'um. That too." Jessy gave a curtsy before turning back toward the kitchen to find Elijah. They shared a room at the back of the house. The Evanses had deepened the crawl space underneath the room's floor and had placed a hooked rug over a trap door, which gave fugitives a quick exit.

Upstairs, Sara knelt by her bed. At first, she could only voice pleas to God to provide safety for Terry, for Tom, her guardian, the fugitives, the household, and herself. But before sliding under the mosquito net, she added—*Merciful, Almighty God, please give a quick victory to the Union. Help the soldiers ... and us. This family is kind, but we are in a trap, far from where we want to be.* She pushed away an image of cannon firing at a field of men, and pulled the sheet over her head, trembling.

CHAPTER 14

After pulling out his pistol, Tom bounded down the stairs. Behind him, Mr. Pendleton, likewise armed, descended more cautiously. Sara brought up the rear, carrying a lantern with its night shade open a crack. The collie's growls grew more insistent as the group approached the kitchen.

Elijah rushed out of his back room, wearing an old black coat from off the coat rack and carrying a sheet. "Saw two men creepin' across the gardens," he said in a loud whisper. "I gon' show up beyond them. Somebody best hold Shep back, and nobody here shoot me, please. I'm using this sheet. I need five minutes to put fear in 'em." Elijah was out the door before anyone could object.

Mr. Pendleton shook his head. "I'll try to cover for our friend." He extinguished the lantern Sara had set down. His pistol glittered in the moonlight as he pointed it in the direction of the pigpen and chicken coop, where two shadowy figures with a smoky torch were moving.

Tom turned the dog over to Jessy to keep in their room. Cocking his gun, he took a position at the other end of the kitchen window from Sara, who had retrieved her bow and arrows from the storage room. "We can't wait five minutes," he whispered, tying back the curtain next to him. "They can take off with pigs or the horses or whatever they're after. Even torch the barn any minute."

Tom stepped aside as an arrow flew from Sara's bow, followed immediately by another. The shafts both zipped inches above the men's heads and struck the side of the chicken coop.

The two figures stopped and turned toward the coop, then stared at the house.

"Raise your hands, or I'll shoot," Tom shouted, just as a white, headless figure, moaning, moved on the edge of the woods.

The fake ghost grabbed the men's attention as it slipped behind a tree. They yelled, fired one shot toward the house, and took off toward the road, the sputtering torch growing dimmer.

Tom fired a shot after the fleeing men, aiming high to send a message.

Mrs. Evans, clothed in a dressing gown, appeared next to Tom. After looking out the window, she lit a large oil lantern and placed it on the small kitchen table. The lady often looked careworn, but in her pink-and-blue dressing gown, she made Tom think of a wilted hydrangea bush dragging the ground. As the lantern brightened, the rest of the Evans family rushed into the room, including Mr. Evans, who had gotten home from Baton Rouge after everyone retired.

"Oh, we were almost killed! Roasted alive!" Marylou wailed, tears rolling down her face."

"Hush, Marylou," her mother ordered. "You're not hurt. No one's hurt." She set a kettle on the stove. "I believe a cup of tea will calm our nerves." She squealed a second later as Elijah walked in, still wrapped in a sheet. The lady edged up to him and looked him in the face. "My goodness, Elijah, you almost stopped my heart. You did look like a ghost for a second there … although I don't believe in ghosts."

"An effective trick, Elijah." Mr. Pendleton pocketed the cartridge from his gun. "You may have helped prevent bloodshed tonight. A phantom's threat in the dark would scare the wits out of most people. I doubt those two will venture onto this property anytime soon."

"Unfortunately, those villains may question the supernatural aspect," Mr. Evans countered, "when they have time to think it over. But thank God for how all of you helped us."

Tom pulled out two stools for Sara and Mr. Pendleton at the table and one for himself. "Seems like I didn't do much. Elijah, Sara, and Mr. Pendleton could have carried it off by themselves."

"Miss Ogawa's better than William Tell." Robert, squatting by the doorway, made a gesture of shooting an arrow. "Thwack!"

Mrs. Evans turned from the stove. "Yes, I think she is." She faced Sara, who smoothed her *yukata* robe after settling on the stool. "I wasn't fair to you earlier, Sara. I've come to see archery as a splendid skill."

Sara tilted her head, offering a sheepish smile. "In my country, too, my ability would—how do you say?—raise an eyebrow. I could not show it in the open."

Tom scanned Sara's face. She looked a little embarrassed, but not put out. Her shyness and reticence—easy blushes, a tear on her lashes—made him want to protect her, care for her. Yet she always handled herself well, and with extraordinary bravery when necessary—having those girders of steel.

"So, Mama …" Marylou had completely calmed down after Elijah made his appearance.

"Not now, child. We'll discuss it later. You and Robert go back upstairs." She motioned for them to leave.

Elijah and Jessy asked Mr. Evans to excuse them, too, and left the kitchen for their room.

Tom yawned, aware of his own weariness. It was nearly midnight. Time to sleep. Before he could act, however, Sara suddenly struck her forehead with her palm.

"Oh, there is something I must tell everyone." She dropped her hand to her chest.

"What is it?" Mr. Evans turned from helping his wife with the cups of tea.

"While Tom and I were teaching Robert how to shoot, I saw something yellow in the woods. Just for a minute. I thought it could be a person's shirt, but then, I thought maybe it was an animal. I am sorry. I should have told you earlier."

Mr. Evans pursed his lips. "Doesn't sound like a cougar. Most likely, one of tonight's visitors, looking the place over." He took a seat at the end of the table. "This is serious, although we wouldn't expect you to be wise to the danger. An afternoon observer would have seen you and Tom. Since we haven't openly spoken of anyone boarding here, our family could be suspected of secretly harboring Union spies … if the word gets out."

"Do we need to leave?" Mr. Pendleton wiped the side of his cup, which had sloshed when he set it down.

"No, that would be a severe loss for us and a hardship for the three of you, as well as a big risk for your two fugitives." He tapped his chin. "I'll tell the sheriff about the intrusion and how our brand-new boarders prevented a tragedy. That should nip the community's suspicions in the bud since our sheriff and his deputy have their noses in all the parish goings-on."

"Thank goodness you can stay." Mrs. Evans balanced on the last available stool and looked around the table. "Being surrounded by so many Southerners opposed to our principles makes for loneliness, but having you here brightens up our lives."

"We treasure your hospitality and friendship," Mr. Pendleton said.

"Now, I'm sure everyone wishes to resume their rest." Mrs. Evans blotted what could have been a tear. "So, I wish each of you a much more pleasant night."

Tom excused himself right after Sara left the kitchen so he could have a little time with her. But when he reached the hallway, she was halfway up the stairs.

She raised her relit lantern and gave a firm "good night." In the lantern's glow, she appeared to float up the stairs, the bottom of her Japanese robe disappearing in the shadows.

Tom stood still, transfixed. Did she know how lovely she was? If only he could share his thoughts—how much he admired her, and how he was struggling about breaking his word.

But maybe keeping his frustrations to himself was better. She'd remind him of his promise and claim the Evanses needed him although the night's events said otherwise. Was it right for him to be comfortable, enjoying Sara and Mr. Pendleton's companionship as well as the household's hospitality while Terry suffered?

Unquestionably, it was not.

CHAPTER 15

Tom accompanied Mr. Evans, who had just told him to call him Thad, into the Baton Rouge feed store, one of the few buildings still intact after the previous summer's cannonade. As the clerk laid out batches of snap bean seeds for Thad to examine, the parish sheriff strode up.

"Hear you have an extraordinary marksman at your place nowadays. Word is the bowman can hit anything at twenty or thirty yards."

Thad cocked his head. "Where'd you hear that, Kenneth?"

"Uh, well uh, from several people. Glad no injuries reported at your place. With the war going on all around us, I've come to expect out-of-control passions."

"I made a trip in to see you last week about the midnight intrusion we had, but chose a bad day. Only found your deputy, who was in a big hurry. I didn't tell him or anyone else about the particulars of the attack, just that our boarders helped." Thad handed one of the seed bundles to the clerk, who had the sense to step away. "So, no one outside our household should know about that extraordinary archery skill save the two hoodlums. If you'll find who began the rumor, we'll know who fled when the bowman nearly scalped them. A gunfire exchange happened when one man shot at my house on his way to the gate. Mr. Ballard here returned fire, but the men were racing like scared rabbits. These men need to be caught, Kenneth. Trespassing. Endangerment. Attempted assault with a firearm."

"I hear what you're saying. Needs to be looked into all right." He turned to Tom. "Now, Mr. Ballard, how did you come to be visitin' the Evans' place? I assume since your weapon was a gun, that you're not the fabled marksman himself."

Tom nodded. "That's right, sir, I'm not. My two companions and I are temporarily boarding at the Evans' home because of the river's closure for upstream, civilian traffic. I'm pitching in wherever I can."

"New to the area and to the South, too, from your accent. Seems you came at the right time to help the family out." The sheriff's face took on a sly look. "Also heard there was a phantom that showed up. 'Course, no smart feller believes in ghosts. Any idea, son, 'bout the dark spirit, roamin' around outside while it seems you were all inside the house?"

"I wonder if someone's making the gossip more interesting, sir. Talk of a phantom and that kind of thing." Confronted by the sheriff's skeptical look, Tom searched his mind for a better explanation. "Also, people sometimes describe an illusion from rising vapors, don't they? Lots of mist in the marshes. I didn't see any phantom among the intruders myself."

"I see." The sheriff pulled a cigar stub out of his pocket, examined it, then pitched it into a nearby can. "What do you think those men were after?" he asked Thad.

"Guess they could'a wanted my two horses and the mules along with the wagon since both armies have been taking any animals they can get hold of."

"Why you reckon yours haven't been taken before now—conscripted by our troops or stolen as contraband by our enemy?"

"I stopped some Union soldiers from making off with my mules a few months ago. Told them we had to have them for hauling cotton upriver in the fall. Northern mills are desperate for cotton, you know. Had the horses hidden."

"Who's selling you cotton?" The sheriff's question had a sharp edge to it.

"Jack Carter at Twin Oaks. Says he has to scramble to buy just the basics with prices of everything sky high. You know he's a died-in-the-wool Southerner—as I am. Both sides let the cargo through. North wants the cotton. South wants the greenbacks."

"Can't say I agree with Carter. Wouldn't want my cotton going up north. But guess that's not my business. Hope you manage to keep your animals and wagon, though. Your fresh vegetables are a help to our townspeople. The missus is mighty dependent on your produce."

"I'll appreciate your apprehending the men who're at the rumor's source, so we can keep the vegetables comin'."

"I'll see what I can find out." The sheriff tipped his hat, then left.

"His intention to help is about as convincing as a drunkard's vow," Thad muttered when the man was out of earshot.

After loading the seed and fertilizer, they stopped at the shabby building temporarily housing the Baton Rouge Mercantile. While Thad searched for the items on Mrs. Evans' long list, Tom took advantage of the extra time to study an area map posted near the front of the store.

Thad handed Tom several of the heavier packages to carry, then scanned the map too. "See, this is where the farm is." He pointed to the spot. "Best we get started in that direction."

One hour later, Tom shifted on the seat, trying to ease his soreness. The four plodding mules hit bump after bump on the dirt road. Like some of the worst days on the island, the muggy heat was sucking his strength right out of him, as if leeches crawled along his skin. If only Terry were with them, they could leave the wretched climate, clouds of mosquitoes, hostile citizens—other than the Evanses—and looming battles. They would be drawing close to home and family. He should have refused the colonel's proposition and headed for Jackson that day.

When the mules finally stopped by the barn, Tom waited in the yard while Thad greeted his wife, who was shelling beans on the porch with Sara and Mr. Pendleton. Sara looked especially pretty in a pink gingham gown that slightly taller Marylou was said to have outgrown. She glanced up and waved. Returning the wave, Tom wished for a minute—ignoring his good senses—that he could peck Sara's cheek as Thad had his wife's. In fact, he wished he could hold Sara in his arms and give her a real kiss. But such a thing would never do.

"Want me to start unloading?" Tom walked closer to the porch.

"Thank you, but not now." Thad turned toward his wife. "I have news I'd like everyone to hear. I'll share it around the dining table."

Once the sassafras tea had been served and Marylou and Robert sent to check on their barn kittens, Thad set his glass to one side. "Our farm is in the Confederate's crosshairs more than ever. Rumors are flying about our marksman."

"I thought you didn't tell anyone about Sara's skill." Mrs. Evans cast a perturbed look at her husband.

"That's just it, Agatha." His voice rose. "Those intruders are talking far and wide. They aren't worried about who else knows they troubled our farm. And Sheriff Potts probed about a report of a phantom's appearance that night."

"Oh!" Mrs. Evans huffed. "With those kinds of sensational rumors, the sheriff, the church ladies, and no telling who else will be nosing around here before a week passes. How can we keep Elijah and Jessy hidden day after day?" She looked from the two fugitives to her husband.

"We can't," he answered. "So Tom, Elijah, and I will have to harvest enough beets, cabbage, and butter beans today to make a wagon load. You ladies and Mr. Pendleton will need to clean off the dirt and pack the baskets. I'll drive the wagon to Port Hudson tomorrow and conduct our two passengers to the *station* there. Tom can ride along to keep a watch toward our rear, if he's willing."

"Yes, sir. I'd be happy to go along." Tom gulped down the rest of his lukewarm tea while making a mental list of what he'd need for his journey to rescue Terry. Port Hudson wouldn't be much closer to the prison, but even the eighteen miles would help.

As Sara took his glass to the sink's washbasin, Tom gazed at her. Would she think less of him after tomorrow? She had sure been critical—actually horrified—when she'd first met him and found out he'd broken deals with his father. But his brother was in a prison's torment. He couldn't stay at the Evans' home to please Sara no matter how much he valued her opinion.

CHAPTER 16

April 1863

The next morning's sky was turning from black to grayish-white when Tom climbed over the buckboard wagon's sideboard for his supposed roundtrip to Port Hudson. Thad held the reins, and Elijah, playing the part of a loyal slave, perched on a milking stool in a rear corner of the wagon. "Good morning," Tom offered to both men, as cheerfully as he could. "Nice weather for our trip."

"Nice enough until the sunshine makes the vapors rise," Thad replied, "but sweating won't kill us." He looked at the revolver holstered at Tom's waist. "I trust your good sense not to escalate any confrontation into a shootout. Now that *could* kill us. And, of course, we'll slide our weapons, cartridges, and percussion caps into this bench's fake bottom before we reach Port Hudson."

"I understand, sir. My pistol's strictly to deter any threat we meet along the way."

Tom stepped across the wagon bed to the low barrel that was to be his seat and greeted Jessy with another "Good morning." With only her upper body visible above the baskets, she sat at the very front of the wagon bed, where Thad judged she could dive beneath the tarp and squirm under the half-filled, flanking baskets of unshelled butter beans. The other baskets, jammed together in the rest of the seven-foot bed, were completely full of beets, heads of cabbage, and the remaining butter beans—all doing double duty in hindering a search near Jessy.

"I'm afraid we're in for a rough ride, bouncing on boards directly over the axle." Tom gave Jessy a sympathetic smile.

"We're thankful to Master Evans and you. I'm praying the bouncin's the only bad thing."

"Don't worry. You can completely disappear fast, and Elijah won't attract attention by himself." Tom smoothed out the tarp. Muggy weather, the rough ride, and even the couple's bounty hunters weren't what bothered him the most. His guilt about taking off had kept him awake for hours during the night. The others didn't know about his Union pass and the silver dollars tucked in his pocket or the knife in his boot. He hated deceit, but it couldn't be helped.

Thad turned on his seat. "Remember, Tom, avoid talking to anyone until we're with our contact, Jeremiah Brubaker. Your attempt at a southern accent leaves much to be desired."

With a snap of the reins, Thad called "gee around," and the mules pulled the wagon to face the road. Tom viewed the house as they drove away, disappointed Sara hadn't stepped onto the porch with Mrs. Evans to see them off. Maybe he should have confided in such a good friend. However, plenty could have gone wrong if she'd raised a fuss. Besides, if everything went miraculously well, he'd return in four weeks or so with Terry, alive and free.

"No boundary markers, but we're definitely outside of Union-held territory," Thad announced after an hour-and-a-half of travel along the dirt road parallel to the Mississippi. To rest the mules and have a break themselves, they had pulled onto an adjacent, grassy area. "This coming section unfortunately has a reputation for lawlessness," he added. "The scarcity of Confederate patrols helps and hurts us."

"I'll keep a sharp eye out." Tom pointed to his pistol. "I'm ready."

Thad handed three cloth bags to Elijah. "In the thirteen miles left to Port Hudson, we'll encounter steep ridges. At the steepest ones, you'll have to dangle pieces of these dried apples— probably with additional help from Tom—to get the mules to pull their hardest. You can reward them at the top." He glanced at the sun's position. "All right. Better get rolling. Don't want to leave the ladies alone much after dark."

At the first steep ridge, the mules, living up to their reputation, dug in their hooves. Tom and Elijah held the apple treat in front of the lead pair. The mules didn't budge. Finally, Thad tapped the lead pair's rumps with the buggy whip. The animals snorted indignantly, but the team lumbered toward the summit.

Three hours later, having stopped only long enough to eat their picnic lunch, they rattled up another ridge in a seemingly unending parade of ridges. At the crest, Tom drew in a sharp breath. Beyond a series of wooded ravines, the winding road climbed toward the Confederate bastion of Port Hudson. Military earthworks on the rough terrain fronted the fortified town. The town itself stood on upland bluffs rising a good eighty feet above the river.

The mules required handfuls of treats to keep them plodding through the final vine-choked ravine, then up the steep incline. As Tom climbed back into the wagon at the last crest's clearing, Thad jerked around toward Jessy and him. "Tom, hand over your weapon and all your ammunition. Then help Jessy take cover fast!" he ordered.

Tom groaned. An entry checkpoint loomed straight ahead with only one other wagon in sight on the empty road.

As soon as Thad reined in the mules at the barricade blocking the way into the town, a Confederate army lieutenant and two grunts headed for their wagon. Tom righted the four baskets Jessy had slid under and adjusted the tarp. Then he slowly stood as if he'd been half asleep.

"Mules look tuckered out. Must be a heavy load back there," the officer was saying while scrutinizing the animals and Thad. "Take a good look," he told the two men with him.

"Not such a heavy load, lieutenant," Thad replied, his voice surprisingly confident. "Ridges took a toll on the animals."

"See you've got a lookout back there as well as a man to mind the load." The officer pointed at Tom, then to Elijah, who had jumped down behind the wagon.

"Yes, indeed. Think the extra men helped dissuade any lurking highwaymen. Didn't know what they'd face."

Tom nodded and rested his hands—obviously not holding any weapon—on top of the sideboard.

While the privates dug deep into several baskets, Tom pretended their scrutiny didn't concern him even though he could hardly breathe. If Jessy were discovered and the couple recognized, the consequences would be horrific, not only for the fugitives and the Evanses, but also for him. If he were held to be a collaborator and a spy for the North, his life and Terry's rescue would cruelly end.

After the two men rolled the tarp farther back and ran their eyes over more baskets, the taller of the two muttered something about a waste of time.

"Only carrying vegetables, sir," the shorter one reported to their leader.

Thad picked up the reins. "Guess the mules'll be happier at Mr. Brubaker's stable."

The lieutenant raised his hand to keep them there, and Tom's budding relief vanished. "So Jeremiah Brubaker can vouch for you, eh? Appears to me," the officer drawled, "you've traveled an unusual distance today to deliver produce. Where *is* your farm?"

"About eighteen miles south of here."

"Bloody close to Baton Rouge and them Yanks then." The officer's eyes flicked to Elijah as he retook his seat on the stool. "So, if you're not a lover of Yanks, how'd you manage to hold onto your mules and wagon that close to their encampment?"

"Not just my vegetables need haulin' for our people." Thad nonchalantly flicked away a fly. "In the fall, I haul several loads of cotton to sell on the river front."

The lieutenant's face softened. "I know how that works. So, you're a two-man blockade runner, supplyin' our loyalists badly needed funds. Permission to proceed. But don't linger or snoop where you don't belong. If you do, you'll find your next interrogators much less accommodating." He spun on his heel and approached a cart that had drawn up behind them.

As Thad drove the team along the town's main street, Tom lifted the tarp a few inches to reassure Jessy. "Better stay where you are a few more minutes, but the worst is over."

"Praise the Almighty!" Jessy managed to say while sniffling.

Thad drew the mules to a stop behind the town's general store. "Let Mr. Brubaker know he has guests, will you?" he called to a boy coming out of the stable.

"Yes, sir." The stableboy hurried through the store's back door.

The merchant came out, close on the boy's heels. "Wait right here a minute, Royce," he ordered, then sped over to the wagon.

"Welcome! Welcome, my friend!" The red-cheeked, robust man glanced over the sideboard, then shook Thad's hand. "Never know when to expect you. It seems you've got a valuable load."

"Yes, with a need of extra-special handling," Thad murmured.

"Ah, I see." He turned toward the stableboy. "Hold up unhitching the mules. Run over to Miss Barlow's tea shop double quick and pick up a tray of pastries for us. Tell her to put it on my account."

"Yes, sir." Royce took off, no doubt with a waterfall of saliva.

"Tom and I don't want to be any trouble," Thad said, stretching his back. "We have to do a quick turnaround, get back to the ladies before too late tonight."

"No trouble at all, and here I am, not sayin' a word to my other callers." After the introductions and firm handshakes, Mr. Brubaker brought them all inside. After pointing the way to his office, he led Elijah and Jessy up the staircase to his family's second-story home.

While waiting at a table for their host to come back down, Tom tried to chat with Thad in a normal voice about the farm, their trip, and the Union's slow progress in gaining control of the rest of the Mississippi. Then when Mr. Brubaker served them the sweet-potato "coffee" and pastries filled with blackberry jam, Tom took as much time eating as he dared. But finally, he couldn't delay the storm any longer.

"Would you have a map of local railroad lines handy, Mr. Brubaker?" he began. The map in the general store in Baton Rouge had included the lines.

"Have one right here." The merchant took a folded one out

of his desk drawer. "A good way to familiarize yourself with the area."

Tom glanced at the map, then turned to Thad. "I'm sorry, sir. I have to find Terry. I can't return with you."

Thad banged his fists on the table and leaned toward Tom. "No, I won't have it! You wouldn't live to see your brother's face even if he's eventually released!"

"Please let me explain. At least, show you my plan." Tom tapped the map.

Their host raised a restraining hand. "Let's listen to the boy. A lot of good plans have been ridiculed at their start."

Thad folded his arms and glared at Tom.

"I know there are swamps and bayous, impassable by all accounts. But I figure to follow the Clinton—Port Hudson line to Clinton." Tom slid the map where both men could see it and traced the railroad line. "From there, I'll cut over to Amite using the wagon road, then follow the New Orleans, Jackson, and Great Northern line. I've got enough money to buy a mule and supplies. I'll travel by moonlight and avoid other travelers."

"Let's consider the plan, why don't we?" Mr. Brubaker's quick response cut off Thad's. "The Bible's book of Proverbs tells us that wisdom lies with the 'well advised' and 'every purpose is established by counsel.' I'm sure we're agreed on that."

"Yes, sir. I believe what the Bible says is true." Tom handed the map back to their host, while thinking that men's advice could still be wrong.

"Now let me say why I'm qualified in the advice area." Mr. Brubaker took a swig of the coffee. "All types of people frequent my store—mainly soldiers, but also farmers, fishermen, bushwhackers, bounty hunters, and ordinary ruffians too—and each of them jabbers to the others around them. Some of these men spend all their time roaming the outlying areas. They know what's going on, and while I'm stocking shelves, I'm listening. Understand, son?"

"Yes, sir." A knot formed in his belly.

"Now, here's what you need to consider. First, you can't be sure your brother's at Jackson. Camp Moore near Vicksburg is known to have prisoners too, ones in transit. And if he is at Jackson, he could escape or be exchanged while you're on your pilgrimage."

"I have thought of that, sir." He glanced at Thad, who still looked ready to throttle him.

"The next consideration is that no mule, ox, or horse is anywhere to be bought. Folks complain about it all day long. Farmers are desperate for animals so they can plow and plant seed. Army's taken them all. So, you'd be walking more than one-hundred miles, and through a red-mud quagmire every time it rained. Blisters are painful and get infected."

"I'd have to persevere, sir, no matter what." Tom kept his gaze steady, despite the awful news.

"Speaking of health, you'd be exposed to swamp fever, cholera, dysentery, and legions of mosquitoes. More soldiers in the area's camps die from disease than battles. If you had to duck into a swamp, you'd attract alligators, which are active at night, and you'd risk meeting cottonmouths. Rattlers can be anywhere, under rails, in the grass, you name it."

"I survived two months marooned on a Pacific island, so I'm not too worried about wild creatures." The half-truth caused him a pang of guilt. The worst wild creatures on the island had been huge bats. However, the bloodthirsty pirates he faced should more than make up for that slightly misleading reply.

"You should be plenty worried, Tom," Thad growled. "Louisiana wilds are worse than you can imagine."

"I'm sure that's so, sir." He had to agree as much as he could.

Mr. Brubaker clucked his tongue. "If you're still unsure about the impossibility of heading toward Jackson, let me tell you who these travelers are that you'd meet. Most of them would be soldiers. Soldiers who shoot before they're a target themselves. The Union wants to clear out a route to Vicksburg, and General Johnson's regiment at Jackson's a thorn in the side. The Yanks are sending out feelers all the time. These pickets and cavalry companies get into skirmishes with the Rebels' counterparts, and woe to an innocent bystander. Also, a pass that one side honors is poison to the other side. Suspected spies are eliminated on the spot."

"That is a huge danger, sir. In fact, everything you've said makes my plan sound impossible."

"It *is* impossible, Tom." Thad's pulse showed in his temples. "It's as impossible as flying to the moon."

"I guess I'll have to pray hard that God helps me make it." A good answer since his challengers were strong Christians. "Elijah and Jessy and other fugitives' journeys must be worse. Our runaways have made it here, even with slave hunters hot on their trail."

"You won't have a mere dozen men after you," Thad said through clenched teeth. "You'll have *hundreds* of Rebels opposing you on your route. Doesn't it bother you at all, Tom, that you'd not only be committing suicide but also leaving my family in a lurch? And you've already seen the hard road I'll have to take back home. I was led to believe you signed an agreement in New Orleans to assist in the farm's defense if we took you in. And didn't you give your word that you'd stay until officially released from the pact?"

"That's right, sir. That's why I apologized. But Mr. Pendleton and you are good with guns. You saw Sara's skill. And if I'm not mistaken, you have driven today's route back home a number of times by yourself. Terry needs me more than your family. Surely you can see that."

Thad huffed out a breath and shook his head.

"Well, young man, short of handcuffing you, I guess we can't stop you. If you come with me, I'll help you buy supplies. You comin' with us, Thad?"

"Go ahead," he muttered. "Thought the boy had more sense and character."

With his host's guidance, Tom filled a new knapsack until it bulged with jerky, dried apples, a change of clothes, five pairs of socks, a small mosquito net, a tinderbox, and a copy of the area map.

Having received permission to say goodbye to Elijah and Jessy, he wished them well and urged them to get in touch when they made it to Canada—the only safe destination due to the Fugitive Slave Act.

After Mr. Brubaker prayed for his safety and success, Tom shouldered his knapsack and walked down the town's main street, heading toward the rail tracks and an old grove that Mr. Brubaker had described. He'd rest there until he could slip out the town's east side under the cover of darkness.

Was he an idiot? Was this another rash decision, worse than one he'd made in signing on to a sail ship when he'd just turned eighteen? But that time he'd led his brother into a miserable stint as a sailor. This time he was trying to do the right thing by Terry. Wouldn't God help him?

CHAPTER 17

Tom looked over his shoulder. No one was following him. His black clothing, the dark night, and the ability to tread softly, honed by hunting on the island with Sara's brother, had made it simple to pass the town's sentries. Reddish heat-lightning flashed far away to the south, not close enough to be a concern. The night was definitely as muggy as the daytime had been, though. Sweat trickled down his back, and mosquitoes swarmed, some already feasting.

He walked at a fast clip to make good use of the absence of travelers until a slithering snake intercepted his path. While pausing to give it space, he peered farther down the track, studying shadows that were wavering in the distance. They were increasing in size. No doubt about it.

He slid down the embankment in the same direction the snake had gone, hoping it had been a harmless one.

"Hey you! Halt!" a voice shouted. The sound of pounding boots reverberated down the rail ties.

Tom bent over and ran through the tall grass brake until he splashed into a swamp's standing water.

Bullets zinged into the grasses behind him.

He waded in a good deal farther, trying not to splash while

disentangling his feet from underwater roots and stumbling over unseen stumps. Finally, he squatted, hating the smelly water that seeped into his britches.

"Maybe got him." The man said something else Tom couldn't hear.

"If we didn't, the swamp'll do it ... not goin' ..." The second man's voice was even less distinct.

Someone agreed. Then the men's voices became an indistinguishable murmur.

Although his muscles cramped, Tom waited a good fifteen minutes longer. He wasn't taking a chance.

Finally, he sloshed in the direction he'd come from, trying to see his surroundings. Had there been trees so close to him? He hadn't been aware of any. But tree branches brushed his head, one or two so low they seemed claws grabbing for him. Had he gotten turned around?

He stopped. Woodsmen coming into Albany back home had told tales of city folk getting lost—going in circles, falling down ravines, then attacked by bears or wildcats. He hadn't heard of bears or wildcats inhabiting swamps, but that didn't mean there weren't any nearby in the woods. Of course, alligators could be a danger right where he stood.

He sat on a log caught in the mud next to him. Waiting until daylight would waste hours, but not as much time as getting thoroughly lost.

Suddenly the log moved! And hissed!

Tom launched himself off the live log and grabbed the branch above him. Squelching the scream in his throat, he swung onto the cypress' trunk and rocketed up the tree.

The alligator's unblinking, red eyes stared up at him.

A second one joined the creature, its low growl sending shivers from Tom's toes to his scalp.

Without question, he'd wait for daylight now. Eventually the monsters would have to sleep if they didn't leave for more accessible prey. He twisted until he could straddle a branch, then slid his feet onto one under him and leaned back against the trunk. No way could he sleep, and even if he could get into his knapsack, lodged between his upper back and the trunk, his stomach wouldn't handle food.

The two pairs of glowing eyes disappeared less than an hour later. Were the gators sleeping? Or awake, hiding under the low branches encircling the trunk? He couldn't tell no matter how intensely he stared at the blackness swallowing up the area directly under him. One thing for sure: his "advisors" had been right about the danger from swamps. But he'd survive the night and get back to the rail line. He and God would make it through.

The dawn's light infiltrated the darkness after untold hours, revealing no lurking gators. The ground toward the rising sun looked drier, more substantial than the ground to the north, so he climbed down and headed east. He'd go parallel to the tracks for a short distance, and then turn to the north to intersect the railway.

He plodded through brush, vines, and thorny brambles into what became dense woods. The rare openings to the sky revealed more and more of an overcast. He couldn't risk getting turned around again and losing the tracks. He turned sharply to the right, then stopped mid-stride.

Voices! He couldn't catch any words, nor tell if the men were stationary or moving. But since they were off the beaten path, they had to be criminals, fugitives, Southern bushwhackers, or Union pickets. And there was no telling which.

He turned to backtrack.

From out of nowhere, a hand grabbed him and held a knife to the side of his throat. Another man walked out of the shadows, pointing a pistol. He wore the butternut shirt of a Confederate!

Tom searched his mind for the right words. "Let me ex—"

The first attacker removed the knife and stuffed a cloth into Tom's mouth. He secured it with a leather strip. "Jack's got you covered. Follow me. Don't try anything, and you'll live long enough to give your story."

The two men brought Tom southward through the trees to a small clearing, where three other men squatted around a fire smoldering in a pit. A tin coffee pot hung from a branch over it.

"What have we here? A lone spy? A courier?" The apparent leader stood and approached Tom. "What's your name, boy?" He yanked out the dirty cloth gagging him.

"It's, aah, Tom Ballard, suh."

"Well, Tom Ballard, if you want any chance to keep your sorry life, you're gonna have to tell the truth. You can drop the fake accent. What's your real name?"

"It's really Tom Ballard, sir." His voice shook, countermanding his effort to sound confident.

"Where you from, Ballard?"

Tom hesitated. The Rebel didn't have a southern accent either. Was he from a border state?

"Tongue-tied, are you?"

"From a farm 'tween here and Baton Rouge." The less they knew, the better.

The Rebel spit next to Tom. He'd come close to spitting in his face. "And we're to credit a Louisiana farm although your speakin' says you're a Northerner?" He knocked Tom's legs out from under him. "Jack, you and Benjamin frisk him," he ordered.

Benjamin, who had held the knife at Tom's throat, tossed the knapsack to the side and took charge of rolling him onto his back. Jack ran his rough hands all through Tom's clothes. Then they yanked off his boots. Tossing his knife to the side, they worked down to the boots' soles.

Following that, Jack picked up the knapsack. "Got clothes. Extra socks we can use. Coins. Map. Food to last one man maybe a week."

Tom shut his eyes. He wasn't going to get to rescue Terry. Or apologize to his parents. Or see Sara again. But any minute, he would see Jesus.

"Hey, he's got a pass, Levi." Jack held up the telltale paper. "A Union pass. Signed by a colonel, no less."

"What colonel?" Their leader sounded surprised, rather than irate.

"Colonel Irwin. Army of the Gulf."

"That's New Orleans." The leader Levi stood over Tom. "Sit up, boy. We can do a procedure of cutting off ears, fingers, toes, arms, left leg, right leg, or you can tell us why you're in these parts. One way or the other, we'll get the truth."

Tom ran through the possibilities for the "truth" while his heart threatened to jump out of his chest. Clearly, since he couldn't come across as a Rebel, death by a bullet would be better than one by torture.

He risked sitting up. No one moved. "The truth is I'm trying to reach my younger brother. We're both sailors, and we were headed home when a storm damaged the mail steamer we were on. It ended up in New Orleans, where bushwhackers captured my brother. My two companions and I reported his abduction to the ones in charge, hoping he could be in a prisoner exchange. To be as close to the prison as possible, the three of us took an offer to help at the farm. My brother and I were thousands of miles away when the war started, but now we're caught in the middle of it." An unwanted mist came to his eyes. His extraordinary rescue off the island, his new friendships, his attempt to reach home—all coming to naught in seconds.

Levi looked at Jack, who shrugged. Then he asked, "And

where you reckon your brother is now?"

"The prison at Jackson."

Jack's mouth flew open.

"That's where the kidnappers said they were taking him. Maybe the information was meant to be a trap, but I can't leave my brother to rot, can I?"

"You were intendin' to *walk* to Jackson?" Jack's tone dripped with contempt. "That's the foolhardiest idea I ever heard!"

Tom felt his face burn. "Foolhardy or not. Can you let me try?"

"You're out of luck, Tom." Levi shot a look at the others. "We couldn't face our captain if we let a Union sympathizer go. And that's what you are, clear as the nose on your face. You've got one minute to get right with your Maker. Your people shouldn't have invaded our peace-lovin' land."

Anger boiled up inside Tom. These hoodlums were just as responsible for the Southern outrage as Elijah and Jessy's master. "You goin' let me have my final words?"

"Go ahead. You can use your one minute to rant to these woods."

"I reckon the two fugitives I helped escape slave hunters yesterday wouldn't agree about this *peace-lovin'* land! Their master, claiming the right to own and torture them, body and soul, is a demon in human form. Maybe you believe you're decent, goodhearted Confederates, but then you're ignorant. You're fighting for the devil, and that's the truth!" He clinched his jaw and waited for the shot.

Levi unbuttoned his shirt. A blue uniform showed beneath it.

Tom blinked. His head fell backwards, and the world turned black.

When he came to, he'd been pushed up against a tree trunk. Levi was slapping his cheek. "Here. Take a sup of this." He held a canteen smelling of whiskey to his lips.

Tom took a sip. It burned, but he could think again. He shook his head, looking from one man to another as all but one of them showed glimpses of their Union uniforms.

"Guess we carried our charade too far, but we had to be sure you weren't a spy who was some kind of great actor. After all, our own mission is to deceive the other side."

"So, you'll help me get to Jackson?" Tom let out a gasp of joy. "The Almighty be praised!"

"We'll help you, for sure. But not to Jackson."

"But—"

"Listen up, Tom! If you want to praise God, praise him you ran into us. Another five-hundred yards, and you'd be in a nest of real Confederates, if you even made it that far. You wouldn't live long enough to get a mile from here, let alone a *hundred*, even if you avoided those first Confederate scouts."

"But I've got—"

"How old are you?" Levi interrupted again, sounding more annoyed.

"Nineteen."

"Then we can't conscript you. Of course, you could join up voluntarily for six months." Levi glanced at Jack. "Or, you can agree to go back to that farm, and we'll see that you get there. We are NOT turning you loose."

Tom exhaled. "I guess I don't have a real choice."

"Jack has a cousin who owns a flat-bottom boat and fishes both directions on the Mississippi. He claims to be neutral about the war. Knows not to ask questions. Where is that farm exactly?"

"Four miles northeast of Baton Rouge, near the river."

Levi turned to Jack. "Reckon that's possible?"

"If the boy pays Byron two of his silver coins, I reckon he'd get him about six miles north of Baton Rouge. He's not gonna want to get closer to the Union's camp and tempt fate."

Levi nodded. "All right, then. It's in your hands."

"I'll make arrangements when I give our report today." Jack turned to Tom. "That boat'll beat walkin' the bandit-infested road. You're in luck more than you prob'ly gather."

Levi tapped the coffee pot with a stick. "Want some of our make-believe coffee? Our other provisions are kinda tight. We'll let you keep your own supplies, except for the socks and four of the coins. Those are payment for *our* help. You'll still need to pay the fisherman. Feel free to chug down all the sweet potato peels you want. Better move closer to the pit anyway and dry out."

"Thank you," he managed to say despite his soul's emptiness. He'd failed in less than twenty-four hours. And while muddling it all up, he'd infuriated Thad, who could hold a grudge and report him to his buddy, Colonel Irwin.

He squatted near the fire. While he drank the fake coffee and ate a piece of jerky, he scrutinized his captors. They looked tough, wiry, determined. Levi gave the impression of hard-earned leadership. Was there any chance he'd been right about praising God for falling into their hands? Or had Levi been mollifying him? Being shot at, the alligators, his colossal failure—all that didn't seem to be what even Mr. Pendleton would term providential, let alone downright praiseworthy.

But he was still learning about God's ways. So maybe God had intervened. "God, have mercy," he mouthed as he lifted the tin cup again. "Keep Terry alive. Please let him be in the next prisoner exchange. Please!"

CHAPTER 18

Tom grasped his bamboo pole and pulled in the gut-string line. A black crappie was thrashing, trying to slip the hook. He leaned against the boat's side and captured his catch with the net that one of the fishermen thrust at him. After removing the hook, he tossed the fish into the barrel behind him. Once the barrel was full, Byron and his three sons would set him ashore north of Baton Rouge as agreed. At present, the four fishermen and he were trolling along sandbars, no faster than a turtle. In fact, while they had drifted in a side current, one of the sons had entertained himself by tossing pieces of chicken liver at a snapping turtle trundling at the same speed along the sandy bank.

In between sandbars, the boat moved into the Mississippi's main channel, where the current was so strong that no rowing was needed except when guiding the boat to the next sandbar. If he weren't so worried about his reception at the Evans' farm, he'd enjoy the good fishing, the spurts of rowing, and the scenery. On the way to Port Hudson, he'd been completely engaged in guarding the wagon. Now, in addition to the thickets and swampland, he could observe the stately plantations set far back from the river, the plowed fields already showing tassels of yellow-green corn plants, the small farm houses closer to the river, and the rows of willows. He couldn't see the plantations' slave shacks, no doubt built in places that wouldn't mar the owners' views.

As the sun started its descent, Byron called for the boat to be rowed toward the shore. It bumped against the pilings under a wooden dock belonging to a plantation, its white mansion garnishing the top of the hill.

"This marks six miles from Baton Rouge." Byron wrapped a rope around one of the dock's posts. "Reckon you can find your way from here?"

"Sure. Thanks for the ride." Tom handed over the two silver coins, then hoisted his bag and himself onto the dock. At the top of the levee, he gave a wave and hurried down the flagstone steps to the road. He couldn't dawdle, as his mother would say, if he was to reach the Evans' place before dark. Who would have thought a trip downriver would take ten hours? But he'd made it back. Now if only those at the farm would be happy to see him.

The twilight's shadows darkened as he walked through the yard to the house. Shep saw him first, probably because everyone else was at supper. The collie let out one bark of alarm, then ran to him and danced in circles around him.

Thad was next, coming out the front door with Robert on his heels. He stood on the porch, hands on hips, not uttering a word.

Robert grinned and waved, but sobered after looking at his father.

Marylou and Sara came onto the porch together. Sara gave a little jump, then clasped her cheeks and disappeared into the house.

Tom flinched. Was Sara so disgusted with him that she couldn't bear even to greet him? Her welcome would have been like a lifeboat for a sinking ship.

Marylou tilted her head and batted her eyes at him. "Welcome home, Mr. Ballard. We were worried to death about you." She came off the porch.

"Go inside, Marylou." Her father's tone brooked no objection.

She showed a pouty face to Tom before walking past her father.

Tom stopped short of the porch. "Please forgive me. You were right. My plan was impossible."

"And that's what brought you back? Not sorrow at having broken your word? At having deserted my family?"

"I am sorry. Very sorry." Tom swallowed the lump in his throat. "I didn't *want* to desert you … *or* Terry."

Mr. Pendleton stepped out of the door. "If you're agreeable, Thaddeus, I suggest Thomas come inside and we discuss the situation around your hospitable table."

Thad turned toward Mr. Pendleton. "I don't know how much there is to say. But since he's your companion, I can't forbid him to stay with you if that's your desire."

"Indeed, it is. I hope you will allow me to share my views on the subject."

"Of course. I know to respect *my* elders." Thad stepped to one side and beckoned for Tom to enter.

When Mrs. Evans met Tom in the dining room, a big smile blossomed, but instantly disappeared. She motioned toward a chair. "Please have a seat. We've plenty of ham and hominy left if you're hungry."

"No thank you, ma'am, but I appreciate the offer." During the long day he'd eaten only a quick snack with the fishermen, sharing his jerky and fruit with them and sampling their slabs of grits dunked in molasses. But he couldn't have swallowed a bite with Thad glaring at him.

Mrs. Evans turned to Marylou, who had taken a chair next to Tom. "This is a conversation that doesn't concern you." She faced Robert. "Nor you. Both of you are excused. I'd like you to find books to read if you've finished your studies."

"Oh, Mama. Can't I stay?" Marylou remained seated when Robert stood. "I'm practically an adult."

"You heard your mother." Thad gave the table a couple of sharp raps.

Mr. Pendleton cleared his throat. "Miss Marylou, would you please ask Miss Ogawa to join us since you are going upstairs?"

"Yes, sir," Marylou muttered, heading toward the door.

Tom felt a little sorry for the girl. Being replaced by Sara had to be salt in her wound. And in a minute, he reflected, he could have a double dose of that salt himself.

Mrs. Evans finished carrying the dishes from their meal into the kitchen, then brought a tray with teacups and the teakettle to the table.

Sara entered and bowed. "Excuse my loss of—what do you say—calmness." Her eyes were red-rimmed.

Tom glanced away. Had she cried because he'd hurt her? Damaged their friendship? He'd give anything not to have caused her distress—anything except abandoning Terry.

"Your loss of composure, I suppose you mean." Mrs. Evans patted the chair's seat next to her. "It's all right." She turned to Tom. "I for one rejoice to have our prodigal back. You're an excellent tutor, and I didn't want that responsibility to fall on the rest of us, who already have a day full of chores. And I think we should recognize your contribution to the farm work too." She raised an eyebrow at her husband.

Thad's frown deepened. "I don't see resuming his chores as the issue."

"With Easter the day after tomorrow, I'm afraid those of us responsible for an array of dishes to prepare, toiling from dawn to dusk, *do* see an issue." She took a breath. "Tom can carry on with his work as well as aid us women by collecting eggs, plucking the chickens, and helping with the other chores we usually handle. I'm sure you see how thankful I should be for his fortuitous return."

Thad gave a disgusted nod.

"If no one minds," Mr. Pendleton intervened, "I'd like for Thomas to tell what happened after he left Merchant Brubaker's store, so we have all the facts. I appreciate having heard the thorough account last night of what happened at the store before Thomas left."

Tom briefly recounted how he eluded the men on the track, nearly became food for alligators, and had to persuade the band of disguised Federals that he wasn't a Rebel sympathizer. During his account, Sara had moaned, then blushed several times. Mr. Pendleton had exclaimed, "Do tell!" Mrs. Evans had said, "My dear boy" and "Thank the good Lord you're alive!" Only Thad had appeared unmoved.

"I also give credit to Providence that you survived," Mr. Pendleton added as his own assessment.

Afraid of aggravating Thad more, Tom bit back his tongue to keep from sharing how he had pondered that possibility.

"Now here are some points—or questions—I'd like us to consider." Mr. Pendleton gave a wan smile to Thad. "Being the eldest, I dare to propose these first. As most important, I wish to examine motivation as the primary consideration, for our Savior cares deeply about what is in our heart. For example, why we contribute to the church—to please Him or to look good. Isn't that correct?"

Although Thad's face had a quizzical expression, he uttered his agreement along with everyone else.

"Let's recognize that at times we must choose between two evils. I'm sure we agree that a good person will choose the lesser one." He paused to allow Mrs. Evans to replenish their tea, then continued. "Here is the first evil: we choose to break an oath, which by so doing, could harm the other party, even seriously harm him. And here is the other evil: we abandon a member of our family who we believe will *die* unless we break that oath. So I ask, which is the lesser evil?"

"Forgive me, but it's a flawed question, Richard." Thad sat straighter, as though a judge rendering his verdict. "Breaking the oath could have brought about my death by highwaymen, not just possibly *harmed* me, and the action undertaken was futile. Tom ignored the advice of those much more knowledgeable than he."

"True enough, but I asked us to consider *motivation*. Let me repeat the question."

"That's not necessary, sir," Thad said, his tone sharp. "If the oath breaker *truly* saw things as you have described, then breaking the agreement would be the lesser of the two evils in his *opinion*. But in Tom's case, he had a wrong basis for his opinion and was extremely foolish."

Tom's ears were burning, and his mind spun. Had it really been so wrong and foolish to try to slay a *Goliath*? In the Holy Bible, David's elders had advised against his action too, but God had enabled David to succeed with a mere slingshot.

"May I address this point also before I yield the floor?" Mr. Pendleton asked.

Thad folded his arms and muttered, "Certainly, sir."

"None of us can claim infallibility, can we? We all may have given erroneous advice at times. Yes, Thomas should have done a better job of evaluating what he was told. But Thomas, and Miss Sara, too, were in dire danger on the Pacific island from some of the most wicked men plaguing the earth. Although they fought for their lives, without God's intervention, they would have perished, having been greatly outnumbered. Why couldn't someone with that experience have expected God to aid him again, even though it looked impossible? Even though he had to discount well-meaning, expert advice?"

"All right, all right. Point taken, sir." Thad glared at Tom as though to block his response. "I'm not eloquent enough to refute it. So, Tom is back. Excused for his *mistake*. We resume our lives and prepare for Easter." Thad blinked with a lost expression for a second, then pivoted toward Tom. "Is that good with you? I've heard your apology."

"Yes, sir. I appreciate it." He didn't dare state that Mr. Pendleton's explanation had been accurate or ask for forgiveness a second time. At least, there was a better likelihood that Thad wouldn't report him to Colonel Irwin and remove any chance Terry had for an exchange.

After vain efforts were made to talk about less-charged topics, the group dispersed. Tom caught up with Sara in the hallway's fading light and matched his steps to hers.

She stopped and faced him. "I was worried, Tom. You could have told me your plans before you left. I can keep secrets. I would have worried the same, but not felt deserted." She pulled out her fan and fanned her face.

Tom grimaced. "I'm sorry. Because of you, I almost couldn't take off. But I thought I'd make it. I really did think the Almighty would help me make it. And then I could return to you … and, of course, to Mr. Pendleton and the Evanses."

She gazed at him, wide-eyed.

More than ever, he wanted to take her in his arms and kiss her. But that would be as rash as his taking off had been. He had to learn to keep consequences in mind, starting with Sara's heart and his.

"It's been a long day," he said softly, regretfully. "Time to turn in." He lit a candle for her and gestured for her to take the stairs before him.

She reached for the candle. "Yes, a very long day. And we have a long way to go. We need to keep our minds straight." She glided up the stairs.

"Much easier said than done," Tom murmured while lighting his own candle.

Mr. Pendleton joined him a minute later. "What's easier said than done?"

"Oh, uh, all that's going on." He glanced at Mr. Pendleton's face. How much had the man observed? "But what I do realize," he hastened to say, "is my need to thank you, sir—for your defense."

"It's easy to make allowances for someone you deeply care for. I regret that your plan to rescue Terrence didn't work out ... although I, too, had insisted that you not pursue such an undertaking." He paused, obviously waiting for a response.

"I was wrong not to keep my agreement with you and the colonel. I betrayed your trust." He hung his head.

"You are already forgiven." He extended his open palms. "And let's not give up hope. God is sovereign, powerful. He is with us *and* Terrence. As for that defense, like we said in New Orleans, we're a team. Team members support each other. Furthermore, we care about each other's minds ... and hearts, don't we."

Tom shot a questioning look at him.

The elderly man picked up his own candle ... and smiled.

CHAPTER 19

Confederate Prison on the Pearl River at Jackson, Mississippi

The iron gate attached to the Pearl River bridge at Jackson grated open. "Any more dead in there?" a Confederate guard yelled at the entrance of the make-shift prison—the miserable quarters where Terry ended up.

"No, only the three out by you." The reply came from Colonel Fletcher, the prisoners' spokesman. "But other sick men lie at death's door unless they get medicines. And those of us not sick are close behind. We need enough food to live! Christian decency requires it."

Terry frowned at the useless petition. The colonel and everyone else knew these hardened Rebs wouldn't care if every last one of their captives died from disease or starvation. The prison superintendent could have turned a nearby empty house into a prison hospital. Instead, he had kept all three-hundred-fifty prisoners crammed together in the dilapidated, covered bridge, part of which had already fallen into the muddy river surging beneath them.

Terry sat still with the others—an unbending rule for getting any of the wretched food. Twelve Confederate privates, complaining of the bridge's stench, as they did every morning, handed in buckets of gruel and replenished the water barrels.

When the bucket of runny, boiled oats reached Terry, he filled his tin cup to the brim to get his full allotment. He needed every ounce of energy to carry out his plan. Joshua, leaning next to him against the bridge's wall of rough timbers, waved the bucket on. Terry grabbed his friend's cup and filled it too.

"Can't eat any more of that pig slop." Joshua took back his cup and banged it onto the floor.

"Don't be like that." Terry took a swallow of the soupy paste, ignoring the wormy weevils. "It's not so bad," he lied. "You want to starve? Or let your fever burn you up again?"

"Can't you leave that weakling alone?" Their nemesis, sitting two men down, leered at them. "Let him pass into whatever place can stand him."

Terry glared at Jake, but didn't get up. The corporal in charge of their eight-by-twelve-foot area had sworn he'd toss both Terry and the brute into the river the next time they exchanged curse-ridden insults or had a shoving match.

Picking up Joshua's cup, Terry held it close to his friend's face. "Here. Drink. Don't listen to that buzzard. You made it this far. You just gotta hang on a little longer."

Joshua took a little gruel into his mouth, but let most of it dribble out. "Head hurts, Terry. Thinkin' about jumping into the cool water below."

"No! You're not thinking straight. Take some more of that slop. I've got something to tell you."

Once their unit finished their organized calisthenics, spaced by their officers so a few men could struggle through pushups and the others walk or stumble in place, Terry squeezed in next to Joshua again. While those around him watched the neighboring unit's exercises—their only distraction from pure misery—he got his mouth close to Joshua's ear.

"Should have a new moon three days from now. If there's rain, guards won't be able to see more than a couple feet in front of them, or hear suspicious noises. Each time I go relieve myself, I step over two rotten boards. The fellow forced to sit next to them—name's Caleb—is friendly enough. I asked if he thought he'd ever fall through. He said that might not be so bad 'cause one of the bridge's support posts is right under those boards. Caleb and I've decided to pry them up and take our chances going down that post. If we swim fast, we can get close to the far bank before any others decide to follow and attract attention. I told Caleb you'd have to come with us. He agreed."

"Got no strength to slide down posts and swim ten yards or maybe more—across the current, in the dark. You go ahead."

"Not doing that. Lots of branches and logs floating down there. I'll find something for you to cling to, and I'll pull it with you to the bank."

"Across the current? I don't think so."

"It'll be nothing like what I did on a sail ship. Climbing rigging and slushing masts. Besides, whacha got to lose? You were talkin' about *jumping* into the river a minute ago. Scrabbling down a post will beat that to pieces. You'll live, and we'll be free. Away from the sick and dying."

"I'm one of the sick."

"Not right now you're not." He felt Joshua's forehead. "No fever, pal."

"All right. You win."

"So you'll go?"

"If it's raining." He closed his eyes and turned his face away.

Thunder rumbled and sheets of rain and wind rattled the old bridge. Terry listened to the snores, curses, and mutterings around him. When he no longer detected any sounds of wakefulness, he poked Joshua. "Come on," he whispered. "This is it."

They inched along the wall, stepping gingerly between men. Enough light came through cracks from the flickering oil lanterns of the guards outside the entrance to outline the sleepers' heads, flat against the bridge's floorboards. Terry counted bodies until he nearly ran into Caleb, squatting by the decaying boards.

The three of them, using their flattened tin cups' edges, worked steadily for an hour, pausing only for some sleeper's snort or mumble. Finally, the first board scraped out. They pried the second board up almost instantly. A gust of wind blew in from beneath the bridge.

Caleb's neighbor jerked up.

"Leavin' this hellish tunnel, Macon," Caleb murmured. "Watch out for the hole. It's right by you."

Terrified that Macon would wake Jake and the hundreds of other prisoners stuffed together, Terry pushed his hands against the floor so he straddled the black hole. "Give me a minute or two," he told Joshua. He wiggled through the empty space, feeling for the post with his dangling legs. His arms and hands followed his body in a free fall. He swallowed a scream.

His left leg bumped the post the next second. He grabbed hold and panted while he hugged his savior. "Post's to your left," he called back up the hole, counting on the storm to muffle his words. "Riding it down."

"Keep left when you bump into the other post, and keep your boots on," he called up from the bottom. He'd found a log stuck between the two posts, which had been built to cross each other halfway up. With three of them kicking, they could push the log across the current and stay afloat even wearing their boots. He didn't have to worry about protection for their feet in the wilds any longer. Including Caleb was turning out to be a godsend.

"Hey, watch out!" a voice yelled inside the prison.

"Someone down there?" another voice, possibly Jake's, yelled, and then a full chorus of shouts bellowed.

Terry motioned to the other two still clinging to the post. "Help me! Gotta move this log to the far side fast!"

Caleb lunged for the log and wrested it from Terry. Terry grabbed for it, but his fingers slipped off of the log's end. Caleb, with his prize, disappeared into the pouring rain.

Gunshots came from the shore behind Terry. He grabbed Joshua's arm. "We gotta swim for it! Now! Hold onto my left leg and kick yours. I'll get us across."

He plunged into the water and felt Joshua grip him. The current, far stronger than he'd imagined, tugged him downstream, but at least away from the bullets. He fought to angle across the rushing water, but made no headway. His ankle boots filled with water while Joshua became a deadweight. He allowed himself and Joshua to go with the current, just to stay afloat. He'd badgered his pal into coming with him. He couldn't sink.

Suddenly Joshua's hands slipped off Terry. Terry spun around, and the next second he joined his friend in clinging to a bobbing tree snag.

"How far to the bank?" Joshua's teeth were chattering.

"No idea. But the current's acting different here. Tricky. Hold on 'til we get some light."

"Are we far enough away?"

"Maybe. I'd like to wring Caleb's neck!" Terry gritted his teeth. "The thief!"

"Unless the current caught him."

"Then he shouldn't have taken over. Ripped the log out of my hands. It'll serve him right if he drowns."

"Don't wish death onto anyone. We all fall short."

"Whatever." Joshua was about as naïve as they came, similar to Jim Mankin, but Terry wasn't about to argue in the middle of a river, in a rainstorm, in pitch blackness.

"Ugh!" Terry threw his head back. "Something fell on me!" He swiped one hand over his hair, expecting to brush off a tarantula or some other large spider. Instead, wet Spanish moss clung to his fingers.

"It's moss. Wind must 'a' whipped it off a tree."

"Reckon it's a close tree?" Joshua's voice held a hopeful note.

"No way of knowing. Are you all right? Got a good hold?"

"Keep thinkin' of my feather bed in New York. Maybe never see home again."

"Sure you will. We're out of prison. Not drowning. Storm's even lettin' up. Just got to stay awake 'til dawn."

As though taunting Terry, lightning streaked across the sky, accompanied by the boom of thunder. He braced for the oncoming downpour.

"I saw trees!" Joshua slapped Terry's arm. "Right in front of us."

"A mirage. Don't let it fool you."

"No! I could almost touch them."

"An island then? You think?" Terry peered into the darkness, but could see nothing.

"Don't think they were growing completely in water."

Terry edged around to the other side of the snag and pulled himself hand over hand down the old tree trunk, his heavy boots helping him sink fast. When the water reached his neck, he stopped sinking. He was standing on the base of the snag. But he didn't dare let go. Even if there was an island three feet away, the powerful current could sweep him right by it.

"Dawn can't be more than an hour or two from now. We just gotta hang on." Terry reached for Joshua's arm while gripping the snag for all he was worth with his other hand.

Suddenly, Joshua's body flew past him. There was a splash, sputtering, and then fits of coughing.

Had his friend gone crazy? Terry pushed off and swam with all his might.

"I'm on land," Joshua gasped out, just as Terry's fingers slid onto a cypress root.

Grabbing higher on the root, he dragged himself onto the bank. Sucking in air, he stretched out next to Joshua. Finally getting his breath, he pulled himself up, anxious to have the rain stop thrumming against his face.

"I'll find us a better tree than that old cypress." He stretched his arms out in front of him and took a step. A dozen steps away on higher ground, he met a weeping willow already leafed out.

Terry helped Joshua ease under the tree's outer branches, then crouching over, headed toward its center. Squatting by the trunk, he yanked off his boots and poured out the water, then squeezed as much moisture as possible from his ragged socks.

"You still doing all right?" Terry couldn't tell anything in the dark.

"Better'n ten minutes ago." Joshua's arm scraped against Terry as he evidently pulled his boots back on. "We're in for a long, hard trip."

"Yep, no question. We just gotta take it as it comes." Terry felt the ground for leaves to bunch together as a thin cushion. "At least, we're out of the river. A piece of luck, I'd say. And think of Talbot's shock when he hears we're gone."

He started to offer a wet bunch of twigs and leaves to Joshua, but his companion had dozed off in spite of his soaked clothes, wet ground, and the heavy showers from the wind blowing the branches. Laying his own head on the leaves, Terry prepared himself for a miserable night. Imagining his enemy's consternation at his escape took an edge off his discomfort for a few seconds. But then he thought of the miles of hostile territory they had to cover to reach any safe place.

CHAPTER 20

Sara picked up the basket of eggs she'd gathered in the chicken coop and headed toward the house. The sun was just peeping through the woods, but the whole household was up doing chores.

"Good morning," Tom said, on his way to pitch fresh hay for the horses and mules. He looked into the basket. "See you got a good number today."

"Yes, and good morning to you." A sunny feeling welled up in her as Tom walked off whistling. During the three weeks since his "escapade," as Marylou called it, life had speedily returned to normal—if life among strangers on a foreign farm during a war could be called normal. Almighty God, with Mr. Pendleton's help, would have sustained her. She couldn't doubt that. But without Tom, life would have been a hundred times harder.

She kept the new screen door from hitting the basket and entered the kitchen, where Agatha was preparing breakfast. The scent of frying bacon whetted her appetite. She'd grown to like the greasy slabs, as well as the daily scrambled or poached eggs and grits, although nothing could compare with her country's *misoshiru*. She set the basket on a stool by the sink and greeted Mr. Pendleton, who was grinding sweet potato peels for their drink. The family had urged him to take life easier, but he insisted on carrying out an equal share of the chores, even helping pull crabgrass and pokeweed from the garden.

"Miss Sara." He stopped her as she was leaving to fill a bucket with well water at the pump house. He held the screen door for her, then joined her on the back stoop. "Mr. and Mrs. Evans asked me to convey a request they have. Instead of the family remaining home with us for our time of worship, they plan to resume attending their Baton Rouge church to prevent more suspicion. The various Protestant denominations take turns using the church building, and it's the Presbyterians' turn today. Since that's my background, they've asked me to go with them this morning and offer a few words as a lay missionary. Mr. Evans thinks the Southern sympathizers will respect my age and Christian convictions. He'd like for you to attend the service too."

"Me? Why is that, sir?" Mixing with Southern strangers, who might have different ideas of polite behavior, along with other unknown expectations of her, did not sound good.

"Since you're a foreigner, he thinks the congregants won't expect you to be passionate about this country's struggle. In other words, you wouldn't pose a danger to the South. Since rumors continue to fly about the 'marksman,' he'd like to appease the gossipers by giving them the opportunity to meet you—to see the family isn't hiding Northern infiltrators on the farm."

"Will Tom be coming too?" She couldn't help asking.

"No. He's needed to guard this place. Additionally, people who merely had heard of the pistol-firing boarder could ask an awkward question if they met such a strong-looking, young man in person—namely, why hadn't Thomas already volunteered for the Confederate army."

"So, I should not mention Tom?"

"Yes, and definitely nothing about Terrence."

"Might not Marylou and Robert say too much about us?"

"Marylou understands the danger. Robert will stay home with Thomas. It seems he came close to revealing information about a previous fugitive."

"I'm afraid of misspeaking too."

"The good Lord has seen us through our trials so far. He won't fail us now, will he?"

"No, sir. I guess he won't."

She wouldn't face pirates at the church. Or be abducted by one of the worshipers. So why did she feel she was walking into a snare, like the ones Mr. Evans set in the garden for the unfortunate rabbits?

"Then I'll convey your intention to come with us and won't delay you any longer."

"Thank you for your care, as always." She forced a smile, picked up a bucket, and hurried to the well.

Mr. Evans drove the horse and surrey to the stables behind the white clapboard church, whose sharp steeple Sara had glimpsed over the treetops a mile away. After the two men helped Marylou out of the cart's front bench, they handed down Agatha, then Sara, from the back bench. For once, her inconvenient gloves were proving useful, for they concealed her shaky hands' dampness. She smoothed her hooped skirt—still disliking its awkwardness—and strolled with the others to the building's front yard.

Marylou joined three giggling girls beckoning to her by the church's front gate. The two men entered the church to speak with the minister about the program. Sara glanced around, having no idea what she should do. Then Agatha took her arm and conducted her across the churchyard to a small group of ladies talking and fanning themselves in the partial shade of a magnolia tree, a tree giving forth the same sweet smell as the *kobushi* in her country.

The ladies broke off their conversation and stared at Sara, then belatedly welcomed Agatha and her.

"What a lovely young lady you have with you, Mrs. Evans," a grandmotherly woman said, the feathers on her hat bobbing as she wobbled her head.

Before Sara could wade into a response, Agatha patted her arm and said, "Yes, Grandmother Owens, it's our pleasure to have Miss Sara Ogawa staying at our farm. She's a citizen of the Japans and is traveling with her guardian. While they're waiting for the river to clear so they can continue their journey, we are the beneficiaries of their skills, including Miss Ogawa's archery."

The grandmother took Sara's hand. "From the Japans. And skilled in archery. How, ah … special. We are so isolated, with the awful invaders trying to encircle us, that we nevah get to meet someone from another place." She released Sara's hand, then gave the other women a look, apparently urging them to speak up.

"My, you must have had a long journey already," a lady in her mid-twenties remarked, her enthusiasm indicating she hadn't needed any prompting. "How long did it take for you to reach us here?"

Sara took a second to calculate the various times. "Twenty-seven days sailing the Pacific, with an added two-week stay in Honolulu, two days in San Francisco, about three weeks on the mail ships and the Panama Railroad, and several days in New Orleans."

"Oh, I would love to see so much of the world."

"Yes." Sara met the lady's intense blue eyes. "Traveling

brings new sights and experiences." *If you only knew.*

"Mrs. Steadman is a neighbor of ours," Agatha inserted quickly. "She and her husband own the attractive plantation closest to us."

"Yes, and a lonely place with my husband away defending our home and the Confederacy." The lady blinked back what could have been a tear. She turned to Sara. "Please call me Lucille. I do hope you and Agatha can come to my home for tea. We live far enough from the river, town, and main road that the horrible Yanks have left our plantation alone. I'd love to hear more about the Japans and all those amazing experiences."

"It would be our pleasure," Agatha put in, then turned her head as a voice could be heard telling the congregants to "please enter." She patted Sara's arm. "I believe that's the cue to find our seats."

Sara detected a note of relief in her hostess' voice. But how could they refuse an eager invitation from a neighbor who was apparently wealthy and influential?

The service began with the singing of the hymn, "Holy, Holy, Holy." The Evanses and she were seated in the fourth row from the front. First one person and then another in the first three rows managed to cast surreptitious looks at her.

Sara pulled out her fan, but resisted the urge to hide behind it. Were the slight differences of her skin shade and the shape of her eyes so startling? Yet she shouldn't mind, really. Her countrymen acted the same way about the Westerners arriving in the treaty cities—the *henna gaijin*, who supposedly had huge noses and ghostly, owl-shaped eyes. Even her family had gaped at a red-headed man they'd seen go by on horseback. Of course, she'd never imagined then that she'd become a *strange foreigner* herself.

The perusals of her stopped when Mr. Pendleton walked up to speak at the lectern. But when he introduced himself and explained briefly his relationship to her, every head swiveled toward her.

Not knowing what else to do, she stood and gave a quick bow, embarrassed to hear a few titters.

Mr. Pendleton adjusted his spectacles and opened the large Bible on the stand. He read the "Great Commission" Jesus had given in the twenty-eighth chapter of Matthew's Gospel. Looking up, he ran his eyes over his audience. A few people coughed during the protracted silence. Sara sat very still, struck by the commission to *go and teach all nations to observe all that Jesus had commanded*. She could hardly go any farther than she'd already gone. But the part about teaching Jesus' commands? She hadn't at all unless she could count her conversations with Tom about her faith while on the island.

Mr. Pendleton adjusted his spectacles again and pointed to the open Bible. "When my wife and I read this command one day, we remembered hearing that Japan had just opened its doors to Westerners after two hundred fifty years of isolation. We decided to sell our summer cabin and retire in the city of Nagasaki, Japan. The country severely prohibits Christianity, which has forced secrecy upon any Japanese citizen who dares to believe. But that is where we could make a difference."

His face lit with a radiant smile. "You see, the foreign treaties allow people from the outside countries to practice their faith. So my wife and I, along with several other expatriates, including the American consul, began Sunday services and small Bible classes. The area's governor has permitted a few Japanese young people to join with us, ostensibly to study English. These Christian meetings are like small seeds planted in a huge field. But God's Word says such a seed, like that of the mustard, can become a large tree. Isn't that so?"

Murmurs of agreement wafted through the room, to which Mr. Pendleton gave acknowledging nods. "Perhaps some of you would dare to go to the other side of the world, too, and experience the joy of the coming harvest." No murmurs accompanied those words. "And I hope," he said, still with a tone of conviction, "that all of you will pray for us and our friends overseas." Heads nodded in response.

He thanked the minister for the opportunity to give the greeting and took his seat.

The rest of the service passed with a message that impressed Sara as perfunctory, perhaps overly rehearsed. Her mind wandered to Lucille's invitation. How sad they were on opposite sides of the war. Otherwise, they might have much to share, and it would be nice to have a female friend.

Pews creaked as everyone around her rose. She lurched to her feet and joined them in the final hymn.

Clouds were lowering when Sara and the Evanses walked through the vestibule. The imminent threat of rain temporarily solved the problem of dealing with an invitation from Lucille, who waved a hand to Sara and pointed to the sky, then hurried toward her buggy.

While people were shaking hands with Mr. Pendleton, exchanging bits of news with Mrs. Evans, and eyeing Sara, a young boy approached her. He looked up and asked, "Why are you at *our* church?"

"I'm visiting with my guardian, Mr. Pendleton." His haughty attitude stunned her.

"Oh, I know that. I heard that inside. But this church is for White people. People like you aren't supposed to come here."

"Why, Billy! How rude." A middle-aged woman, apparently his mother, had come up behind him. She gave a smart slap to the top of his head. "This lady is from the Japans. I want you to know, young man, that the *Atlantic Monthly*, an excellent magazine, had an article expounding how intelligent and hard-working these people are." She smiled at Sara. "The poet Walt Whitman even wrote a glorious poem about the meeting of East with West when their ambassadors visited our country. You need to apologize right now."

"Sorry, ma'am," the boy muttered.

The lady cocked her head at Sara. "He's probably heard talk about the other Orientals, who are coming in such numbers, and confused you with them. We'll make sure he understands the difference."

She nodded to Sara and pulled the boy toward their wagon.

Sara rubbed her temple. Another person looking down on the Chinese—like the policeman in San Francisco—but this one a church member. Of course, this shouldn't be surprising in light of the slaves' poor conditions, perhaps even on Christians' plantations.

She bit her bottom lip. How about herself and her country's Untouchables that Mr. Pendleton singled out? Admittedly, she had looked down on them as a disgusting class, people to be avoided … but that was before she'd become a Christian. If an Untouchable crossed her path this day, how would she feel? She would *not* tell him to go away, that he couldn't attend the church. But would that be good enough?

She sighed. Life had been much easier living with her family, in its cocoon. But then, a caterpillar that never came out of its cocoon, died. It never metamorphosed. Never flew.

Mr. Evans brought the surrey into the drive, and she joined the others hurrying to get under the cart's canopy. Soon the raindrops turned into a full-fledged torrent. Mud droplets splashed up on her gown, but she didn't care. Thankfully, she was on the way back to the farm, even if it was a temporary cocoon.

After the lunch and cleanup, she slipped into the parlor, dressed in a plain *yukata* robe that didn't require a gown's ridiculous bustle or even the kimono's bow when she chose to omit it. The room was her favorite, with its hooked rug over the pine flooring, two bookshelves, and soft armchairs. Expecting a cool breeze after the rain, she chose a chair upholstered in blue-and-white chintz, close to one of the open windows. She turned to where she'd left off reading Dickens' *A Tale of Two Cities,* ready to lose herself in the story.

"So you're reading another Dickens novel. Guess you liked the Christmas one."

She looked up, surprised to see Tom standing a few feet in front of her. "Oh, I didn't hear you come in." She glanced down at her book and back at him. "I like this book's story, too, but it is very different from *The Christmas Carol.* I worry much for these characters because they could suffer and die. While I read about Mr. Scrooge, the ghosts, and Tiny Tim, I was mostly curious how it would work out."

Tom pointed to the book he took from under his arm. "I keep comparing this tale to what we experienced while marooned. It's about a family that ended up on a deserted island too. Of course, it's interesting, but it's not realistic. They have too many tools and even livestock they saved from a shipwreck."

"The author probably was never marooned himself, but just used his imagination. Maybe you could write a good story about what really happened to us."

"My high school English teachers would find that idea highly amusing, but thank you."

"Are you going to stay here and read?" She certainly hoped so.

"Would you mind?"

"No, I always like your company. In fact, it is too bad you could not attend the church. I was at a loss, as Agatha sometimes says about Marylou."

"You looked a little out-of-sorts when you got home. It wasn't just the drenching from the storm then?" He scooted a chair next to her and sat, holding the book, *The Swiss Family Robinson*, in his lap.

"No, it was the stares and my ignorance of the customs." Tom was frowning, so she didn't mention the boy's rudeness that led to her own jumbled thoughts. "It is foolish for me to care about such insignificant problems, I know. They are ridiculous compared to Terry's imprisonment, the dangers you met, the threats against the Evanses ... and slavery and the terrible war." She swallowed the lump in her throat. "I am sorry I mentioned this morning's small nuisances."

"Small nuisances, like thorns, can be painful too. But are you sorry you came to America?"

She hesitated. If she were honest, she'd say she wasn't sorry, mainly because she was with him. But she couldn't admit that.

"No, I am not sorry." She took a breath, glad for the diversionary explanation that came to mind. "In Japan, it would be hard to disguise myself as Daisuke's young brother while he acted as a masterless samurai. Or if he continued to sail with a ship, I might be a cook's assistant, like Jim was. That would be ... unpleasant." She looked away, wondering for the hundredth time where her brother was. Had he been able to greet their parents? Or—horror of horrors—had the authorities discovered his illegal reentry?

"So, this is the least of two or three evils for you?" Tom was gazing at her, clearly disappointed.

"America is not the dreamland I imagined—a Christian country, where everyone loves God and their neighbor."

"Not by a long shot, I'll give you that. But is everything here so bad?"

"No, no. The omnibus, the carriages, the railroad, the tall, fancy buildings are fascinating. What's bad are the mean people—like Talbot, and the unfair judge, the bounty hunters, the slave owners, and the soldiers killing each other." She took a breath. Tom's furrowed brows told her she'd said too much. "But, of course, there are very fine people too—the Evanses and all those people trying to help the slaves."

"Mr. Pendleton, Jim, Mr. Mankin, Elijah, Jessy, Terry, and I are Americans too, you know."

"Oh, of course, all of you are … grand. And there are many more nice people. It just seems we meet so many beastly people." She pulled out her fan.

"When we left the island, I hoped you'd find the trip an adventure. Maybe find a place that you'd like to live for a good while because … well, you are the type of person many men would want to marry."

She stopped fanning despite her warm face. "Maybe my marriage will be impossible. There are no men from Japan in America, I think. If I reenter Japan someday, maybe no man there will marry me—a lawbreaker, according to our strict rules. Also, my husband must be Christian. My brother is the only Christian Japanese man I know."

"So, you would marry only a Japanese man? A Christian Japanese man? Perhaps you should keep the door open to other possibilities. I mean"—he glanced out the window and back at her—"I don't know what I mean. I'm sorry. I shouldn't have gotten so … personal."

"You are kind to listen to my problems. Yours are so much greater. I pray every day for Terry."

"Thank you." He exhaled. "You know, next to my family, your friendship means the most to me."

"And so does yours to me," she said softly, hoping she hadn't just revealed more than she intended.

He smiled and picked up his book. "A best friend together with an interesting book provides a fine time."

"Yes." She laid aside her fan and turned to where she'd stopped reading. "And now to find out where Mr. Dickens takes me in unlucky, dangerous France."

But the words on the page didn't enter her mind. All she could think about was the splendid person sitting in the chair right next to her.

If only he were Japanese.

CHAPTER 21

Terry woke with a start. Joshua had a finger to his lips.

At least two men were talking right by their willow tree. Thankfully, their Black dialect indicated they weren't Confederates unless they'd been forced to accompany their master.

A hand and arm, followed by a full head of hair, poked through the silvery leaves.

"Hey, friend!" Joshua called. Ducking under the drooping boughs, he approached the face gawking at them.

Terry fell in behind him. At least, Joshua's tattered blue uniform might smooth the way if the men were runaways.

The two men sprang back a few paces as Terry joined Joshua outside the tree's curtain of branches.

"You need our raft?" the older-looking one asked, tilting his head toward the river. "Ain't got much else."

Through the fine drizzle, Terry caught the hazy shape of a raft of bundled sticks and branches resting against the cypress trunk. "Not planning to steal it," Terry answered when Joshua hesitated. "You've got nothing to fear from us. But we'd sure appreciate help in getting across to the shore." He looked around him. "You after something from the island?"

"Willow bark?" Joshua gestured toward the tree behind them.

"Have plenty o' willow." The elder one lowered his hands, followed by the younger. "Goosefoot an' yarrow mostly. Grows thick here."

"How about we help you pick the plants in exchange for a quick ride?" Terry mustered up a smile. The cobbled-together raft didn't look too safe, but better than another attempt at swimming.

"You deserters?" the younger man asked, ignoring the other fellow's shocked glance.

"Got separated from my New York regiment during a battle," Joshua answered. "Ran into Terry here, who'd been bushwhacked. Are you runaways?"

The two men, looking grim, shook their heads.

"We're on your side. All the way." Terry straightened his damp, shabby clothes. "My traveling companions and I were with two fugitives near Lake Borgne when the bushwhackers took me."

"Swamps near Orleans crawlin' with slave catchers an' them Rebs," the elder one said, apparently gaining more confidence. "We're free men now, workin' on a farm east o' here. We'll give you a way o'er the stream. Has to be one at a time. Reckon you kin pole?"

Terry's lip curled. "We've had plenty of practice, where any slip up was deadly, thanks to the two-footed snakes."

"But hold on," Terry called when the men headed toward the raft. "We'll help you pick first. We could use some yarrow salad ourselves." *And whatever else is edible.*

The elder hesitated. "Easy to mix it up with poison hemlock, suh."

"We'll pick the goosefoot then and leave the yarrow to you." Joshua smoothed back his dark hair, and looked the men full in

177

the face. "We're not wanting to bring harm to you folks. You're practically the Lord's good angels."

Terry rolled his eyes at the men. "I'll agree with *good*, anyway. But before we start picking, would you give your names? And call me Terry. Joshua's older and a real soldier, so I can't speak for him."

"I'm not an officer or someone who answers to *sir* either." Joshua smiled.

The older man cocked his head. "Home folks call me Elder John, and this here's my boy Ezra. Can't sound friendly-like when Southern folks nearby. Free or not, we'd be askin' for a beatin'. But here's just us. So we'll call you what you like."

"These Southerners have a lot to learn." Terry drew himself up tall. "Maybe you heard all men in the Confederate states were declared free from the first of January this year. Emancipation Proclamation."

Elder John clicked his tongue. "Masters pay no mind to what Yanks say." He picked up two bushel baskets from the raft and handed one to Terry. "This here's for the goosefoot. If the goosefoot runs out, you can toss in some burdock if your hands kin stand it."

"I've been a sailor, and Joshua's trained for battle. We can handle prickly leaves. Burrs too."

Ezra glanced at their hands and nodded. "One more problem with burdock—it looks like that poison rhubarb. If you see red stems, shiny leaves, best let them be."

The center of the island turned out to have a narrow stretch of rich soil, full of grasses, weeds, and the plants the two men sought. For an hour, Terry did the work of breaking off the bunches of leaves, while Joshua, lagging a little, mainly carried the basket. Once they had enough goosefoot leaves, they piled several layers of burdock on top.

"We're done here." Terry walked toward the two men. "Do you need help with the yarrow?"

"We've plenty." Elder John motioned to Ezra to take one side of his basket. "Best get to the farm before ..." He jerked, then raised his hand for them to be quiet.

Two or three dogs bayed faintly in the distance.

"The owners can't reach us without a boat." Joshua kept his voice low.

"But they can shoot. And they might be portaging a boat." Terry spun toward the closest willow. "Come on. If we lie flat on the far side of the trunk from them, they won't see us."

"The dogs smelled us, though." Ezra was visibly shaking. "They wait 'til we're starvin' or they get a boat."

"They won't be sure we're on the island. Hurry!" Parting some of the tree's

outer branches, Terry motioned for them come.

"Maybe you're the real fug'tives." Elder John remained standing. "Ezra best hide with you. He'd bring the men a right smart sum if taken and sold. I'll tell them I'm Widow Starkly's worker. They leave an ol' man alone. But if they're real mean, don't do nothin'. Keep hiding."

Oh, God, Terry found himself praying despite himself, *don't let Elder John get shot!*

"May the Almighty protect you," Joshua prayed out loud. He pushed through the branches with Terry. Ezra came along after them.

The bloodhounds bayed in earnest as the hunters drew closer.

Terry gripped the dirt and old leaves under him as if they were a life preserver.

"Hey you!" The hunters' spokesman included a derogatory word. "Watcha doin' o'er there?"

"Pickin' weeds for my missus, suh," Elder John answered.

"Speak up, boy! The river's swallowing half your words!"

"Pickin' weeds for my missus, suh!" Elder John called louder.

If the men were conferring, their voices were too low for Terry to hear them.

"Any dead bodies wash up on the island?" A new voice came loud and clear.

Terry flinched. Talbot's!

"Not seen bodies, suh!" Elder John shouted.

Quiet followed. Terry strained to distinguish whether or not the men and dogs had left.

"How'd you get across the current?" It was Talbot's voice again.

"With a pole an' a raft, suh."

Terry held his breath. Could they believe only one elderly person could do that?

"Are you alone? Tell the truth and you'll live!"

"I be alone, suh."

"Louder!"

"I be alone, suh!"

"Old man, you're lying."

A gunshot sounded.

Terry plunged his hand over Ezra's mouth before more than a grunt issued. "Hold on!" he whispered. "Your father said to keep hiding no matter what." His hand became wet from Ezra's jerking sobs. "We don't know he's hit. Just hold on."

The voices and dogs' baying became less distinct.

Ezra half rose, but was tackled by Joshua. "Wait!" Joshua's order demanded respect in spite of his wheezing. "Wait a couple minutes more. If they see us, they'll come back."

Ezra pulled loose, but then sat, shaking violently.

180

Terry put his hand on Ezra's arm and squeezed it. "If I just had a gun, I'd shoot those monsters dead."

A moment later, Elder John slid in through the branches. "Shhh!" he said as Ezra lunged toward him. "I played possum. Not hurt at all. That man a poor shot." He wrapped his son in his arms. "Just give them more time, so they're gone for sure."

"Oh," Terry rasped out, relief sapping his strength. "I'm awful sorry. We almost got you killed. Joshua and I escaped from the prison upriver. The gunslinger's the one who abducted me. An old enemy."

Elder John shook his head. "Never you mind. That man shot 'cause I not say Ezra here."

"They wouldn't have been searching this area if we hadn't escaped."

"Nothing's wrong with gettin' free. We know 'bout that. And we're in the good Lord's hands. The angels made the bullet miss."

Terry stared at Elder John. How could anyone believe God was good when an evil man could go wherever he wanted and shoot at whoever made him mad? There was no use voicing his thoughts, though. The faithful Christians outnumbered him three to one.

Ezra was the first to speak in a normal voice. "They're gone. Dogs don't hush up like men." He pushed his way through the leafy canopy.

Terry followed with the other two. "Reckon it's a good time for us to get that raft ride?" he asked. "Joshua and I have to get far away from here as fast as we can. And before too long, those fiends might return if they come across a boat, looking for the extra man they suspected."

"Should be safe enough for now. We'll be quick." Elder John turned to Joshua. "You go first with the plants. Second trip's harder when tired. Mister Terry's arm kin help us then."

After Ezra secured the two baskets on the still-tethered raft, he slid it into the water and plunged his pole down, bracing against the current.

Elder John motioned to Joshua. "You best come after me an' sit near the back. Mister Terry kin let us loose."

Joshua shot a concerned look at Terry as he followed Elder John onto the shifting raft.

The two freedmen studied the upstream waters for oncoming logs. Then Elder John called out, "Let 'er go!"

After untethering the raft, Terry squatted to watch the crossing. The cobbled-together raft looked far from sturdy, and the river was close to the top of the bank, right at flood stage, explaining the powerful current's strength. But they couldn't stay on the island with men like Talbot prowling the woods.

Fourteen alternating pole pushes took the raft up against the east bank. Terry puffed a relieved breath. After calculating where the raft was most likely to land on the return, he walked along the island's bank to meet it.

The men had brought back a third pole for Terry. After pushing off with the other two, he fought against the grasping current with all his strength. Making progress was as demanding as the grueling swim in the river on the previous day, but the far bank drew closer. Finally, he eyed the weed-covered ground just ahead.

All of a sudden, a partly submerged tree trunk slammed into the raft. The bundle of sticks disintegrated under Terry's feet. He sprang for the bank along with the two men.

A yard from the bank, something entwined itself around his leg. He struggled to get loose. But the demon wasn't yielding. He dove down to attack the entanglement. Instead of unwinding, the thick root held on like a bulldog's grip.

Fear roiled his stomach. He dog paddled and yanked his leg up, down, and sideways. After surviving kidnapping and prison, he couldn't die so close to shore!

A splash jarred him. Joshua disappeared under the dark water. A sharp pain struck his leg right below his knee.

Terry jerked his leg. Wonder of wonders, it came free. His breaths rasping, he scrabbled through the mire for the bank.

"Get him! Look!" Ezra yelled.

Joshua was moving downstream fast, his legs and arms thrashing.

After a dozen strokes, Terry caught up to him. He crooked his arm under Joshua's chin. But the current attacked them like a Tasmanian devil, tugging them downstream.

Joshua slipped from under Terry's wrist.

"No!" Terry thrust his body forward.

The next second, strong arms took hold of Terry. Elder John dragged him onto solid ground.

Terry struggled to stand. He couldn't lose his friend. He had to make it back to the water.

Footsteps crashing through bushes stopped him. Ezra appeared, supporting Joshua, who was shuffling forward on his own two feet.

Terry plopped down and squeezed his eyes shut to block any tears.

Joshua managed to sit under a tall water oak and leaned against the trunk. "That river was out to get us, but here we are," he breathed out

Terry scooted farther from the shore. "The river, a root, Talbot—the whole wicked world worked against us. But I got my life back, thanks to you three."

"We're ... We're a unit, a brigade." Joshua clasped his hands in a victory shake.

Ezra bent over Terry. "Got blood oozin' from a big cut on the side of your leg. If you let us take you to the farm, Widow Starkly kin help you, 'cause you bleedin'. She thinks she's a nurse. She'll let you stay till it gets a good scab."

Terry swiped his hand over the blood to stop it from running down into his boot. "I'm all right. Just got to rest a little. Don't want to bother Widow Starkly. She might not like Yanks."

"White folks round here don't care much 'bout who be Yanks or Secesh." Elder John stopped squeezing water out of his clothes and walked over to take a look at the wound. "What most farmers hate is them conscript enforcers." He squatted beside Terry. "The missus' family—now they cared 'bout secession at the start of the fight. The two boys signed up with them army volunteers, but 'bout then, the whole family took sick. Chol'ra, doctor said. Master and sons passed. After Missus got well, she freed all us slaves and called herself a *Christian pass'fist.*"

"So this pacifist will take us in because Terry's been hurt? And she's good at healing?" Joshua stood, wobbled, and leaned his shoulder against the trunk.

"She's good." Elder John puffed up like a bullfrog. "Long time ago, my ma taught the missus which plants go with what ailments. Missus takes the whole credit for plant smartness now, but Ma don't care. She's smilin' on them golden streets." Elder John's smile disappeared into a frown. "This river water's bad, and your cut's no small thing. If you want to come with us, I got a shirt with my mule. It'll stop the bleedin' if yarrow don't." He pointed behind him toward a clump of pines.

Terry stood and took a few steps to see better. Two mules were barely visible beyond the trees, the tree trunks growing so close together they were like a fence. He sighed. No use being stupid and losing his leg or life. "Guess I better take you up on such a good offer. That all right with you, Joshua?"

"Sure. I'm in no hurry except to get far away from this river and those hunters. You have to get help, and maybe the widow has quinine in her stockpile besides." Joshua turned to Elder John, who had also risen. "Is the farm far?"

"Three hours, dependin' on the mules' speed. Sometimes they laze along. Sometimes they're longin' for the stable." He jerked his head toward Ezra. "So we move now and get these men hid with the mules."

Terry glanced back at the river. "I'm sorry about your raft. We'll help make a new one if you show us how."

Ezra shook his head. "We'll make a new raft here by the river. They're heavy. But the missus, she'll find you plenty o' work. 'Earn your keep' she tells her guests—those that survive an' up to walkin'.'"

When they came to the mules, Elder John reached into the basket of yarrow plants, stripped off some leaves, and handed them to Terry. "First off, you chew this right good. Then take the wad and paste it on your cut. That bleedin' quits faster than you kin kill a fly. We'll sit a short spell. Let the medicine work. Those hunters can't see us here, even they come back."

Terry sat with the others and examined the feathery leaves. At least the rain had washed off almost all the dirt. But could he actually cram the leaves into his mouth? How much did Elder John really know?

"Have you ever used chewed-up yarrow leaves yourself?" Joshua asked the elder, obviously for Terry's benefit.

"Oh yes, Mister Joshua. Works like magic. Should've seen the missus' eyes that first time she used them."

"And you're sure they aren't poison hemlock?" Terry added. "You said they were hard to distinguish."

Elder John frowned. "I'm as sure as my ma's passed through them pearly gates."

Terry started chewing. Coming from himself, the pearly gates might be a joke, but not from Elder John. He ran his tongue over his teeth. The taste was strong and a little bitter, but not too bad.

"That be 'bout right." Elder John slid up Terry's wet-and-torn woolen trousers, once so smart looking on the steamers. "Now, just set the wad o'er your cut. Then push the skin together. Hold it for a bit."

After three or four minutes, Terry took his hand away ... and stared. The wound had puffed together and only a few droplets of blood trickled out.

"It *is* like magic." He eyed the old shirt in Elder John's hands. "Maybe I don't need a bandage."

"Oh, best use it, suh. The path be downright narrow. Pines and bushes rub an' poke. When you get to the farm, the missus gonna take off that bandage and fuss 'bout the muddy river. She'll mash yarrow root with spirits. The whiskey makes folks holler. My ma said the hollerin' scares away the devil. Maybe the missus also takes a stitch or two."

Elder John made quick work of bandaging the wound, then picked up a tin bucket, hidden under a bush. He turned to Joshua. "You want to sit a spell longer with Mister Terry? Or come with Ezra and me to run our limb line? It's 'tween the bank and a sandbar up a way. We'll find out if we caught the missus some fish."

"I'll rest and keep the invalid company." Joshua managed a thin smile.

While Terry was still debating with Joshua over the least dangerous route to take out of the Confederate territory— northwest to hopefully meet Sherman's Union troops or east to less patrolled Alabama—the two men returned grinning.

"Mighty good catch," Ezra boasted, showing Joshua, then

Terry, the bucket's contents of three carp, two crappie, and two small catfish. "We won't clean them here. Missus against usin' river water."

"Can't be too careful," Terry agreed. "I can almost smell disease in the rotting weeds."

Ezra attached the bucket to the saddle of one of the mules. "This mule's for Mister Joshua."

"I'm not wounded. I can walk." Joshua pushed himself up.

"Hope you not mind my sayin', but you look puny." After securing one of the baskets behind the saddle, Ezra gestured for Joshua to mount. "We're fine to walk. Strong 'cause of fieldwork."

Knowing his own objections would be even more futile, Terry mounted the other mule as Elder John fastened the second basket behind him.

The mules plodded fairly quickly along the narrow forest path, covered in thick pine needles. The constant motion jarred Terry's leg no matter how he positioned it against the creaking saddle, but, at least, he and Joshua were with kind men, free from the prison, off the island, and headed away from the river and Talbot. There'd be a fire to dry out their clothes at the farm, surely some food, and treatment for his wound. He tried to set aside worries about the widow's frame of mind—whether she'd welcome Northerners or spring a trap. He'd rather die than go back to prison.

The off-and-on drizzle was letting up. With enough patience, maybe they'd get a few clear days despite April being a wet month in the South. Whenever danger forced travel off the road, sunny days would make keeping the direction easier. So he needed patience. Always patience. And more patience.

But how much patience did Tom have? Or Sara? Or Mr. Pendleton? Maybe they had resumed their journey and were simply *praying* for him to make it home someday.

Did Tom understand how hard he'd worked to rescue *him* from the island? Now that Tom was with Sara, did he still care for his family ... if he ever really had?

CHAPTER 22

The seven-or-eight miles through the pine thicket nearly wiped out what remained of Terry's stamina, but at last the jostling and poking came to an end. Their guides led him and Joshua over a little creek, spanned by rough planks, then up an incline, its red clay supporting sedge grass.

At the top of the rise, Elder John called a stop in a stand of scrubby oaks. He gave three owl-like hoots of the great horned owl, then received an answering one.

"No slave catchers prowlin'," Ezra explained. "Missus can't help us this far from the Big House."

Terry shifted in his saddle and studied the surroundings. Beyond the oak grove, a gate opened into a field of corn, the shoots already three feet high. Except for the roofs of the distant house and barn, he couldn't see the rest of the farm. Bushwhackers could be lurking anywhere. But hopefully the lookout would have thought they were a menace too.

A young boy in overalls, with no shirt, ran from between two of the corn rows and skidded to a halt.

"My grandson." Elder John motioned the boy forward. "After his chores, the missus lets him run free."

The boy dropped his eyes and ambled forward.

"You run to the Big House and tell the missus we're bringin' her yarrow, goosefoot, burdock, an' fish. After that, say we're also carrying a wounded man an' his friend from the river. Ask if she wants to help them. The unhurt man, he be happy to work. If she asks questions, just say you're sorry but that's all you know 'cause your grandpap said to hurry quick. You got that?"

"Yes, suh." He glanced at Ezra.

"Then away with you." Ezra gave the boy—most likely his son—a swat on his rear, and he took off.

As soon as they'd crossed the cornfield and a garden, the boy was back. "Missus says for the hurt man an' his friend to come to the house for now." He gestured toward the farmhouse.

A lady in a dark green gown stood on the front porch, her hand shielding her eyes. Next to her, a yellow cloth fluttered on a pole attached to the porch railing. Terry raised his arm to doff his hat, but stopped. He'd lost the hat weeks earlier. He turned to thank the two men. However, they were already guiding the mules toward the stable.

While limping toward the large clapboard house with Joshua, Terry checked for signs of visitors in the yard. "No tethered horses. No restless hounds—at least not in sight," he reported.

"Just praying we get to stay." Joshua sounded like he was close to a collapse.

Widow Starkly asked their names, then ran her pale blue eyes over them, pausing on Terry's bandaged leg. "You men have a welcome here." She pointed to the yellow flag. "I stand by that neutrality. *All* God's children who need doctoring find an open door at my house. Come this way." She led them through a narrow hall to a small sitting room.

After taking two worn coverlets off a shelf by the door, the widow spread one of them over a Chippendale chair, which must have been brought from the East. "Mr. Reynolds, please have a seat there." She motioned toward the chair. "Mr. Ballard, you'll be lying on the sofa so I can take a look at your wound. Did Elder John already treat it with yarrow?"

"Yes, ma'am." After the widow spread the other coverlet, Terry lay so a pillow propped up his head. "The leaves stopped almost all the bleeding, but the wound is kindah deep." He'd slowed his words to a drawl. "Elder John worried a lot because mah skin tore open in the *very* filthy river water." The injury might not look like it needed much care, but their temporary haven was a gem they couldn't lose. Even a day or two in a house where the world appeared sane would be an incalculable respite.

The lady pursed her lips. "You don't need to hide your accent from me. This is a healing house for anyone, no matter their loyalties. However, I don't want to learn where either of you are from or how you got here. Sometimes our Southern soldiers come looking for conscripts or troop stragglers. If they should pry too much, I'd hate to have to lie about whether or not Yanks were on my property."

"Thank you for your kindness, ma'am," Joshua said from across the room.

The widow faced Joshua, who struggled to his feet. "Young man, you don't look too well yourself, but I'll deal with your ailments later. Would you go tell my servant Maybell in the kitchen to bring my jar of yarrow potion, clean bandages, my needle, thread, and two sheets."

When Joshua returned with the young Black woman right behind him, the widow folded one sheet in half and placed it under Terry's legs. Then she unwrapped the bloody bandage, told the servant to hold the sides of the wound slightly apart, and poured the potion into the open sore.

The fiery mixture roared through his wound. Terry gritted

his teeth against the curses and squeezed his eyes shut. When he opened them, his would-be doctor smiled at him. "You bore that well. If you're not a soldier, I believe you could be—a courageous one at that. But I'm a pacifist now, so I hope you'll walk in peace."

"That's powerful strong medicine, ma'am. Came close to hollering. As for being a soldier, I don't aim to fight in the war if I can help it."

"My, then you're a pacifist, too?"

"Not really. I have an enemy I'd shoot on sight if I got a chance. But while all this trouble between the states brewed, I toiled on sail ships halfway 'round the world. I learned the hard way not to make stupid decisions, like signing on as a sailor. I'm doing all I can to get back to my family." He pushed away the ache that always accompanied thoughts of home.

She pushed a loose strand of her brown hair into her bun. "Then I hope you never see that enemy of yours. Now, you'll need to grit your teeth again. I'm going to take three or four stitches and then wrap your wound."

Terry clenched his mouth. The needle's pricks were painful, but nothing compared to the alcoholic potion's torture. He closed his eyes and forced his muscles to relax while the widow wrapped his leg.

After covering him with the extra sheet, the lady stood, her expression like that of a true doctor, proud of her work. "Supper and a good night's sleep should speed your recovery. You can try changing your bandage yourself in the morning, but tell me if your leg has any red streaks." She indicated the pile of bandages on the nearby desk, then turned to Joshua. "Have you had a bout of swamp fever?"

"Yes, ma'am." He started to stand, but she motioned for him to stay seated. "Every time I think I'm over it for good, it pokes its ugly head back up."

She put her palm on Joshua's forehead. "Hmm. Feels normal. Maybe you're not sick at the present, but getting as worn down as you appear begs for trouble. I'll get you the quinine powder I have squirreled away. Maybell will bring you and our invalid supper trays, and we'll give you a pallet in here for tonight. If you're better tomorrow, you can help hoe the garden and cornfield with my hired folks—no enslaved or shiftless folk on this farm. But I want you to rest at least three hours in the afternoon, every afternoon you're here."

"I'll be glad to help anyway I can." Joshua smiled up at her.

"Oh, you'll both earn your keep. I have a special job for Mr. Ballard after he can hobble around, but he'll need to stay off that leg and in the house for a couple of days." Her eyes twinkled as she picked up her potion, needle, and thread from the desk.

Before Terry lost his effort to stay awake, the last thought he had was that the lady looked ten years younger when she was enjoying herself.

At a rooster's crow, Terry woke and glanced around the room through the mosquito net. He'd lounged on the sofa for two full days, making baskets out of palmetto leaves for Widow Starkly to sell to peddlers who frequented her home. But the widow had said he and Joshua were to move to the barn this day since his wound was healing nicely. They would have quick access to the hayloft if unwanted company was spotted on the road. The barn would also be convenient for Terry's task. The widow's eyes had twinkled again.

Joshua came through the door, pointing at him. "Up and at 'em, lazy bones. Breakfast's on the table. More ham and molasses, with corn pone today. The widow's already eaten, but she's waiting to give you items for your assignment."

"Do you know what it is?"

"No, but she's mighty tickled about it."

Terry rinsed his face and sponged off his body with the washbasin's contents, changed his bandage, and threw on the clothes the lady had provided from her son's farm life. In less than fifteen minutes, he made it to the dining room.

"Good morning, Mr. Ballard." The widow eyed his clothes. "You're looking much more presentable than when you arrived. Does your leg pain you any? Any red streak?"

"No, ma'am. You knew exactly what to do for it. You probably saved my leg … maybe my life."

She chuckled. "You needn't flatter me, son. But you'll be able to reciprocate by helping one of my people for a few days. Have you had any experience with teaching?"

"Yes, but only if being an assistant teacher in Japan for several weeks counts." Did he have a built-in affinity for teaching that others saw, but he didn't?

"Ezra—you remember he helped lead you here—has a son named Samuel, who wants to learn to read so bad, I believe he'd run away if he thought he could get an education that way. Of course, he wouldn't get far before he'd be snatched up and taken into slavery. Now, most of my ailing guests would be horrified if asked to teach a Black child, but I sense you're different."

"I remember seeing Samuel when I first got here. I'm willing to try."

"He's a bright boy. You'll find that out right away. I've gathered materials for you." She picked up a small box from the side-board. "Here's chalk, two slates, paper, ink, and scissors. Let me know if you need anything else. You can send Maybell to my room."

"Yes, ma'am, I'll do that." Terry looked under the loose papers. Instead of the hoped-for teacher's guide, the bottom of the box met his eyes.

She swept up her skirts to leave, then paused. "I do hope Samuel can master simple words while you're here, enough to read a few sentences. You can't imagine how happy that would make his grandparents. They keep talking about the joy they'll have when he can read to them from the Bible. You know, when that happens, I think I'll be as happy as his family. Of course, I do read the holy book to my people on the Sabbath."

She swept up her skirts again, but then paused once more. "Oh, another thing. The lessons will take place in a part of the barn that lends itself to a quick removal of the lessons' *evidence*. I assume you know it's illegal to teach people of color to read and write."

"Uh, I didn't know. But it doesn't matter. There's already a noose hovering over me if I take one false step."

"Then I can rest assured that you will keep a sharp eye out." She swept up her skirts and actually left the room.

After their hostess' steps faded along the hallway, Terry looked at Joshua, who had lit into the food as though it were his last meal on earth. "Gosh, wonder why she isn't teaching Samuel herself. Reckon she's scared of getting caught? Thinks she has more to lose than someone like me? Or maybe thinks it's below her—the mistress of the place?" He kept his voice low, so Maybell couldn't overhear.

"I've no idea. She's a bona fide Southerner, but not a run-of-the-mill one." He took a huge bite and gulped some of the fake coffee.

"You're putting away that corn pone in record time."

"Got to get out to the garden. Don't want Elder John to show me up. You happy with your assignment?"

"I suspect pulling off this job will be an uphill battle, littered with booby traps. How much can I teach the boy in two or three days? But I'll do what I can and try not to disappoint Elder John and Ezra too much."

"That's how I feel with the gardening too." Joshua stood to take his plate to the kitchen. "We really owe those two men."

When Joshua left for the garden, Terry gathered his materials and headed across the yard, moving fairly quickly in spite of the bandage. After his eyes adjusted to the barn's dim light, he found Samuel standing just inside a dusky side room.

"I know my ABC's," Samuel announced. "The missus taught me before she got in big trouble."

"She got in trouble?" Terry headed across the room for the bench on the far side of the cracked table, which not only had a tin lantern and a thick Bible on it, but—surprisingly—a McGuffey reader.

"For teachin' me, my pa, and the other workers." At Terry's signal, the boy sat on the bench across from him. "Sheriff don't care we free. He near took the missus to jail, but she swore on the Holy Bible she not teach us anymore, 'cept the Bible on Sundays. She let me keep the books here, though."

"That explains a lot."

"My grandpap wants me to read him the Holy Bible, so I got to listen good to you."

"A wise thing to do, Samuel."

"Folks here call me Sam."

"All right, Sam."

During most of the morning, Terry had Sam copy each alphabet letter on separate squares of paper while the boy repeated its sound and named words beginning with the sound. Once that was done, Terry wrote one of Sam's words for each letter on the back of its square, and added rough sketches for most

196

of the objects, accompanied by Sam's muffled chortles. By the time Joshua came by the barn to tell Terry to join the workers for lunch, Sam had associated the letters with the beginning sounds of *apple, bad, cat, dog, egg, fat, God, hat, ink, jump, kitten, lick, mat, no, open, pat, quick, rat, sit, top, under, vat, water,* and *yellow.*

While Terry gathered their papers into a stack, Sam picked up the Bible and held it out. "Please, Teacher, show me where it says *God.*" Apparently, Joshua's message about lunch hadn't penetrated the boy's mind.

"Come on." Terry stood. "We can't be late for lunch. There might not be any food left. Anyway, before you start looking in the Holy Bible, you have to learn how letters fit together to make words."

Sam's mouth drooped. "Do we have to stop?" He looked as if he'd heard the world was coming to an end.

"My, you're a fine student," Joshua said from the doorway. "Aren't you eager to show your grandfather how much you've learned?"

Sam jumped up and led the way to the log cabin closest to the kitchen. He ate just a few bites before he started entertaining the eleven workers with his recitation of the alphabet, its sounds, and the associated words. When he finished, the ones next to him slapped him on the back, several agreed he was as smart as a whip, and all of them predicted he'd be reading in no time.

Terry sighed. They had a long way to go.

By supper, and thus quitting time, the boy had learned to fit the sounds together for the easiest words. He had even written his first sentence, *The fat cat ate the bad rat*, with Terry supplying *ate* and *the.* Sam was practically dancing when he read his sentence aloud at the supper table for his audience, all of whom had paused eating in order to catch each word and then insisted he read it three more times.

Terry came close to dancing himself.

As soon as it was dark, Terry readied himself for his new bed—a blanket spread on the other side of the loft from Joshua's. He'd been sitting most of the day, but was as tired as if he'd run one of the famous Greek races. However, as he slipped under the mosquito net and reviewed the day, it wasn't weariness that held his attention. It was something he hadn't sensed since his capture—a hint of happiness.

CHAPTER 23

By midmorning of the next day, Terry had helped Sam locate the word *God* in the Bible's first sentence, and the boy had found seven of the previous day's words in the McGuffey reader by himself. He was working hard to use combinations, such as *ink* to make *sink, pink, wink,* and even *stink.*

In the midst of Sam's hunt for more words in the reader, two hoots of the great-horned owl sounded from outside.

Sam jumped up. "Teacher, hide!"

After grabbing the papers, slates, scissors, and chalk, Terry ran for the loft. "Take care of the rest, Sam!" he called over his shoulder. He pulled the rope ladder up behind him and crawled beneath the hay.

Seconds later, men burst into the barn. Terry didn't dare move to see how many.

Boots scraped across the barn floor. "What's that you got in your hand there, boy?" Talbot's ugly voice with its threatening question struck Terry like a balled fist. If only he had a weapon! The pitchfork near the ladder wouldn't work against a gun.

"Ain't hardly nothin', suh.

Terry's stomach turned. Not the reader, surely!

"Lookee here. We've a lawbreaker right on the widow's farm." Talbot's voice was close to gleeful.

"Oh, no you don't," another voice growled just as the boy yelped. "You ain't goin' nowhere!"

"Lemme go! I ain't done nothin'!" Sam's terror came through each word.

"Where we gonna string him up, George?" Talbot's voice again. "The widow needs to see what happens when she breaks the law."

Terry inched to the loft's edge. Talbot and the man called George, who held onto Sam, were ten feet from the loft. If either one turned his back, he'd jump him from behind, grab the man's gun, and shoot Talbot dead first. Then he'd handle the other man anyway he could.

The two turned toward the barn door, yanking Sam with them.

Terry hesitated. He'd end up getting shot himself. But … But what of it? He couldn't let them hang Sam! He drew up, ready to pounce on Talbot's exposed back.

A shot rang out.

"Hands in the air!" It was the widow!

Terry dropped down on the loft's straw, chilled from sweat.

"Now, now, ma'am. You don't want to shoot someone for upholdin' the law." Talbot's voice had gone syrupy sweet. "That'd be murder, and you'd get strung up yourself. You're a pacifist, remember?"

"I protect my chickens from foxes, and my people from villains. That boy can't read. He likes the pictures. Samuel, you go find your pa. Now!"

"He got my ear, Missus."

"Let him go!"

When the boy's call to his pa came from outside the barn, Terry released the breath he'd held.

"Now, if you two men have come to your senses, you can come out slowly." Fierceness underlay the widow's controlled voice. "I'm sure you have better things to do than steal from a widow. I reckon you're looking for Yanks, not little boys."

"All right, ma'am, but I'll just keep this reader so nobody else misunderstands. And the ignorant slaves don't need the Bible in there either."

Terry fisted his hands. The idiots! The boy was ten times smarter than either of them. What he wouldn't give to have shot Talbot and pounded the other one to smithereens.

"You can take the picture book, but you *cannot* take the Holy Bible," the widow declared. "My workers are Christians. They can't read the Almighty's Word, but they honor it."

"Best not fool with no holy book, Talbot," the partner warned.

"It'd be too bad if the sheriff caught that boy readin' sometime, now wouldn't it, Widow Starkly?" Talbot's voice came from right outside the barn door. "The lawman might ask you and your Black *Christians* embarrassing questions. Answers from someone not careful enough could bring about a jail sentence and the loss of property as well as more hangings than just the no-account whelp's."

"I know the law, and I've kept it." The widow's icy voice could have frozen lava. "And now, you may wish to be on your way so you can capture those Yankees you're after … unless you and your partner wish to stay for sassafras tea in my parlor. I'm out of coffee. Seems the invaders not only want our land, but everything else as well."

"We'll forego the tea, ma'am, and be on our way." One of the men slammed the barn door shut.

The welcome hoofbeats came at last. Terry waited a few minutes longer, then left the barn, nodded to the widow, and looked around. Joshua was approaching from the cornfield with Sam, Ezra, and Elder John.

The widow glanced from Joshua to Terry. "Those scoundrels were after you two, weren't they?"

Terry forced himself to stop thinking about killing Talbot in order to answer the lady. "Yes, and I'm sorry. We were wrong to bring you danger."

The widow dismissed his words with a wave of her hand. "That comes with opening my doors to everyone who needs my help. Evil men don't dictate what I do. But if one of them is that enemy you mentioned earlier, I see why you would kill him if you had a chance. Not that I'd necessarily approve except to save a life."

"I was about to jump the one named Talbot from behind when you fired that shot. At least, that was my intent." He nodded at her weapon, now pointing downward. "Toting a gun wasn't exactly how I featured Southern ladies acting, but you probably saved my life again as well as Sam's. Still, it pains me the snake Talbot will see another daybreak." He sucked in a breath, fighting to keep his rage in check.

The widow clucked her tongue. "Even though the man is wicked, you have to lay aside that hatred. Otherwise, it'll eat your innards, and you'll end up a shell. I've seen it happen."

"Don't reckon I can do that, ma'am. But I appreciate the advice and all you've done—taking in Joshua and me, complete strangers. Speaking of that, it looks like it's high time for us to move on, not cause you any more trouble."

"The trouble's not your fault. I advise one more day for your leg to heal before you take off. You could continue the lessons, and Mr. Reynolds could supply more of his good field work." She nodded at Joshua, who had walked up closer.

Terry turned his attention to Joshua. "Our kind hostess advises us to stay one more day. Is that all right with you?" He hoped it was. He'd like to help Sam deal with the day's unthinkable horror.

"Of course, it's all right." Joshua rubbed his hands together, getting off dirt.

"Then, it's settled." The widow set her gun on a barrel, then beckoned to Sam, standing next to his father. "Come here, Samuel."

The boy dragged his feet forward as though facing a firing squad.

The widow put her finger under Sam's chin to raise his head. "I have good news for you. I have the McGuffey second reader."

The boy's eyes lit up.

"If you study hard the rest of today and all tomorrow, you'll be ready to tackle that book on your own. We're not going to let bad men keep you from reading. God gave you a mind, and he wants you to use it."

"Yes, Missus." Sam mustered a smile. "I'll work right hard. Someday soon, I'm goin' to read more o' that good book."

"That's a fine goal, Sam," Joshua put in. "You keep at it." He offered a slight bow to the widow before heading back to the cornfield.

"Then if you'll excuse us also"—Terry paused until the widow nodded her assent—"Sam and I will tackle the lessons. I can reconstruct much of the first reader's material." He put his hand on Sam's shoulder. "Come on. Time's a-wasting."

Terry led Sam into their not-so-secret classroom. "Now, let's see you write another sentence," he instructed, as though nothing traumatic had happened.

"Teacher, suh, can I ask you somethin' first?"

"Sure. Go ahead." Who wouldn't have a ton of questions after almost being hanged? The boy probably wanted to know if learning to read was worth the danger.

"Did Almighty God really give me my mind?"

Terry blinked. That was the last question he'd expected. And one he was the least prepared to answer. But where'd the boy get a mind if it wasn't from God? It took a mind to give the first people a mind, didn't it? Animals and people had minds that couldn't have sprouted from rocks and plants and dirt.

"You don' think so?" Sam was tearing up again.

"Oh, Sam! God gave you a mind just as much as he gave me or any White man a mind. Don't you doubt that for a minute."

The boy jerked up straight and wiped his eyes. "I'm glad you talked like that. That be from your heart, suh."

"Then we'd better *use* our minds, hadn't we? I'll get our materials from the loft."

"Missus gon' be proud o' me. Grandpap too." Sam firmed his jaw. "An' I aim to make Almighty God proud too."

Terry clambered up the ladder. They needed to leave theology alone and concentrate on reading. These deep questions would have to be confronted later, if at all.

After managing to set aside the issue of God-and-Sam's-mind for the rest of the day, Terry couldn't get rid of the idea as he lay on his straw bed that night, listening to Joshua's snores and a late shower's patter on the roof above him. He'd never considered a question like Sam's before, any more than he'd asked himself why caterpillars became butterflies or birds could fly. Tom was the one who liked nature's puzzles. How strange that the answer he gave Sam had popped into his mind, as logical as all get out. How downright amazing that he'd credited God despite not knowing whether there even was a god. And instead of his conclusion repulsing him, it offered a kind of hope. If God really did exist, then he wasn't as alone in the world as he'd thought.

But then, Talbot had a mind too. An evil mind. The tentative ray of light was swallowed up in a haze of dark, vibrating hate.

CHAPTER 24

Sara stepped through the back gate of the farm's farthest field without a whisper of sound. Tom followed with a barely noticeable crunch. Robert, coming last, sounded like a stampede of wild horses.

"Shh. If you want to surprise a turkey," Sara whispered, "you need to be quieter." To carry out the stealth necessary for the hunt, she'd donned her old sailor clothes, relieved that Agatha had merely scanned her outfit without commenting. Any kind of long gown would have swished and made it impossible to see the ground's hidden noisemakers.

The crescent moon hung low in the sky, but provided enough pale light to safely cross the shallow creek, stepping from one rock to the next. A red-winged blackbird in an oak on the far bank greeted them with a *conk-la-reee*. The woods beyond stayed quiet, as though conserving energy for the upcoming day.

The dawn's light was brightening the trees' hazy silhouettes when Sara crouched with Tom and Robert next to the low brush a hundred yards or so beyond the creek. She breathed in the fresh scent of thriving plants, then caught a glimpse of a pink-flowering azalea bush nestled in grasses beyond a clump of pines. How wonderful to be at one with nature again.

Tom took out the whistle Mr. Evans had loaned them. She braced for the intrusion on the peace. No matter how much she'd like to prolong the quiet, Robert, holding his bow with his arrow notched into place, was already wiggling. She readied her bow, too, since she was to be the backup if Robert missed the target.

Tom blew his crow call twice. A turkey gobbled in reply, not too far away. Tom beamed at Robert and her, then beat his hat against his leg in imitation of a hen's flapping wings.

When he stilled, Sara put her hand on Robert's jiggling arm. A big tom waddled their way, and all three of them gulped air at the same time.

The bird drew closer and closer, gobbling its anticipation of a romantic tryst. At ten yards, Tom gave Robert the go ahead to shoot.

The arrow missed by a couple of inches.

Sara let her arrow fly, compensating for the startled turkey's jerk. It let out a squawk, tried to fly, and fell over.

Robert looked ready to cry.

Tom stood and put his hand on the boy's shoulder. "That was a great shot, Robert! Really terrific. I mean, almost nobody does as well as you did on their first shot in their very first hunt. Remarkable!"

A smile transformed Robert's face.

Tom's unexpected tenderness touched Sara to her toes. Her father and brother, as much as she admired them, would have scolded the boy for missing.

After Tom cut off the turkey's head and bagged its body, he rejoined Sara. "We can go a little farther and see if we can attract another romantic fool if that's good with you."

"Yes, I'm sure Agatha would appreciate ..." A breaking branch caught her attention.

A dark-skinned man jumped from a tree and zigzagged away.

"Stop!" Tom shouted.

The fellow stopped, looked back at Tom, then lit out again.

Sara whipped an arrow from her quiver and aimed her shot above the fellow's head. It thwacked into a tree trunk in front of him. She readied a second one.

He halted, raised his hands, and slowly turned to face them.

"I missed on purpose," Sarah called, pitying the man's frightened look.

"We're your friends." Tom held up the whistle. "Just been hunting turkeys."

"Oh ho!" Robert stepped forward as though lord of a manor. "Bet you're the thief who took two of my piglets."

"N-no! I ain't no thief!" He slid his eyes from Robert to Sara's bow. Visibly shaking, he fell to his knees and tented his hands above his head as if in prayer.

"I'm not going to hurt you." Sara returned the arrow to her quiver. "We want to help you if you're a maroon, even if you have been surviving off the Evans' farm. Are any slave catchers close by?"

"I don' know, miss." His eyes flicked at the trees around him and back to Sara, as though still planning his escape.

Tom scanned the woods too. "It'd be safer to talk at the farm, or maybe in the oak grove till we know a little more." He extended his open palm. "Do you want our help? Or do you want to carry on alone?" He dropped his hand. "We'll let you go if you promise not to take anything more from the farm. We'll even give you this turkey. But I found out recently how hostile the marshland, wildlife, and scouts are, let alone highwaymen and slave hunters."

The runaway stood, looked around again, then said, "I take your help, suh."

As they tramped back to the oak grove, Sara paused partway and surveyed the woods behind them for trackers. The shadows didn't reveal anyone, but then, she hadn't noticed the slave until the branch cracked. She shivered and caught up with the other three, who waited for her.

Rays of sunlight penetrated the grove. Sara knelt on the fallen leaves beside Tom and Robert, then sat back on her heels, relieved to be closer to the farm. The runaway sat, too, in response to Tom's order to sit with them so they could talk more easily.

"Are you from a place around here?" Tom picked a fresh grass blade and sucked on it. Robert copied him.

"I come from the Steadman plantation, suh."

Sara stared at the fellow. "Lucille Steadman's?"

"Yes, miss."

"Then we can urge her to allow you to return to the plantation without penalizing you, and to make changes that will give you a more satisfactory life. She struck me as a kind person."

"Sometimes she kind, ma'am. But she gon' have me beaten forty licks, put in irons, and chained to a pole all day and night for a week."

"You must be mistaken! The lady I met would not be so cruel."

"She not do it herself. But I ran three times already. She told me what gon' happen if I run again. She gon' have her driver 'tend to me.' Exactly like I'm telling you. And she's meanin' it. I know."

Sara's chest heaved as she expelled a breath. The lady was a wolf in sheep's clothing—soft and sweet on the outside, ferocious on the inside.

Tom rubbed his temples. "This makes everything a lot harder to manage. We'll have to see what Thad says."

Robert, wide-eyed, piped up, "You can stay in our woods if my ma and pa won't take you in because Miz Steadman's our neighbor. I'll bring you part of our breakfast every morning, and we'll keep you a secret."

The slave's brow furrowed. His dark eyes studied the boy.

"We already agreed the woods are too full of danger, Robert." Sara glanced back at the thick woods beyond the creek, hair rising on the back of her neck. "But that was a kind offer."

Robert yanked up another blade of grass. "We have to help him."

Tom faced the man. "What's your name?"

"Malachi, suh."

"Well, Malachi, there's a shack at the back of the Evans' vegetable acreage. I've never seen anyone visit it. You can be safe waiting there until we talk to Robert's parents. I feel sure they'll come up with a good plan. They'd never turn you over to be tortured."

"That shack's where the hired men make turpentine when my pa gets enough pine sap. It'll be empty, all right." Robert's take-charge attitude would have been amusing any other time. "But my pa's helping mend the Parkers' fences. He told Ma he wouldn't be home till late in the day, and Marylou went with him to see silly Anna May Parker. Ma's maybe at her circle's quiltin' bee, but she'll come home to see about the noon meal since it's Annie's day off."

"I'll be waitin' in that shack," Malachi mumbled.

"Since Mr. Evans isn't home, you'll probably need to wait all day." Tom shifted into a squat and picked up the bagged turkey. "I'll let you know what he says."

"I'll be prayin'."

After they pointed Malachi toward the shack, Sara accompanied Tom and Robert to the back stoop, then headed for Mr. Pendleton's room. He'd want to know about the runaway and the threatened torture. But could he or anyone suggest a way to confront the evil without jeopardizing the Evanses' work with the underground railroad? Everything was so complicated, so awful.

She stopped at the top of the stairs to catch her breath while one thought chased another. Only two hours earlier, she'd relished her harmony with nature. Yet the woods' beauty had concealed not only a hunted man, but possibly his wicked hunters too. How little she knew, like Buson's haiku implied that she'd learned as a girl. *Asa-giri y; e ni kaku yume-no; hito-dōri* echoed in her mind.

> *In the morning mist*
> *as if in a painted dream*
> *men go on their way.*

A simple idea: ordinary people, unaware of their dream-like appearance in the fog. Yet her philosophical mother had claimed the poet hinted that life itself could be an illusion, as a painted dream would be. Sara still couldn't wrap her mind around the possibility that everything she knew wasn't as it appeared.

A stab of homesickness made Sara's eyes water. What would her dear mother think if she could see her daughter in America? If she observed her archery showmanship? Her jiu-jitsu skills? Her Westerners' clothes and dealings with slaves? Those waltz *gyrations* she'd carried out in Tom's arms? Sara closed her eyes, imagining her mother's shocked face.

"Aah," she breathed out the next minute. How could she have overlooked the most important truth about the poem—at least, for her? And it wasn't that life was an illusion. The people in the mist were unaware of the *poet* who actually did observe their situation. And the world had a far greater Observer—an Observer who wouldn't scold her for investigating a new way of life and who could intervene in the fog.

"Heavenly Father," she whispered. "Please help! Show us and the Evanses what to do."

As Sara expected, when she told Agatha about Malachi, the lady couldn't think of any way to proceed, other than for him to continue to hide. The two men and Robert joined them in considering various solutions as they ate their lunch of pinto beans, seasoned with ham drippings, accompanied by fried okra, dried apples, and rice pudding.

"Maybe we could say we saw men with tied-up slaves while we were hunting turkeys in the woods, and we helped Malachi escape," Sara suggested.

"But," Mr. Pendleton responded, "the men would have been armed and tough. Such a rescue, presumably using only bows and arrows, would be hard to believe. In addition, the slave hunters' possession of Malachi implies he had left the plantation's safety."

"How about producing the turkey and claiming that Malachi had been hunting to atone for his recent faults and got lost in the woods?" Tom proposed.

Agatha shook her head. "A slave wouldn't dare go hunting without permission."

"Doesn't it look like the only solution, then, is to send Malachi on to Port Hudson and pretend ignorance if ever questioned? Seems to me a little deceit would be justified." Tom voiced what Sara had silently concluded.

"Oh, Lucille has been such a kind neighbor to me," Agatha lamented, "overlooking our difference in prominence. Someday she will face God's judgment and be mortified about her mistreatment of her plantation's people. How I wish we could help her take steps toward the path of righteousness—for her to forgive Malachi, even up to the seventy-times-seven standard, and then allow him to work toward his sought-after freedom."

"I hope Miz Steadman doesn't come here looking for

Malachi before she takes those steps," Robert said between bites of his pudding.

"Yes, indeed." Mr. Pendleton glanced out the window and sighed.

Agatha rose. "It seems we'll need my husband's guidance." She picked up the tray for the dishes.

Sara helped her hostess clear the table, freeing Tom to finish dressing the turkey and Mr. Pendleton to rest in his room. She picked up a towel to dry the dishes when the sound of running feet made her pause.

Robert dashed into the kitchen. "Ma, Miz Steadman's carriage turned into our road!"

Sara's heart lurched. The wolf herself! And they had no plan.

Tom swept up the plucked and washed turkey and pivoted toward Agatha. "I'll get this bird started in the smokehouse, then change into something decent if you'd like me to help entertain the lady."

"Yes, yes, Tom. Do join us." The lunch plates rattled as Agatha set them aside. "There's strength in numbers. But Robert, you need to tend to your studies."

"I'll be quiet, Ma. Could I just stay and listen? Please."

"No, and I don't have time to repeat myself."

Sara wordlessly agreed.

"If I mind really well, could I go turkey hunting with Miss Ogawa and Mr. Ballard again this week? As a reward?"

Agatha rolled her eyes. "We'll see. Now be gone!"

Sara smoothed her hair and removed her apron, thankful she'd changed into one of her nicer gowns. Truth be told, she'd chosen the green one because Tom liked it, but it didn't hurt to look her best for the coming skirmish. "I'll get the tea things together," she offered as Agatha was rushing into the breezeway, her gown and cap askew.

"Add the macaroons in the pantry," the lady called back.

Sara brought the tray into the parlor at the same time Agatha, who had managed to change into a flouncy yellow gown, conducted their guest into the room. As Sara set the tray on the coffee table, Lucille swiveled toward her. "Oh, I hate to interrupt your day and make a visit under such trying circumstances." She straightened her ruffled skirt and took Sara's hands in her gloved ones.

Sara squeezed Lucille's hands before withdrawing hers. "I'm very glad we can meet again, but sorry to hear it is because of some distress." Had she conveyed a welcome without any hint of her censure?

Lucille seated herself in one of the armchairs, and Sara and Agatha set about serving the tea and the precious macaroons, saved for the most special occasions. Then Agatha sat on the divan next to Sara and leaned forward. "Do tell us your trouble if you think we can be of help. We ladies need to support each other during these difficult times."

"Oh yes. These times are terribly trying." Lucille looked upward as though appealing to the heavens. "It's especially hard being bereft of my family, and now one of my slaves has run away for the fourth time. I threatened the fool within an inch of his life if he left again, and now I'll have to keep my word once the trackers find him. Our driver tends to go somewhat overboard with the whip and manacles, so I wish the boy had made an effort to maintain an ounce of loyalty. Even my dogs are more faithful."

And better treated, no doubt. Sara looked down and stirred the nonexistent sugar.

Tom entered the room and gave a small bow. He had made himself presentable, attired in a gray frock coat—a good color for the South.

"My goodness! You have another house guest, Agatha?

Have you and your family been hiding him? Or, is he the mysterious boarder I heard about, the one who fired at your intruders weeks ago?"

Before Agatha could answer, Tom walked toward Lucille and gave a deeper bow. "I'm the third member of the travelers staying here, madam. Thomas Ballard, at your service, but sorry to be tardy in welcoming you. I'd been out hunting with young Robert, and wished to wear clothes appropriate for meeting a southern belle."

Lucille's sour face broke into a smile.

"Miss Sara told me she'd met a delightful friend," Tom continued, taking a seat in the straight-back, cane chair near the desk. "Mr. Pendleton will want to greet you too. He begs to be excused a bit longer so he can finish the message he's preparing for his next opportunity at the church."

"I wouldn't want to impose on his time." Lucille patted her cheek. "In fact, I do hate to impose on every one of you. I know you have many tasks. We're all short of help, and now I am one man shorter still. It is so aggravating."

"It's no imposition, dear friend." Agatha glanced at the door and waved Mr. Pendleton in. "Here's the man himself, fresh from his Bible studies, I suppose."

"Mrs. Steadman, a pleasure to see you again." Mr. Pendleton bowed, balancing on his cane, and took a seat in the other armchair, catty-corner to their guest. "I'll risk intruding on this good company's fellowship for a few minutes before resuming my efforts upstairs."

Tom turned toward Mr. Pendleton. "Sir, I believe we have the perfect person here to give you the advice you wished for your message. Didn't you mention basing it on a runaway slave?" He smiled at Lucille, who frowned. "Excuse me, Mrs. Steadman, I'm still learning my way around the holy Scriptures, but I'm sure you are well acquainted with them. Since none of us has a plantation with enslaved people, it seems you might be able to share some insights."

"What advice might that be? I'm also in immediate need of help as I've already explained to my hostesses." Lucille's pained look said she wasn't eager to follow a possibly unpleasant rabbit trail.

"Ah, yes." Mr. Pendleton looked over his spectacles at Lucille. "A kind Southerner who has experience with the enslaved is just the person who can give guidance. You see, in the Bible's book of Philemon, the Apostle Paul has addressed a letter to a Christian slave owner, and the letter is being carried by the owner's runaway slave himself."

Lucille looked as though she faced a skunk that had raised its leg.

"Now, as we'd expect," he continued, unfazed, "Paul told the owner that the enslaved man, who had also become a Christian, should be *welcomed* back as a *brother* in God's family."

Sara sat fascinated. If she'd ever read Philemon, she'd forgotten it, but it was perfect—absolutely perfect—for the situation.

"I know many plantation owners practice Christian principles." Mr. Pendleton pushed his spectacles higher on his nose. "I worry, however, if one of the less principled owners in the congregation—a non-Christian visitor perhaps—would take offense at hearing God's command to forgive a runaway slave's transgressions just as all their own transgressions were forgiven through the Lord's sacrifice."

Lucille, frowning, shook her head. "This is a strange coincidence and somewhat upsetting since I have a missing slave. But as you have asked for my advice, I would strongly suggest you choose a different topic since you are a Northerner and an *outside* observer of our culture. Select a topic less controversial, or frankly, one less irrelevant to our situation."

A challenge perched on the tip of Sara's tongue, but she held her peace.

Lucille scooted around in her chair to face Agatha more directly. "I've come to ask my cherished friends to keep an eye and ear out for any news about my runaway. You and Mr. Evans will need to be forceful if the opportunity comes to capture him. He may resist, having been warned of the consequences."

"I understand." Agatha took a sip of her tea. "We'll certainly be on the lookout."

"We will keep you in our prayers, too." Mr. Pendleton adjusted his cane, preparing to rise. "If the boy should show up on this property, we would assure him that his treatment by every good Christian would be compassionate, obeying God's Golden Rule."

"I covet prayers, even from those who don't understand our situation here." A tear rolled down the lady's cheek. "These slaves have no idea how their dereliction of duty harms me and themselves. I've had to sell off ten acres of my land just to make ends meet." A second tear joined the first.

Tom handed her his handkerchief. "The war is making life harder and harder for everyone, isn't it? I understand the situation in Vicksburg is deteriorating much more quickly than here. If that city should fall to the Union, it seems the condition of all the area's plantations will become even more dire."

"Oh, I can't bear to think of it—how the civilians in charming Vicksburg have been reduced to living in caves within the bluff and eating their pets and rats." Lucille shook her head. "Imagine!"

Tom made a face of disgust. "Terrible indeed, madam. I

suppose the slaves will all have their freedom if the Federals take over. At least, there wouldn't be any more runaways, would there? It almost makes granting them their freedom in advance seem a wise move."

Lucille gasped. "Why on earth?"

"Because the freed slaves would appreciate their former owners—maybe even stay to work the land, with pay, of course—instead of giving *all* the credit to Mr. Lincoln."

"Oh, I'm afraid you are quite naïve, Mr. Ballard. You non-Southerners! You'd best miss the Sunday gatherings as you have been doing, young man. Such ideas could ire a number of the congregants. Seriously ire them." She blotted her forehead. "And now, I must be on my way. Thank you, Agatha and Sara. I'm confident of your common sense. Perhaps you can share some of your wisdom with the men. After all, we women know what it takes to hold a place together these days."

Sara pasted on a smile.

"We'll certainly see what we can do." Agatha rose and gave Lucille a hug.

As the men quickly stood, Lucille turned to Mr. Pendleton. "At least, I can trust that a man who references the holy Scriptures would not approve of harboring a runaway. Would he? That would be a form of stealing property."

"I assure you, Mrs. Steadman, I would never steal another person's rightful property."

After all the farewells, Sara joined the others in the parlor. Her stomach still turned at Lucille's hypocrisy, but at least Mr. Pendleton and Tom had given the lady the chance to reform her thinking.

Agatha passed the remaining macaroons to the two men, then smiled at Mr. Pendleton. "You are a sly person for such a dedicated soul."

"The lesser of two evils—a minor twist of words to rescue an innocent man from a horrific evil. But I congratulate each of you for being equally sly."

"Yes, we did our best." Agatha gathered the teacups, then addressed Tom. "Could you bring Malachi to the house. We'll have him stay in our room for fugitives. I'm sure my husband will be taking him to Port Hudson in the next day or so." She caught Sara's eye. "After we all change clothes, we'll need to start bringing in enough harvest for a wagon load. Tom and Malachi can join us too."

"As will I," Mr. Pendleton said. "And I'll take the tray and care for these dishes."

Tom followed Sara up the stairs to their rooms. He stopped her at her door. "Would you like to share some of your female common sense with me?" The twinkle in his eyes betrayed his solemn tone.

Sara tried to think of a teasing response, but her mind hadn't shifted from the horrors of the Steadman plantation. "I can't tease like you," she said, "but I hope you will be careful. Please remember Mrs. Steadman's warning about the 'ire' of plantation owners. I don't want you to get shot when you and Mr. Evans go back to Port Hudson."

"Why, my lady, I think you almost care about this barbarian."

"Oh, I do, Tom!" *More than I dare say.*

Tom spread out his arms.

Sara hesitated, fighting her urge to fall into his embrace.

At that moment, Mr. Pendleton coughed as he stepped from the stairs.

CHAPTER 25

On a road between the Pearl River and Westville, Mississippi

The road running east and west lay before Terry and Joshua. But which way was the quickest route to reach a Union refuge? Both directions teemed with danger.

"Maybe heading east toward Alabama would be best," Terry ventured, "away from the Pearl. The river's like a dragon with its claws out."

"A dragon river with bushwhackers lurking besides." Joshua shifted the six baskets he carried on the pole across his shoulders. "How about going as far as Westville and selling some of these? We can still turn back west if we hear of Confederate troops ahead of us."

"All right." Terry shifted his load of baskets to a better position, too. "East, it is."

The steamy mist gradually dissipated as they headed toward the brightening sky. After rounding a curve, Terry squinted into the light to make out an approaching dark shape.

Joshua slowed his pace. "Looks like a donkey cart's coming, pulled by someone on foot."

Terry groaned. "A peddler, then. He'll be nosy. Every one of them's born a chatterbox. Your fake accent beats mine."

When they drew even with each other, the bearded, long-haired peddler stopped his dingy cart. "Got rust-free tools, and a like-new harness, too." He eyed the baskets swaying on the poles. "Reckon y'all got yer hands full, though, with what yer peddling."

"You're rahht about that." Joshua coughed and spit phlegm, a poor effort to account for his unauthentic drawl.

The peddler stepped to the far side of his cart. "Hate to tell you. It's a ba-ud time to be on the road. Yankees ahead. Heard they burned Newton Station. Locomotives too."

"Why cain't the Yankees leave us alone?" Despite the incredible news, Joshua had managed a disgusted tone. "If they're not too close, we gotta make a few quick sales in town. Git some vittles. Is the bridge o'er the Strong River good to cross?" He had another attack of coughing.

"It is now. Them troops ain't made it through the piney thicket this side of Raleigh yet. But they're sure comin'. Better hitch up yer britches and turn 'round soon as you can. Or lay low somewhere if you don't aim to git robbed along with the mules, horses, and food the Yanks been stealin' from every farm. Word is, plantations don't escape their thieving neither. They pitch camp on the grass. Empty storehouses and barns down to nothin'. Pitiful!"

Terry shook his head and steadied his pole.

Joshua rubbed his growth of new whiskers. "Much obliged for the warning. Guess we best hurry on. Git done in town."

The peddler picked the cart's handles up. "Best o' luck then."

As soon as the cart disappeared over a rise, Terry shot his hands into the air, nearly dropping his load. "Can you believe it? Yankees a-comin'!"

"If the old fellow's right." Joshua wasn't jumping for joy at all. "How can Northern troops be this far into Confederate territory? They should have been surrounded by Rebs in the first twenty miles into the state."

"But Secesh troops wouldn't burn a Southern Railway's train station. Although I guess they'd resupply their troops from hapless civilians along their march."

"Might not have been Yanks causing the fire. Just getting the blame."

"At any rate, it sounds like we still have time to get to Westville. Make our exchange. We got to get food." Terry jerked a nod to Joshua, who fell in step beside him.

Halfway up the next hill, Terry stopped to listen. A horse? "Did you hear that?" he called to Joshua, who still trudged ahead.

The next instant, three men rode out of a narrow path skirting the hill.

"You men, hands up!" the one out front shouted. The riders were pointing Colt revolving rifles, yet wore civilian clothes.

His heart sinking, Terry raised his hands at the same time as Joshua. If these were rabid Confederate sympathizers, they signified deep, deep trouble.

The apparent leader dismounted. "What's that you're carrying?"

"Thar empty baskets, suh," Joshua drawled, moving back by Terry.

The man frowned. "Where you from?"

"Up Jackson way mos' recently."

"And you?" He pointed at Terry.

"Same, suh."

"Put your poles down over there." He pointed to the side of the road, then turned toward one of the men still on horseback. "Luke, make sure there's nothing of interest in those wares.

Check for false bottoms. Messages." He faced Joshua again. "Hand over that knapsack. Unusual bag for a peddler."

Terry worked to analyze the man's accent. It didn't sound southern. These could be Union men, ahead of the main company, spying out the land. Or they could just as easily be former Northerners with southern sympathies. After setting down his wares, he hunched his shoulders, like an innocent, unaligned peddler might, worn down from toting goods day after day. With any luck, his shaking knees fit the part of a rustic bumpkin facing a gun.

Joshua shrugged the pack off his back. "A widow's payment for mah week's farm work."

The man pawed through the items on top of the bag, then stopped. "I'll be darned if there's not a blue coat here!" He pulled out Joshua's tattered jacket and held it up for the other two to see. "What's behind this, peddler?"

"A prisoner of war, sir." Joshua had entirely dropped the drawl.

Terry cringed. What was Joshua thinking? Along with the New York accent, prisoners coming from Jackson *most recently* clearly identified them as Union soldiers or sympathizers. No wiggle room there. Even if they could make a case for having been paroled, how could they explain their guise as peddlers? And their location, traveling *south* of Jackson, precisely as a disguised Union spy would do?

His inquisitor looked puzzled. "Loyal to which side?"

Terry held his breath. Surely Joshua would try to resurrect their neutrality. Somehow.

"Union, sir."

Fire ran through Terry's veins. He eyed the woods next to him. He'd run, zigzagging, before being captured.

Joshua raised his chin. "Taken by bushwhackers near New

Orleans while serving with the New York 128th Regiment at Camp Parapet. Sent to the Jackson prison."

The man still on horseback lowered his weapon.

Terry's heart slowed its pounding.

The leader looked at Terry. "You a prison escapee too?"

"Yes, sir." If he was reading the lowered weapon wrong, he'd opt for a bullet, not a rope. "Also taken by bushwhackers near New Orleans."

"Then let me relieve your minds." The man cracked a smile. "I'm Sergeant Yeats. You've managed to fall in with a nest of Federal cavalrymen."

Terry slapped his chest. "Man! That's the best news ever!" A flash of lightning made him twitch, but nothing could lessen his exuberance. They wouldn't be hunting for an empty barn or a cheap room in return for the baskets this night or any night if they could tagalong with the cavalry. Best of all, no hanging or a bullet in the back.

"We're pickets with the 7th Illinois Cavalry, part of the Grierson Raiders." Yeats handed the knapsack back to Joshua. "Our captain will want to talk to you men."

Joshua beamed. "I figured Illinois from the way you said 'I'll be darned if.' Just like my Chicago cousin."

The third man, Matthew, doubled up with Luke on one horse and took the lead. Terry and Joshua were given the vacated horse. By the time they had turned west and ridden into the cavalry camp at the Smith plantation, a heavy downpour had soaked Terry to the bone. But they were among fellow Yanks, who surely had some plan to escape the Confederates, preferably a lot sooner rather than later.

Captain Trafton interrogated Joshua alone in his canvas headquarters for a good twenty minutes. When he got to Terry, the interview was more like a get-acquainted chat. After questions about his kidnapping, family, age, and any fighting abilities he might have, he invited Terry to sit on a stool while he prepared a paper for him to sign.

"If I may, sir, I forgot to mention one talent, especially since this is a cavalry unit." Terry felt his face redden.

The captain raised his quill. "Go ahead."

"I've been told I'm talented with horses."

The captain came close to rolling his eyes. "How about this then? I'll let you muster in as a temporary volunteer until we get to ... er, where we're going. You can fill in as an assistant herder. Would that suit?"

"Yes, sir. And I'll do my best."

"Don't get attached to any animal, son. So far, our men have avoided anything more than villagers' half-hearted potshots, but after our action at Newton Station, we have the Rebs' full attention. We care about the horses and mules—don't get me wrong—but we care about men a heck of a lot more. We push the animals without mercy. You gotta accept they're expendable in a race for our lives."

"I'll remember that, sir."

It was already dark when the captain ordered the quartermaster's assistant to outfit them. Since Joshua belonged to another Union regiment and had experience as a marksman, he'd been transferred in as a regular cavalryman. As such, he'd have a horse already trained for battle. Terry's mount would be one of the horses confiscated from a farm that morning. The assistant supplied Joshua with a full uniform, replacing his tattered one in the knapsack. Terry received a used pair of the regulation trousers, but a civilian shirt. They were each provided a thin bedroll, poncho, ill-fitting jackboots, socks, a moth-eaten blanket, a pocketful of salt, a tin cup, and a saddlebag for their animal's feed. Additionally, Joshua was equipped with a musket and a saber in an iron scabbard, seventy rounds of ammunition, and a two-person tent he could share with Terry.

One of the guards on duty led them to their squad and left them to pitch the tent in the still pouring rain. They finally got situated around midnight.

Terry changed from his wet clothes into the dry ones from within his poncho, wrapped his blanket around his shivering body, then lay on the damp inside of his poncho, which was better than the muddy ground. "What a day!" He directed his words toward Joshua's sounds in the inky blackness. "Seems like a month since we left the widow and Sam."

"Yeah. Maybe two months. God was good to us today, Terry. You know what I'm happiest about?"

"No idea. Being alive, maybe?"

"Getting my own horse."

"Seriously?"

"Yep. I had a Shetland pony when I was eight. Spent every afternoon with her after school and chores. But when money ran scarce the next year, my father sold her. Each Christmas after that, I asked only for a horse—no special breed, even a broken-down nag—but never got one."

"Then I'm happy for you. Being in a Union cavalry in the middle of Mississippi isn't a slice of paradise, but it sure beats slinking by ourselves along roads and swamps and especially prison."

"You bet." Joshua made the snuffling noise of wrapping in his blanket. "And I've got you to thank for getting me loose."

"And I've got you to thank for not getting shot today. We're still a team, aren't we?"

"That's why we'll make it through—through the valley of shadows, like the Bible says."

"Guess it's good one team member has belief. Good night, o' faithful one." Terry took a deep breath and turned on his side.

He'd concede meeting the scouts had been amazing. An extraordinary coincidence. But beyond that? Who knew?

<hr />

The next morning at the Pearl River crossing, Terry's black Arabian snorted, impatient at being tied to a tree. "Easy, boy." Terry stroked the horse's forehead. "We're next."

A fellow herder led the first half of their assigned horses and mules off the ferry and onto the river's far shore. Once the ferry had made the trip back to his side, Terry mounted and drove the remaining twenty horses and five mules onto the vessel, amazed at how easily he managed the animals. Someday he'd awe his family with his newfound herding ability—if he ever got home. He pushed away the pang.

Their fifty head were only a small part of the stock of five hundred already amassed by the Raiders during their dash from the Tennessee border. Terry and his animals were at the tail end of the 7th Illinois companies' crossings. Next would be the 6th Illinois.

Terry stared down at the Pearl, whose waters surged under the ferry with even more ferocity than when he and Joshua nearly drowned in them a week earlier. If the Raiders' two-hundred advance men hadn't gotten hold of the ferry in the middle of the night, the brigade, along with him and Joshua, would have been trapped on the wrong side of the river. The Confederate battalions closing in on them would have annihilated them. He glanced back at the troops still waiting to cross over what had become their deliverer. Joining up with the brigade hadn't taken him out of danger liked he'd hoped at first, but somehow, belonging to its fighting force made the extreme peril less terrifying.

Later that morning, the Raiders' vaunted luck held again.

Upon reaching Hazlehurst on the New Orleans, Jackson, and Great Northern Railroad, the brigade's scouts managed to send a false telegraph to the Confederate commanding general, alleging the Yankees had been unable to cross the Pearl and had turned north—the opposite of the true direction.

Terry rode along with the whole cavalry into Hazlehurst. While other men cut telegraph lines and burned railroad cars, he got permission to work with Joshua's contingent, tearing up a large section of the railroad track. During a break, he squatted next to Joshua under an awning to avoid the off-and-on, spitting rain. "Nice payback for the mutilation the bushwhackers carried out on the Mexican Gulf Railroad, isn't it, Josh? Reckon it'll take the enemy three times longer to restore these tracks than it probably took the Union to undo the Rebs' damage."

"Our boys are going to wrap the rails around the telegraph posts. Won't be any restoring for a long time." Joshua's grin disappeared the next second. "Oh man! That building down there's on fire. Must've spread from the locomotive."

Joshua ran to his horse and galloped after the other men heeding the order to report at the depot.

By the time Terry made it to his horse, farther away, he could tell the fire was out. So, he rejoined the herders at the unit's temporary mess tent. There, greatly appreciating the decent meal, he wolfed down his allotment of the eggs and ham the brigade had confiscated from the town's larders.

After wiping up the last crumbs with a biscuit, Terry looked up as Joshua sat down beside him. "What alignment of stars brought me a cavalryman's renewed attention?"

Joshua laughed. "Sergeant gave leave to check on you since you're a *young tenderfoot*. Said to be back in fifteen minutes."

"Well, here I am. Still alive and downright stuffed. So, how's your quarter horse? Did the fire spook him?"

"Not at all. You should have seen him at the Pearl, too. Fearless. I'm calling him Champion."

"Champion, huh?" Terry set down his empty bowl. "Are you sure you should've named him? What if the worst happens?"

"He deserves a great name. I might get to keep him permanently so long as I do my duty. You know, it's because of people like you and your chief herder that he's trained so well— and that we've got mounts at all."

Terry shrugged, trying not to like the praise too much. "Feel sorry for the animals, though. After they're ridden nearly to death, it's a hard lot for them to get cast aside." He paused so the underlying warning could soak in. "One of the discarded mares followed after her old master for miles. Finally collapsed on the road."

"Better not happen to Champion. He'd have followed me here like a pup if I'd let him. Can't see I'd ever leave him behind."

"The captain told me it was a fact of war. Not to get attached."

"Strong ones like mine'll make it. We will too, huh?"

"That's our intention." Terry fought against the persistent yearning for home. "Breaking records now for speed. That's for sure."

"We'll get out of this mess real soon." Joshua stood. "Gotta get back before the sarge gets his dander up, and the bugle makes us ride like there's no tomorrow. Champion's bound to be wondering where I am." He chuckled and strode off as though he owned the world, then turned and gave a cheerful wave as he threaded his way along the company's perimeter.

Terry returned Joshua's wave. If only he could be as optimistic.

The following day, Terry's chief ordered him to ride along

228

with Captain Trafton's battalion when it was detached and sent twenty miles out of the way. His excitement at having a part in the deceptive raid on the railway fizzled during the long day and disappeared entirely during the midnight return. He and his horse, along with the rest of the column's bone-weary troopers, galloped, then plodded, galloped, then plodded.

"Not again." Terry grimaced at the rider next to him as the line slowed to a near halt. A tent wasn't a featherbed but it sure beat the back of a horse. Were they being led by idiots? Couldn't their leaders hit a steady stride and keep at it?

"Rumor is we're ridin' into a trap." His fellow rider peered at the trees on both sides of the road, then leaned toward Terry. "They're saying our main force is already cornered. A Secesh battalion caught up and is fixin' to outflank both our companies. Don't know if our captain is waiting on orders for us to turn tail, or meet the enemy—gallantly and all that."

Terry stiffened. So, the Raiders' boasted luck had vanished. But no matter what, he wouldn't go back to prison. He'd get shot first.

Every unusual noise in the woods made him cringe. But hour after hour no bullets came as they alternately sped and crawled through the darkness. Finally reaching the bivouac and his tent, he slid into his sleeping bag, too tired to wake Joshua to hear the latest rumors, or to calculate his chance of survival.

The morning reveille sounded, waking Terry after a mere catnap. He lay still. Obviously, he was still alive. Furthermore, the Raiders still had to be intact. And Joshua, squatting near him, was pulling on his uniform as though everything was normal.

Terry propped himself up on an elbow. "What's going on?" He tried to set aside his jealousy of his friend's much easier night.

Joshua stopped grooming his scruffy beard and faced him.

"I'll tell you what. You're one of the heroes. Those late hours you kept with that detachment? Well, that saved the whole brigade and probably our lives, too."

"Our detachment? Impossible. I heard the Rebs outnumbered *all* the Raiders at least five to one. Our detachment was like a group of toothpicks."

"Yeah, but you guys thundered up the road in the pitch dark at 3 a.m. That so unnerved the Confederate officers, they ordered their troops to withdraw."

Terry sat up, searching for words.

"Colonel Grierson's like a magician," Joshua mused. "The enemy catches up to us, but gets mightily confused because they can't guess what's up his sleeve."

"The problem is," Terry rejoined, his relief replaced by irritation that he'd face another long, perilous day, "they know *exactly* where we are now. The colonel needs to have a lot more tricks, or we're all gonna be corpses when his last deception folds."

"You have a way of putting things too succinctly, as an old teacher of mine used to say."

"If it's any help, I'm still counting on Lady Luck a little."

"No help at all."

"About the same as counting on a magician." Terry pulled on his Union pants.

"You got me this time."

Terry gave Joshua a friendly shove out the tent. It was thoughtful of his partner not to mention what he was really counting on. Talk of God might be the straw that broke his exhausted back.

CHAPTER 26

Gunfire! About a mile away! Terry spurred his Arabian into a trot and wove through his herd, cutting horses to take with him for replacements. By the time he had his herd of ten in hand, the whole 7th Illinois were moving fast.

"Trouble at the Tickfaw bridge," a sergeant called to his privates as Terry came up behind the man's unit.

Gunfire erupted again. Terry gripped his reins harder. Was Joshua at the front? He passed the first dead horse as his Arabian's hooves clattered onto the wooden planks of Wall's Bridge. Reaching the far side of the fifty-foot span, he stopped cold. A horse that looked exactly like Champion lay on its back in a gully, its four legs in the air, not moving.

"No!" His shout had been guttural, like his soul was emptying out.

But no crushed rider lay beneath the horse. He needed to keep hold of himself. Joshua's belief they'd both make it had been strong, seemingly unshakeable. Shouldn't that have counted for something ... maybe with some kind of higher power?

Easing onto the edge of the road, he spotted two men up ahead holding a man's body. An ambulance wagon passed him and stopped. More men carrying the dead or wounded hurried to the wagon.

His scalp tingling, he ran his eyes over the men being loaded. Four of the wounded and dying were the enemy. One was a Raider. "Are these all the casualties?" he asked a nurse tending the men. He hoped desperately to get a *yes.*

"No. Three of ours are already on their way to a farmhouse. It's our field hospital. Belongs to a Newman family."

"Near here?" Terry swallowed hard. He looked back at the horse. If it wasn't Joshua's, it was his twin.

"About a mile from here. Turnoff's back behind us."

The doctor giving orders paused. "You think you got an older brother there, son?"

"Not sure, but he's someone who's like my brother, sir. We escaped a Rebel prison, joined the Raiders together."

The doctor glanced behind Terry. "Discharge your duties with that little herd following you." He waved his hand at the horses Terry had forgotten. "Then tell your sergeant that Surgeon Yule could use an extra hand—for a very limited time. If he approves, meet me at the farmhouse."

"Yes, sir. Thank you, sir." Terry saluted with a trembling hand.

After assigning four horses to replace the fallen and helping the riders assemble their horses' bridles, saddles, and stirrups, Terry took the remaining animals back to the herd and checked in with his chief herder, who gave his approval.

While he pushed his horse to a gallop on the rutted lane to the farmhouse, he fought his panic. *Don't think the worst. If it was Champion, Joshua could have jumped free. Fought on foot, found another horse. And even if he's wounded, it could be a cracked rib, a broken bone. We'll both make it, like he said.*

At the cottage, he was directed down the hall to a parlor that had been changed into a hospital room for the wounded privates on both sides of the war—Grierson's Raiders and the 9th Louisiana Partisan Rangers.

Joshua, lying faceup on a cot, raised a hand when he spotted Terry.

Terry bit back a curse. *Why?* he aimed at nonexistent God.

"You were right about Grierson's limits." Joshua inched up on the bunched pillow when Terry reached his bedside. "The magic ran out on me and a few next to me."

"Sure wish it hadn't." Fighting down the acid wanting to erupt, Terry looked away from the bucket next to the cot, holding a swath of bloody bandages. "Surgeon Yule's gonna tend your wound any time now. He let me come when I told him you're like my brother."

"I'm real glad you're here, Terry, and still in one piece. Didn't know how the fight would go for you if it started up again—you being unarmed."

"It was over by the time I got to the bridge." Terry took a step back, seeing the surgeon heading their way.

Yule circled the cot toward Terry's side. "It seems you found your adopted brother."

"Yes, sir." Terry moved back several more feet to be out of the way. His mind reeled while the doctor inspected Joshua's bloody leg. Could he help somehow? A suggestion of yarrow? But every military doctor already knew about the herb.

Joshua gave a series of deep groans.

Terry gasped for breath, wanting to cover his ears. If only he was having a nightmare. He'd wake up, and Joshua would give him a hard time about having thrashed around inside his safe tent. But it wasn't that kind of nightmare. It was a true-to-life one, its claws burrowing into him. He'd insisted Joshua escape with him, and look what happened.

Yule straightened his wiry body and put his hand on Joshua's chest as Terry moved closer to the cot. "I'll be back to take care of your leg after I tend to the men teetering between life and death. You'll get more laudanum when I come back."

Once the surgeon left Joshua's bedside, Terry squatted next to him, his fear easing a bit. At least, his friend wasn't one of those on the verge of dying.

Joshua made a face. "Champion was a champ to the end. Seems I won't be needing a horse after all."

"Champion's not suffering anyway. I passed him on the way here. What's Yule think about your leg?"

"Gonna lose … the bottom half." His voice faltered on the last part. "Bone's shattered to pieces. Puts an end to our plans to ride together in New York."

Terry blinked back tears. He wanted to object, to argue the doctor was wrong. But the evidence in front of his eyes stopped him. Fragments of bone poked through the skin of Joshua's lower leg, trickles of blood running down onto the open bandages left under his calf. His lower leg looked as though it'd been through a meat grinder.

Joshua was staring at him, his eyes tight with pain.

He had to say something. "If, uh, if you do lose your lower leg," he managed, his voice squeaking at the start, "I reckon you can still ride. I've seen men ride with an artificial leg. They use a special stirrup that unlocks in case of a fall. Only you'd never fall with all this experience we're getting."

Joshua frowned, and Terry flinched. He should have known better than to spout words about something he never experienced.

"I've already been told I'm out of the cavalry." Joshua flung his arm to one side. "No jumpin' in the saddle and galloping away with a split second's notice. Soon as I'm able to hobble around, I'll be carted to the nearest Union town."

Terry lowered his voice. "Isn't this a Confederate sympathizer's home?"

"Yes, but Colonel Grierson himself made Newman swear to treat us well. The farmer and his wife's given their own bedroom to Colonel Blackburn, who's barely alive, a lot worse off than me. Colonel Grierson expects the Secesh to parole any of us who recover enough for transport. The enemy won't want extra men to feed who aren't a military threat."

"I'm sorry, Joshua. Awful sorry! I shouldn't have hounded you to leave the prison. You'd probably have been exchanged by now and kept both your legs." Terry fought back the threatening tears.

"Messed up again, didn't you, Ballard? Always messin' up," a voice growled from the four Confederate cots across the room.

Terry stiffened. "Talbot?"

"The same. But if you wanna do a good turn for a change, I could use a cup of water."

Terry snorted. "You've got some gall after the torture you put us through. Worst of all, in case it's slipped your rotten memory, you shot at an old man for nothing and nearly hung his grandson." He thought about spitting in Talbot's face—giving him the kind of *water* he deserved, but an attendant was watching him.

"The no-good, Black boy? Word gets around. Now where's the water?"

"Give him a cup, Terry, for your own sake," Joshua mumbled.

"That monster's on the way to hell if there is such a place— the sooner, the better."

"Don't do this to yourself," Joshua pleaded.

"Don't want your stinkin' water anyhow." Talbot coughed and looked toward the window next to him.

The surgeon reentered the room and headed toward the man lying in a cot beside Joshua's. Two nurses followed in his wake.

Joshua turned his head away from Terry. "Sergeant," he called to the nurse carrying a tray with a pitcher, "could you give that man in the second cot over there a drink of water?"

Terry restrained his indignation at Joshua's interference. Pain and religion could do strange things to a person.

The nurse poured a cup and took it to Talbot. "Here you are. Doctor will be with you soon. Bullet wound doesn't look bad."

Terry clamped his teeth together. Why couldn't Talbot be losing his leg instead of Joshua? In fact, both legs would be even fairer. Losing his worst-than-worthless life—the fairest of all.

Joshua sighed. "When I joined up, I thought I'd help right the world. Didn't know how hardhearted people could be."

Terry stiffened. "Including me?"

"I was thinkin' of only Talbot. I didn't want him to get water either, but figured I'd better be right with God before the surgeon put me under." Joshua waved his hand in a dismissal. "You've got to find that brother of yours and get home. I'm gonna be all right. And stop kicking yourself for rescuing me from prison. The swamp fever would have finished me off in that rathole." Joshua raised a hand as if to keep Terry from disagreeing. "And if I'm paroled, I might beat you to New York." His effort at a grin amounted to a grimace. "But if my time's up in this world, we can ride together in heaven." He hesitated. "'Course, you need to get acquainted with our Savior first." His eyes locked with Terry's, undeniably extending an invitation.

Terry searched for words. How could he refuse what could be Joshua's last dying wish—especially since he deserved the blame no matter how Joshua wanted to twist things? But virtuous Joshua wouldn't want anyone to lie just to please him, would he?

"I, er, I'm counting on our riding together in New York," he finally stuttered, moving farther aside as the surgeon joined the nurse at Joshua's cot.

After Yule gave Joshua the promised laudanum from his flask, he ordered Terry to bring a pot of boiling water from the kitchen on the double. Terry rushed off, yearning to do more— plead that his friend could keep his leg, or, he thought bitterly, use some of Grierson's magic to restore it. Or how about magically transporting them back in time to Widow Starkly's farm or even to the Jackson prison, where they could make different decisions? He let out a sob. How could he leave without his friend?

The drug was already making Joshua incoherent when Terry returned with the boiling water. The doctor had Terry help slide the "operating table," which was actually a door taken off its hinges, under Joshua. After the assisting nurse placed a keg of whisky on the board, Yule took his scalpel, Caitlin knife, and bone saw from his bag and dipped his stained instruments in the pot.

Terry's stomach threatened to empty itself as the lower half of Joshua's leg came off. The nurse left to deal with a patient screaming for help in the hallway, so Yule showed Terry how to hold a flap of skin over the leg's exposed flesh. Then the surgeon sutured it into a smooth stub below the knee.

Terry shut his eyes against the sight although he knew he'd never be free of it.

Yule wiped his hands on his bloody apron. "He won't wake up for several hours. It's high time for you to get going. The colonel's keeping me here, so I'll take care of this young man. Unless infection sets in, he'll recover."

"Sir—"

"That's an order. You'll have to ride hard before the

Confederates get between you and our troops, their trap snapping shut with you inside. What's more, our brigade's bound to use more feints to confuse the Johnny Rebs. You better have caught up before they confuse you too." He pointed to three guns, ammunition, and two sabers lying on a desk against the wall. "Take a pistol and some ammo with you. These men won't need them anytime soon."

Tears running down his face, Terry picked up the weapon and cartridges. He ignored Talbot's taunts, and with one last glance toward Joshua's face, left the room.

Mounting his horse, he stared back at the house. Someone moved in the parlor's window, but the sun's glare blocked more than a dark figure. Then he spurred the Arabian and galloped off.

CHAPTER 27

"Whoa, boy." Terry reined in his horse and dismounted. The old wagon road he'd followed through the piney woods for over an hour had narrowed down to nothing but a footpath. The hundred or more riders he'd thought were ahead of him on a shortcut had vanished even though hoof prints, broken branches, and a lost Union cap caught in thistles had clearly marked where a large number of cavalrymen had left the main road. Despite his own previous participation in Grierson's magical feints, he'd obviously been stupid enough to fall for one of the Raiders' deceptions himself—and when every minute counted.

He had no choice but to return to the cut off. Even now, Confederate scouts could be closing in. But first he and his horse had to have water. He walked the Arabian along the footpath until they came to a creek. After filling his canteen, he stroked his horse as it continued to thirstily drink. Although he'd probably regret the fondness someday, he'd become more than a little attached to the magnificent steed.

Once he'd gotten back to the main road, he halted to listen for approaching troops. Hearing only bird calls, buzzing insects, and rustling leaves, he settled his horse into a steady trot southward. Was the enemy behind or in front of him? If in front, he could be riding straight into a trap.

In the later afternoon, the north/south road ended at a still broader road running east and west. He peered in both directions. Nothing guaranteed Grierson had chosen the most logical route. And anyway, which way was most logical? Nothing was there to guide him—no map, no hoof prints, not even lost items this time. He hesitated, then tightening his jaw, turned to the west. He'd aim for Union territory farther southwest on the Mississippi River, even if the magician hadn't.

Facing the sun that dipped toward the horizon, he let the scene's solitary beauty free his mind from the danger for a while. Clouds streaked high above the dark green pines covering the hills. He'd paint the scene if he were home in New York. He swallowed hard and spurred his horse to a faster trot.

After another mile, the road started trending downward toward a valley. An awful thought struck him. The Tickfaw River flowed southward, and it probably moved in a westward drainage too. So soon, he'd meet up with another of the treacherous river's bridges. It'd be a guarded bridge, most likely defended by Southerners. But if he was lucky enough to be catching up to the brigade, it could be guarded by Raiders. Clearly, he had to scout ahead. Utilizing a gap in the thicket lining the road, he threaded his way into the woods.

After hitching the horse to a tree far enough back to be hidden from unfriendly eyes, he crept through the underbrush.

The river and its bridge appeared after half a mile, with eight armed men standing guard. He moved closer to get a better look through the tall brush. Five men wore gray, mud-splattered pants. But three wore blue. So, some of the men had to be wearing uniforms confiscated from the enemy. But which ones?

He scanned the rest of the area, halting his gaze at a spot deep in the piney woods across the road. A camp had been pitched, poorly camouflaged. His rising relief plummeted as he surveyed the small number of tents. The camp wasn't big enough for even a Raiders' detachment, so a local unit of Confederate volunteers had to block his route.

His fake accent and Union blue pants would be dead giveaways. If the Rebels captured him and judged him to be a Raiders' scout or a Union spy, imprisonment or a hanging followed. Shuddering, he felt under his shirt for his newly acquired pistol. Before he'd fall into enemy's hands, he'd shoot himself—if he could pull the trigger.

A belfry tower rose among the pines a couple of miles off the road to the right. He backtracked to his horse and followed an overgrown trail to the country church. The cemetery behind it promised seclusion along with temporary safety. He tied the Arabian to a fencepost, loose enough to allow grazing, and slipped into the silent grounds. In the unlikely case of watching eyes, he chose a moss-covered headstone to kneel at before resting in its shadows.

Could he swim his horse across the broad river at some other spot? Or might the eight guards retire to their tents later at night, without replacements? Neither looked like possibilities.

He pulled out the pistol. Deep in vast Confederate territory with no idea how to reconnect with his brigade, was it time to give up? It shouldn't be too hard to pull the trigger. If he did it right, the pain would last only a few seconds. But was he willing to stop existing? To become a nothing? To never see his family again? Never see his stallion, Admiral? Never even have the unlikely chance to ride with Joshua on earth, let alone in heaven?

He jerked his hand from the pistol's grip. No, he couldn't do it. A lump the size of a walnut clogged his throat. He didn't even have the courage to free himself from the earth and its suffering.

The buried person's partial birthdate showed on the

gravestone he faced. Had the deceased been young like him? Or an old codger, thankful to shed a meaningless life? He rubbed off enough moss to read, *1785 born. 1833 died.* So, neither young nor old. He used a stone to scrape off the remaining moss covering the inscription.

Here lies Nehemiah Eason. Beloved husband, father, and brother.

Saved by grace. United with his Savior.

"United with his Savior?" The words were probably mere platitudes to soothe the family. Yet from the "spiritual axioms" Mr. Pendleton had asserted as truth—much to Terry's dismay at the time—Nehemiah Eason might not have become a nothing. He just might be with Jesus.

And Joshua had spoken with the same certainty. Could such a heavenly future make up for the loss of a leg? Compensate for having a handicap as long as his friend lived on earth?

Terry jerked his eyes off the tombstone. So what if Nehemiah Eason, Joshua, his buddy Jim, and the likes of them got a heavenly afterlife? Such a future was not for someone like himself. He'd not given this supposed *savior* one ounce of respect... or even credit for existing.

The sun sank below the horizon. Frogs croaked, and mosquitoes whined. Terry slapped at a mosquito by his ear and leaned back against the stone. He'd wait a few minutes longer in order to check the bridge between dusk and the full moon, hopefully while the bright disc still had cloud coverage.

An owl hooted, bringing to mind Elder John, Ezra, Sam, and the widow. They had believed in Jesus too, "trusting God" despite heaps of trouble. And, of course, there were Mr. Pendleton, Sara, and "defector" Tom. It was almost as though the real God had been dogging him, more than even Talbot had. As if God hadn't quite given up on him. An inexplicable warmth flickered through him.

Terry scooted around to face the shadowy tombstone again. "I wish I could hear from you Nehemiah—get filled in about all those pearly gates and golden streets." A tear streaked down his face, and then a lot more until a thought arrested his tears. If he had gone through with killing himself, Talbot would have caught him. He'd have ended up in the same place where Talbot would eventually—either decaying in the ground until nothing was left or facing hell itself. Those options would be worse than prison. And a whole lot worse than giving his life over to God—if it wasn't too late.

He stood up and tentatively raised his hands to the darkening sky. "Jesus, far as I can tell, you did die … on purpose for people … even for strangers like me. And your tomb was empty, like Mr. Pendleton proved. So … if you'll take me, then save me."

He lowered his hands and ran more of Mr. Pendleton's words through his mind. His elder had emphatically declared that Jesus offered forgiveness as a free gift. "But a gift must be received," he'd said.

Raising his arms again, Terry added, "I receive your gift … and thank you for it … I mean, I thank *thee* for it."

He looked up at the sky a minute longer, then at the cemetery around him. Everything appeared the same, of course. But, anyway, he'd accepted what was offered, the best he knew how. Undeserved, for sure. But a *gift* was a gift.

Tom and Sara would bounce up and down with glee if he told them he'd chosen to believe after all his skepticism. He laughed at the scene his brain conjured up, but sobered at the next thought. If he were hung by the Rebels, the two *wouldn't* hear. He supposed he could tell them once they all reached those golden streets. He shook his head. He'd better keep his mind on the here and now.

And that meant he needed to see if his new Savior could get him across the bridge somehow. Maybe in the middle of the night, after all? He started to brush the grave's dirt off his pants, but stopped and smeared more dirt on instead. The less seen of Union blue, the better. Untying the Arabian, he walked the horse down the lane, warily approaching the road through the dark woods.

A distant thunder made him halt. When his horse nickered, he clamped his hand on its muzzle. Goosebumps rose on his arms as the sound grew louder. Definitely not thunder—rather the pounding of approaching hooves. He tripped and nearly fell in his rush to get himself and his horse farther away from the road.

Minutes later, butternut Rebels were sweeping by. Terry stole along the edge of the woods until he had a view of the battalion's last company crossing the bridge. When the noise faded and the dust settled, the road and bridge looked deserted. Nothing stirred where the camp had been either. Obviously, these troops were some of the thousands chasing the Raiders, trying to hem them in. Were they hot on the trail or as lost as he was? Anyway, the Confederates and he were headed in the same direction. He might as well follow behind—but at a fair distance behind.

As though he were one of the injured tail-end troopers, Terry began limping next to the Arabian as two horsemen galloped across the bridge toward him. Neither stopped to question him in the deepening shadows. Amazed at how well his pretense succeeded, he surveyed the road beyond the river. No one was traveling in either direction, so he mounted his horse. From time to time, when night noises in the woods caused the horse to break into a nervous kind of prance, Terry calmed it with reassuring words. He tried to reassure himself also, but failed, too aware of the danger in all directions.

The road entered a hamlet after half a dozen miles. Terry dismounted, hunched his shoulders as if bone-weary, and kept a slow pace. When townsmen, out past suppertime, raised their lanterns to see him better, he nodded and added a weak salute. Again, no one questioned him, apparently used to stragglers in the wake of troop movements.

On the far side of the town, the road led close to a plantation mansion whose windows glowed with lanterns. At its driveway, four guards with their backs to him were jiggling their hips to a band's rendition of "Dixie" issuing from the house. Tents and small campfires littered the spacious grounds as far as he could see.

Terry held his breath as he rode past the men at a trot on the far side of the road, dreading to hear a *halt*. But the party had the guards' full attention. And that was not the only effect of the splendid Southern hospitality. The Confederate officers who had thundered by Terry earlier were no doubt dancing the night away while their underlings took it easy, writing home or perhaps enviously peeping at the party.

A quarter of a mile later, he gave his horse free rein. The animal galloped down the level road like a bat out of hell, which seemed appropriate. Maybe its master was moving out of his own kind of hell.

His Arabian slowed its pace to a fast trot after a mile or two, but still pressed forward as though haunted by a demon. The wind in Terry's face as well as the menace of bushwhackers, scouts, and pickets kept him alert, and grateful for the muscular legs pumping beneath him.

Close to midnight, the last of the high clouds vanished, and a full moon's brilliance lit up the road. Terry reined in his horse to a walk. Had he become too visible—a man on a stallion in front of, or even between, troop movements? Should he wait the night out in the forest of tall pines and pick his way forward in the early dawn?

All at once, his horse gave a shrill whinny, then took off again, bucking when Terry tugged on the reins.

"Halt!" came a gruff order.

"Don't shoot! I'm tryin'!" Terry yelled.

His Arabian slammed to a stop, and Terry grabbed the saddle horn to stay off the fool horse's neck.

"I know him, Sarge" came another voice. "He's one o' ours."

Shaking as though he had the swamp fever chills himself, Terry swung down. His horse nickered as though to say, "Take it easy. I got you here."

Nat, a fellow herdsman, rushed to him. "Thought them Secesh got you for sure. But here you are with your fine horse besides."

"Thanks, Nat. I … I can hardly believe it too." A weight, like that of an elephant's, fell off his shoulders.

The Raiders' rear guard escorted him and his horse to the temporary bivouac, where his company's men were eating a late meal. As heads turned to see him, he held back tears of relief. He was among friends. Not yet completely safe and no longer with his best friend, but he had escaped the inescapable trap.

His chief herder found him while he was sprawled on the ground, having eaten his fill after giving his horse a supplement of corn and a drink at a stream. "Hey, Ballard," the man growled, scowling down at him in the moonlight. "'Bout time you showed up. Straggling's not allowed even when a friend's hurt."

Terry shot to his feet. "Yes, sir. Not intentional straggling, sir. Got separated by the enemy."

His superior stared at him. "The enemy, you say? What do you think you're doing, lying around like it's a sunny day at the beach? Report to Captain Trafton on the double. After your debriefing, get your bones in shape, trooper, and be ready to ride. The colonel's not gonna keep us here like sittin' ducks."

The chief swept his arm toward a mass of Black men at the edge of the camp, squatting around their own small campfires. "The officers tried to tell all these tagalongs that the ride was too hard, that they'd have to keep going all night. But the colonel couldn't deny them their liberty." He pointed to the right side of the throng. "You'll take that half of the trainees. Keep the mules, wagons, horses and riders in line."

Terry saluted with a "Yes, sir," then strode toward the captain's dominating tent on a section of higher ground. He'd almost said it would be his honor to help the tagalongs. How strange that would have sounded to the chief herder and to most White men.

Yet, how true.

CHAPTER 28

May 2, 1863, Baton Rouge

S ara put her gloved hand in Tom's as he waited to help her up
the steps to the boardwalk's rough planks leading to the
Baton Rouge Mercantile. Although not feeling the least bit
feeble, she leaned into Tom's support. This chivalry was one
American custom she'd come to enjoy more and more, especially
with that certain gentleman next to her.

"Thank you, Tom." Sara surveyed the crowded walkway. "It
looks like people are making the best of what they have left.
Agatha said the Mercantile occupied an 'impressive' building
before the Union cannoneers destroyed it."

"So I heard. The business still serves as a gathering place for
the whole area." Tom guided her toward the entrance. "This is
where Thad bought some items on his wife's shopping list before
our first Port Hudson trip. But he couldn't afford the astronomical
prices of the store's one bag of sugar or its two bags of salt.
Coffee and wheat flour were not for sale at any price. Today, I'm
guessing improvised tools, cornmeal, a few vegetables,
houseware articles, and maybe homespun clothes will be the

main things for sale. Of course, the farm doesn't need any of those."

"Even if I cannot find much that is on Agatha's list, it will be interesting to see American items in a real general store. I'm happy to do my part in giving you and Mr. Pendleton an excuse to 'roam.'"

The two men's "roaming" had become necessary when Colonel Irwin's assistant, visiting the port, had sent word for them to meet him on his Union ship's long boat. Tom had driven the surrey conveying them and Sara since the Evanses chose to stay home rather than risk being associated with the Union rendezvous. Of course, everyone in the house was curious—and a little nervous—about what the meeting would reveal.

Tom tipped a make-believe hat to Sara. "Then I'll leave you to your exploration of the spike-tip harrow for planting, if it's still in stock, and the hay-cutting scythe. Of course, you *might* gravitate toward more feminine items." One corner of his mouth curved up.

"I just might." She gave a small bow to Tom and then to Mr. Pendleton, still in the surrey across the street. Anticipating the chance to browse aisles displaying kitchen crocks and teacups with handles, quilted bed coverings, and the like, she gaily stepped inside the noisy store.

Lucille Steadman, fingering a scarf for sale, stood not two feet away. Before Sara could duck out, Lucille spied her.

"Why, Sara, what a lovely surprise. But are you here without your guardian?" Lucille peered around her.

Sara smiled despite the tightening in her chest. "Uh, no. Mr. Pendleton and Tom conducted me here before taking care of their own errands. I must buy as many items on Agatha's list as possible."

"You'll be lucky to get even one or two of them." Lucille

waved her arm at the empty shelves. "Mr. Stafford apologizes over and over for the measly supply and places all blame on the blockade. Rightly so, I imagine, but unproductive apologizing doesn't make it easier to bear. I do so hate how the war has rooted up everything." She glanced at Sara's dangling reticule and empty arms. "But didn't you bring something to barter?"

"I have a few coins to make the purchases."

"Gold?" She'd lowered her voice to just above a whisper. "Did you and your fellow travelers strike it rich in the California gold fields?" She gave a suspicious laugh.

"No, we did not get outside of San Francisco. The coins are from a payment for simple items my brother and I made while marooned."

"Now, that sounds interesting. We must really have tea where we don't talk about the battles, shortages, or slaves. I'm tired to death of those subjects. Your experiences must have been fascinating."

"Yes, I guess you could say they were." *If you enjoy being marooned, under the threat of pirates.* She drew her shopping list from her reticule and perused it. Perhaps Lucille would take the hint and attend to her own shopping.

"Do you hear that?" Lucille turned toward the door, then took Sara's arm and pulled her into the exodus of shoppers flooding the boardwalk.

"It sounds like cheering and a band, does it not?' Sara extricated herself from Lucille's grasp.

"I believe it's some kind of parade. Let's go see. Come on. We're getting left behind." Lucille raised her parasol.

"Mr. Pendleton—"

"They'll meet you back here. I'm sure they'll head toward the excitement too. You know how men are." Lucille put her hand to her chest. "Oh, Sara. Wouldn't it be the most wonderful thing in the world if the South has won this awful war!"

Sara nodded with what she hoped was a naïve expression.

While they headed toward the town's center, walking past the rubble of other businesses not yet rebuilt, the music and cheering grew louder. After several blocks, they came upon a long line of mud-covered cavalrymen on equally dirty horses, parading four abreast, with sabers drawn, around the public Royal Square.

Sara studied the men's muddy uniforms. "I think they're wearing blue uniforms. Am I wrong?"

"Huh!" Lucille stretched her neck forward, staring. "Looks that way, so our men must have stripped them off the Yankees' dead bodies."

"Excuse me, ma'am." A short, balding gentleman standing next to them in the crowd bowed to Lucille. "I couldn't help overhearing. This *is* a Yankee parade."

"I beg to differ." Lucille looked down her nose at the man. "The despicable occupiers would doubtless cheer for their fellow Yanks, but not these citizens here with us."

"Look, I should know," the man persisted. "I'm a reporter with the *Jackson Mississippian* newspaper, and I've been riding like the dickens trying to catch up with these raiders. But like our infantry and cavalry, I was always a day or two behind until this morning."

"Then why in heaven's name would our people cheer? And I believe you were also." Lucille's lip curled.

"For their bravery. Their amazing accomplishment." The reporter's tone implied she'd questioned the obvious. "They won the race. Rode six hundred miles through enemy territory— enemy for them, you know. They tore up track and telegraph wire but with few killed or wounded on either side. Respected the womenfolk, which can't be said about enough men in wartime.

Didn't burn farms or plantations."

"I'm sure they stole plenty of things, didn't they?" Lucille gave an icy look in return to the reporter's nod. "No doubt they were like the biblical plague of locusts."

Sara gave an audible gasp. A passing rider's profile looked exactly like Terry's. But it couldn't be. She kept her eyes glued on him, but he never looked fully to the side.

"Do you recognize someone in that appalling spectacle?" Lucille's eyes glinted with distrust.

Sara shook her head. "One of the men resembled a man I last saw in New Orleans. That is all." She cautioned herself not to get carried away by wishful thinking. Or say too much.

"These men, known as the Grierson Raiders, set out from Tennessee." The reporter was more than eager to show off his knowledge. "They rode south and struck Newton Station on our Southern Railroad line first, 'tween Jackson and Meridian, then headed southwest. Long, long way from New Orleans, miss."

Sara's heart resumed its pounding at the mention of Jackson. She drew in a breath, then forced a smile. "Thank you. I knew he had to be just a lookalike, I think you say. I suppose the men are very tired, headed somewhere to clean up and rest?" She paused as if expecting to hear more—like where the men might be bivouacked.

"Rode the last miles all day and all night, I heard. That's why our men never caught up. Some of the troopers had to tie themselves onto their horses last night so they wouldn't fall off in their sleep. They'll have to rest a day or so before another mission. Already saw tents going up couple miles south of town, next to the river."

Sara nodded to the reporter and turned aside from viewing the riders to face Lucille. "Now that we know what the excitement's about, I had best get back to the store. I would hate to make Mr. Pendleton worry. But I do not want to rush you either. I'll be all right by myself."

"Oh no, I'll go with you. I'm not about to cheer for Yanks. And a virtuous, unmarried young lady in this land shouldn't walk through town by herself. My carriage is close by the Mercantile. There's a stall with fabric I noticed on the way. I'll stop for just a minute and see if they have any lace."

Sara hesitated, but could think of no way out. "Thank you, then. You are very kind." A few more minutes with the fiend wouldn't hurt. After all, it was extremely unlikely she'd really seen Terry no matter how much she wished she had.

The stop for lace turned into twenty long minutes as Lucille vacillated between several lace trims, but they finally arrived back at the store. A quick survey of the nearly empty shop revealed that Mr. Pendleton and Tom still hadn't returned.

Determined to rid herself of Lucille, Sara drew out Agatha's shopping list again. "I'm thankful we could investigate, uh, the unusual parade together. Now, excuse me please. I must hurry to fulfill Agatha's order. But I will look forward to another time when we have a better chance to chat." She bowed and turned toward a small pile of work gloves.

"All right. We both need to be about our business, don't we?" Lucille swished her skirt and moved a slight arm's length away.

The work gloves were the only item Sara found on the list. A clerk almost laughed in her face when she asked for sugar or salt, wanting to give a bag to their hosts as a special treat. While she was paying for the gloves, the men returned.

"Could we please leave town now if you have no further errands? I feel a headache coming on." Sara wiped her brow.

Lucille, busying herself with a set of corncob dolls, had remained close by as though positioning herself to eavesdrop.

"Why, yes indeed." Mr. Pendleton took Sara's right arm with his free hand. "Thomas can bring the surrey. It's at the stables two blocks away."

"Oh, I'm not feeling faint. I can walk that far. There was such a lot of excitement today that I am eager to lean back in the surrey and close my eyes for a spell."

Tom gave her a questioning look, then took the lead as they walked to the stables, making sure they avoided horse droppings at the crossings and other obstacles on the way. When they had the horse and surrey in hand again, he scrutinized Sara's face before helping her onto the bench. "I've never known you to complain of too much excitement. Are you really feeling poorly?"

"No, I am all right." She ran her tongue over her dry lips. "I don't want my imagination to get your hopes up, but I have to tell you something others do not need to hear, especially Lucille Steadman."

"What is it, Sara?" His brow furrowed.

Mr. Pendleton, already seated, put his hand to his ear to hear.

"While you were both on the long boat, a Union cavalry paraded through the center of town. I know it could not possibly be Terry, but one of the troopers resembled him from the side."

Tom turned pale. "Oh God, please let it be."

"Amen," Mr. Pendleton added.

"But how could it be him?" She was almost sobbing. "The person was riding with a brigade that came all the way from Tennessee. He had a beard. He just partly looked my way, and from a distance. I'm only mentioning this because I know we have to check every possibility, far-fetched or not."

"Do you know the direction of their camp, my dear?" Mr. Pendleton reached out, handing her his handkerchief.

"A spectator said a couple of miles south of the city, next to the river." Sara blotted her cheeks and accepted Tom's help into the surrey, wishing she could comfort *him*.

"There's no time to lose, Thomas. Let's get underway." Her guardian patted her hand, but refrained from more words.

She returned the handkerchief with her thanks, while thinking how her brother would scold her for lack of self-control. Moreover, she'd forgotten Tom's own strength. He had persevered after being disappointed before, hadn't he? And didn't he recover well from his failed rescue attempt?

As their surrey's wheels turned beneath them, they passed Lucille's stationary carriage. The driver was stowing packages while Lucille observed the process. When Tom slowed the horse and surrey to turn the first corner, the carriage still hadn't moved.

Evidently, Lucille had more interest in her purchases than in spying any further. Sara breathed a prayer of thanks. *And please,* she added, *watch over Terry and keep him alive ... if he isn't the cavalryman I saw.*

Tom raked his eyes over the tents covering the grounds at the Magnolia Mound Plantation. Could his brother really be in one of them? He told himself to calm down. Lots of people looked like other people. Terry had no inclination to join up with Federal troops. His single-minded goal was to reach New York and their family. Even if he'd somehow escaped the Jackson prison, he was as likely to have joined the Union raiders as their loyal dog Tuffy would join a wolf pack.

He brought the surrey to a stop on the lane fronting the field of tents. To his left, hundreds of horses were in a straight line. Two guards ahead were checking passes.

One thing was going right anyway. Colonel Irwin's assistant

had given him four passes for the group, expressing a hope they would still be reunited with Terry, regretful he had not been in either of the prisoner exchanges. The passes gave them unlimited freedom to pass through Union-held territory. The rest of the meeting on the boat had been a shock, but Tom put it aside for later.

He handed three of the passes to the guard for his inspection.

"Signed by a colonel under General Banks." The trooper pursed his lips. "These passes allow you to proceed, but I wouldn't advise the lady to do so."

"Yes, I'll pull out of the way." Tom gestured over his shoulder. "The lady and her guardian will stay in the surrey. I'm looking for my brother. All I know is that bushwhackers took him near New Orleans and planned to throw him into the Rebel prison at Jackson."

"All the men in the company I'm with started out in Tennessee, and I ain't heard of no additions to my regiment. But I don't know 'bout the 7th Illinois. Also, former slaves with their mules an' sway-back mares joined in along the way. He could've helped with their herding."

"Were they and the herders in the parade?"

"Yes, Colonel Grierson wanted the folks here to see the slaves' desire to be free. If you want to check with the 7th Illinois, they're camped on the far side. You're welcome to check with the herders too. Good luck." He returned the passes.

Tom moved the surrey onto the edge of the field. After securing Thad's horse, he walked around to Sara and Mr. Pendleton.

His elder waved his hand at the layout before them. "Searching through all those men? Not as bad as hunting for a needle in a haystack, but it's going to require a lot of patience." Leaning on his cane, he climbed out of the surrey and placed his hand on Tom's shoulder. "Let's pray the Almighty leads you to Terrence if he's here. I feel as though we've forgotten he's our Good Shepherd."

Tom bowed his head, but mostly whispered his own pleas for help before joining in the final *amen*. He turned two of the passes over to Mr. Pendleton, then took off.

Two hours later, the sun was setting while he still peered into one tent after another and walked between dozing troopers, lying on the grass with their boots still on. Frequently, he leaned far down to check under the blooming magnolia trees. He could make much quicker progress if the men weren't in such deep sleep. After waking a few men and being growled at, he'd determined to carry on without anybody's help. He shouldn't have allowed himself to have hope with such an improbable possibility.

He moved the next tent's flap and gazed inside.

His heart skipped a beat. There lay his brother's twin if he wasn't Terry.

"Terry?"

The man didn't move.

His blood ran cold. Could he be Terry—dead?

"Terry?" he said louder.

The man next to the still body nudged him.

The next second Tom was sobbing with joy.

Terry was hopping around outside the tent as if he'd gone crazy. Then they hugged.

"Oh, God! Oh, God," Tom cried, collapsing on the bedroll, "at last!"

When they'd both regained a little equilibrium, Tom thought to ask Terry about his duty to the Raiders.

"I was mustered in temporarily—if that's the right word for a volunteer—and mustered out before the captain dozed off.

Everyone was a walking zombie 'cause we rode days without stopping except to water or replace worn-out horses. I don't know how we made it through the parade. The captain gave me a kind of certificate and wrote a note on it, stating I could keep the Arabian horse I rode 'cause I wouldn't get any pay. That was fine with me. I would've paid the Raiders for letting me tagalong. That poor horse has about seen the last of its days, but I'd like to take it with us. Don't want it turned into horse meat by the Secesh. Heard they eat anything that moves 'cause of Grant's anaconda squeeze."

"Sure." Tom blinked back more tears. "I know how you love horses. Let's get the animal. Sara and Mr. Pendleton are in a surrey at the edge of the camp. They're gonna be half out of their minds when they see you." He could hardly wait for the moment.

After the chief herder wished Terry and his horse well, Tom led his brother and the Arabian to where Sara and Mr. Pendleton waited. When they were about twenty yards away, Sara looked up. The next second she had leapt from the surrey, and Mr. Pendleton was climbing out the other side. For a second, Tom thought Sara was going to throw her arms around Terry, but she stopped and bowed instead. Forbidden tears wet her cheeks.

Mr. Pendleton, hobbling up, swung his cane in the air and shouted *Hallelujah* before he grabbed Terry's hand and shook it as though he couldn't ever let it go.

On the way to the Evans' farm, Tom repeatedly looked back at Terry riding his horse after them. It wasn't a dream. But still, he had to check again and again.

CHAPTER 29

A whirlwind of introductions, questions, and explanations swirled from the minute Tom, with Terry and the other two, arrived at the farm. Everyone wanted to hear everything about his brother's experiences, especially how Terry had ended up as a Grierson Raider. But Thad held up a hand to stop the chatter when Mr. Pendleton passed him a letter from Colonel Irwin, marked "confidential."

"This has to be important. Give me a few minutes, please." Thad unsealed the envelope.

Mrs. Evans eyed the letter for a second, then beckoned them toward the dining room. "We didn't wait on our meal for you, except for the dessert. However, we saved good portions, so there's plenty for Mr. Ballard too. Why don't the four of you wash up, and take your time eating. We can have our coffee—such as it is—and brandied-peach meringue together in the parlor. That way we can hear the details if our guest will save them for us."

Terry smiled. "Yes, ma'am, I'll do that. And please call me Terry. Tom may be a *mister* now, but I'm younger than him."

"All right. As you wish … And Terry," she added after a minute, "the laundry's rinse water is still in the tub right outside the kitchen if you would like to make use of it until you can have a real bath. Your brother can bring you a change of clothes from your valise stored upstairs."

"I'm sure the air will be fresher after that." Terry chuckled, then followed Mrs. Evans.

After Terry had washed up and rejoined them in the dining room, Tom assessed his brother's lean figure. "Are you doing all right? I bet you're still completely played out." How often he'd had nightmares of Terry suffering and dying. Yet, his brother was alive, breathing right there in front of him.

"Yep, I'm tired, but a whole lot better today than I was yesterday." Terry gave one of his good-natured grins, like when they'd gone hunting with Tuffy—a grin that had disappeared even before San Francisco. "I just hope I don't splat my head in the sweet potatoes or whatever we're having."

While the good-smelling food, including sweet potatoes, was being passed around, Thad joined them at the dining room table. "Please, don't let me stop you from eating, but I'll take this chance, after all, to speak with you. We've already explained the letter's communication to the children, who don't need to hear it a second time. I assume the colonel's decision was relayed during your meeting with his assistant today?" His gaze moved from Tom to Mr. Pendleton.

Mr. Pendleton looked over his spectacles and nodded. "The news distressed us at the time, thinking we'd be forced to move farther away from Terrence and also leave this fine family. Now, however, the orders for us appear beneficial to everyone, and the Union passes are a godsend. We haven't informed Terrence or Miss Sara, however." He gave Sara an apologetic look. "While in the surrey, I could think of nothing but our locating Terrence."

"I'll summarize the contents then." Thad tapped the letter. "Because of growing suspicion among the community as well as the army's needs, Colonel Irwin has ordered four officers of the Army of the Gulf to be billeted in our home, starting two days from now. Our family is to tell the Confederate sympathizers that the Union requisitioned our farm, but is allowing our family— and only our family—to stay in order to carry on the farming. The most upsetting part to the children is losing Miss Sara's archery lessons and, unbelievably, the arithmetic lessons by Tom."

Tom caught a look of surprise cross Terry's face.

"My wife and I will miss your fellowship and kind assistance," Thad continued, "and she isn't a bit happy in having the men take charge of the house. We're hoping their presence won't interfere with our aid to fugitives."

"You've been tremendous hosts, and we care for you and your family ... a great deal." Tom took a swig of tea to compose himself.

Sara offered a short bow of agreement.

"Indeed. Well put." Mr. Pendleton raised his glass. "To our hosts. We couldn't have asked for a greater kindness than what you've provided."

After the meal was finished and they had all joined together in the parlor, Tom ached as Terry related his appalling experiences. First, the grueling trip to the prison—even worse than Tom had feared. Then, Terry's desperate plunge into the Pearl River with his new friend Joshua and their close brushes with drowning. The hairs on Tom's nape rose at Talbot's attempts to kill the elder freedman and then his grandson at the widow's farm. Yet, Terry's intention to rescue the Black child at the risk to his own life confounded him. What had happened to his brother's lifelong faintheartedness and his vacillation with the issue of slavery?

When Terry described how he and Joshua had met the Raiders' pickets, Tom couldn't contain himself. "Glory, Terry, glory!" He smiled at the surprised group. "That's what our fugitives would say if they were here. Right? They knew how to express themselves, and *glory* is the perfect word."

"Fugitives? The two at the cabin?" Terry cocked his head.

"Yes, and one more. I'll tell you later." Tom rubbed his cheek. "Sorry to interrupt."

After nodding, Terry recounted his hard ride with the Raiders, his heartbreak at Joshua's amputated lower leg, and the irony of Talbot's less severe wound. Then his face reddened and he paused, glancing around.

"Don't stop now," Robert put in. "How did you get to Baton Rouge?"

"Hush," his mother ordered. "He's going to tell us."

"Sorry, Robert. I'm sorting things out in order to include just what's most important." Terry angled his body toward the rest of the group. "Anyway"—his voice shook a little—"I got separated from the brigade by the Secesh troops. I was trapped. Really trapped, and didn't see any way out. While I hid in a church cemetery, trying to find a solution, I, uh, well, had some deep thinking to do. A choice to make. But"—his face brightened—"about that time, a Confederate battalion went thundering past, picked up the local unit, and then turned in at a plantation for the night, letting me sneak by—like it was providential, to use my elder's word." He tilted his head to Mr. Pendleton. "After that, I caught up with the Raiders. We rode straight through at breakneck speeds, and here I am."

While Tom groped for a way to say how proud he was of Terry, without sounding older brotherish, Mr. Pendleton pronounced, "What a wonder this is! The Lord God sustained Terrence and brought him safely through trials beyond our worst imaginations." He beamed at Terry. "Without question, you're right to mention Providence."

Terry looked abashed. "Actually, sir, I should have credited God more directly. I did leave out something awfully important."

"You're crediting God?" The words slipped out of Tom's mouth unbidden.

Sara and Mr. Pendleton looked just as stunned.

Terry turned toward Mr. and Mrs. Evans. "The three of them know how I opposed Mr. Pendleton's efforts to win me over to God's side—and I'm sorry I didn't listen."

Mr. Pendleton waved off his words. "Don't trouble yourself about my part."

"So, here's what I didn't tell. While I hid in the cemetery, a thought came from nowhere. Well, maybe it came from a tombstone. Anyway, the thought struck me that *God* had been chasing me down. I mean, the Almighty himself had actually been chasing *me*. So, I decided he had to care for me a little." He glanced around the circle at the nodding heads.

"And something else," Terry continued. "I figured if I kept battling him, I'd end up like Talbot, in the same place with the brute. So, I called on Jesus. Like Mr. Pendleton explained once, I took Jesus' offer to be my Savior. I figured a gift was a gift, even undeserved."

"That's right, Terry!" Tom had a hard time staying seated.

Mr. Pendleton chimed in, "Yes, indeed. Indeed, it is!"

Terry beamed. "Then, I decided to see if my Savior could get me out of the Secesh trap. And as I told you, I rode right out. Guess that sums it all up."

Tom smacked his chair's arm. "Terry! Nothing in the wide world could ever make me happier!"

"Daughters of a samurai can't cry," Sara sobbed out, "but I can't help it."

Mr. Pendleton wiped his eyes. "Oh, my boy! I can hardly

contain myself. It's as though I've already reached the pearly gates and am dancing with the angels."

Both Marylou and Robert looked up at the ceiling as though they might see the dancing.

"This is certainly a reason to rejoice—a light in the darkening skies." Thad eyed his wife. "It's our privilege to be witnesses."

"Oh my! Yes, it is!" Mrs. Evans affirmed. "And if only we lived in a normal time, y'all wouldn't have to rush off. We could get to know Terrence, er, Terry better. And when you did finally have to leave us, we could bless your travels homeward with a grand neighborhood send-off."

Thad stroked her hand. "Changes come, whether we like it or not."

"Yes," Mr. Pendleton said, "and so suddenly—both blessings, as we've so wonderfully just heard, and also the new challenges we learned about today."

Tom jerked at the word "suddenly." The two days remaining was no time at all. Before they knew it, they'd be ushered out the door. "Do we have a plan for our departure?"

Mr. Pendleton drew out his Union pass. "These precious papers are smoothing the way. Of course, they look like passports to the world, but we're actually blocked in every direction but one. New Orleans is a dead-end until the war is finished. Going east would take us into enemy territory crawling with Rebel troops. However, since General Grant moved his vast army down the *west* side of the river before transporting them to this side, I believe we can follow the army's route in the opposite direction, up to Milligan's Bend. From there, according to the newspaper, civilians can board steamships traveling north on the upper Mississippi and then onto the Ohio River. How does that sound to the rest of you?"

Tom tempered his enthusiasm, not wanting to hurt the Evanses. "It sounds like a good route to me since we obviously must be on our way."

Terry and Sara agreed.

Mrs. Evans wagged her head. "The four officers billeted here are unlikely to pitch in like you folks."

Marylou's eyes grew large. "Four officers? In gold-braided uniforms with brass buttons?'

"Most likely married," her mother advised, "and when the war's over, they'll take off like rabbits before a fox."

"Do not think for a minute you'll be fraternizing with them." Her father scowled at her. "A stay at Aunt Nell's is in order, but we'll discuss this later."

Marylou made a face, but didn't argue.

"We'll all help you prepare the place for the men," Mr. Pendleton offered.

Mrs. Evans looked more put out. "And how does the colonel think we can sleep four officers here? We can have three upstairs if Marylou leaves by their arrival. But can we put the other one in the room for the runaways?"

"We'll need to take that room ourselves, my dear." Thad screwed up his mouth. "A minor sacrifice for the men in blue, and we can hide a fugitive more easily in a pinch. Terrence here will occupy it for the time being, however. After what he has experienced, its small size probably won't distress him. In fact, I imagine he'll want to retire as soon as the linens are spread."

"You're right, sir. My eyelids keep trying to shut like they have a mind of their own. Much as I want to hear about everything that's happened while I've been gone, I guess it'll have to wait. Otherwise, you'll have to drag my body to bed."

Tom walked with Terry to the fugitives' room, then lingered at the door. "At last, we're going home, brother. Home!"

"I'm kind of scared to count on it." Terry grimaced. "You reckon it's wrong for me to feel that way now that, you know, I'm supposed to have faith."

"I'm sure God understands. It seems like lots of saints in the Bible were worried, but they kept going. And that's what we're doing. And he knows how happy I am right now. I can't think up good enough words to describe it."

"If the superior communicator can't come up with words, it's a sure bet I can't either 'cause I feel the same." Terry crawled onto the cot. A minute later, he was snoring.

CHAPTER 30

Mid-May, 1863, Mississippi River's Greenville Bend

The Mississippi River steamboat, requisitioned by the Union Army to transport its soldiers on emergency leave and its wounded toward northern hospitals, vibrated with the roar of cannon. Smokestack plumes mixed with the acrid smells of battle. Tom sat cross-legged on his cabin's berth. Terry paced, and Mr. Pendleton had taken the room's one chair. None of them tried to speak over the thundering blasts.

Tom, along with Terry, had offered to help defend the boat, but its first mate, U.S. Army Lieutenant Grayson, turned them down flat. They had been ordered to their rooms along with everyone else who was not an active-duty soldier or part of the civilian crew.

The river's Greenville Bend was living up to its infamy. The river narrowed beside a peninsula of dense woods, thus providing the ideal place for Confederate partisan rangers and local guerrillas to lurk while watching for vulnerable steamboats. The zings made it clear the attackers' bullets still riddled the cotton bales piled along the boat's railings. Yet the roar of cannon, shouted commands and pounding boots had begun to diminish.

This was most likely due to the addition of firepower from a Union ram that had caught up with their boat. This ram, owned by the Mississippi Marine Brigade, had been fortified by iron plates to enhance its ability to ram enemy boats and made a formidable escort.

Tom figured the passengers would be safe enough so long as the steamboat's boilers functioned and the boat didn't ground on a sandbar. But if the boat and ram floundered, the guerrillas would rush on board, and hand-to-hand combat would ensue. He wouldn't stand down then, and he knew his brother wouldn't either.

As planned, they had first caught a ride on one of the wagon trains returning north after supplying General Grant's army. Reaching Milliken's Bend, a town next to a Union army post, Colonel Irwin's passes enabled them to board the steamboat. To Terry's gratification, his Arabian had been stabled with other horses on the engine deck. Everything had been going swimmingly well until the morning attack.

The whistles and booms of cannon fire finally stopped altogether as did the battle cries.

Mr. Pendleton stood. "I believe the boat has made it through."

"We thrashed 'em," a passing cabin boy called to Tom and the other two when they stood in the doorway, observing the boat's forward movement. "Pilot's taking us up river."

"Good to hear," Tom called to the boy, then turned to the others. "How about we see for ourselves that the boat's secure and seaworthy, then check on Sara?" He'd almost said to check on Sara first, but the responsible act was to make sure the vessel was intact.

Their investigation showed the boat to be in fairly good condition. They found the side paddle wheels turning unhindered, men hard at work patching the bullet holes in the bulwark, seams being recaulked, and the carpenter's assistant replacing damaged planks in the main deck. So, Tom set a quick pace in leading the group toward Sara's stateroom.

Dressed in a navy-blue morning gown, she stood under an awning in front of the ladies' salon, which had kept its title despite becoming part of the boat's sick bay. As they approached, she gave a weak smile. "I thought we were out of the battlefields when we left Baton Rouge. Danger seems to catch us wherever we go."

Mr. Pendleton adjusted his spectacles. "Let's hope that word doesn't get around and we're thrown overboard like the biblical Jonah." His eyes shown with mild amusement.

Tom exchanged a knowing look with Terry since an unwanted "Jonah" was precisely what several of the crew had called Tom on their original ship. But those awful days were behind him, and hopefully, no more obstacles would rear their heads on their way home.

"Two men were brought here with serious wounds," Sara said, motioning toward the salon. "I offered to help, but the doctor said only married women or widows, like the other ladies onboard, could nurse the men. Those four ladies assured me they had things 'well in hand' and that I was 'too young' besides."

"It was thoughtful of you to offer, nevertheless." Mr. Pendleton used his cane to tap the salon door closed after two men came out with an empty litter. "And resilient, I might add. Few people could act with so much strength and courage in a foreign country and culture. You are a rare gem."

Tom caught Sara's appealing blush, then glanced at Terry. Did his brother still resent their friend, see her as some kind of threat?

"I couldn't agree more, sir," Terry declared. "And I'm sure that's true for Tom too." His lips gave a hint of a wicked smile.

Before Tom could do more than utter *Well, yes*, Terry went on. "Now, if you three will excuse me, guess I better check on my horse. Make sure no bullet made it to that deck."

"I'll join you if that's all right. Looks like things have smoothed out here." Tom looked at the other two.

"You can all come if you want." Terry gave an inclusive gesture. "You might like getting to know ol' Commander a little better."

Sara chose to join them, while Mr. Pendleton said he needed a rest to regather his strength.

"Commander, is it?" Tom asked, descending the stairs with Terry on one side and Sara on the other. "When we picked up your steed, I remember you hadn't given it a name. Didn't you say that was on purpose so you didn't get too attached?"

"The problem is, I already got attached anyway. He may not last the trip, but I'd sure like to turn him loose in our pasture if he does. No gunfire. No hard rides that siphon all his energy. You should have seen him when he was in his prime. A real beauty."

After entering the aisle leading to the horse stalls, the group drew up short at the sight of dark blood oozing from under the gate of Commander's stall.

Tom groaned, and Sara laid hold of his arm.

Terry jerked open the gate. The horse lay on his side—his throat cut. Terry knelt and put his hand under the horse's nostrils, murmuring, "No, no, Commander!" Stroking the horse's forehead above the glazed eyes, he sobbed, then wailed, while still talking to the horse. "You worked so hard! Such a good horse! I'm sorry. Sorry." He swiped at his tears, then stood and looked at Tom. "How could anyone do this to a helpless animal?"

A boy jumped out from behind a hay bale across from the stall. "Teacher Terry, I'm sorry. I didn't do it!"

Terry gasped. "Sam, what're you doing here? What happened?"

"The Secesh, he killed your horse. I was hidin'. He's the one wanted to hang me at the widow's. Called me to come out or he'd kill your horse. I'm sorry. I didn't come out."

A shadowy figure stumbled out of an end stall, cursing.

Tom stared in disbelief. Talbot! He prepared himself for a fight to the finish.

The fiend stopped.

Terry had drawn a Colt pistol from under the saddle hanging next to them on a pole. "Drop the knife!" he ordered.

Tom gaped at his brother, then managed to say, "Horse thieves hang. Goes double for horse killers." He waited for Talbot to lunge and the gun to fire.

"Go ahead. Finish me off, Turd," Talbot ground out when nothing happened. He hadn't dropped the knife.

"Sam, bring a uniformed officer. On the double!" Terry's voice had become cold, professional. He kept his pistol trained on Talbot. "You're gonna get a trial by someone who doesn't despise you. Guess a man's life is worth more than a horse—even a great one like this one. Maybe you'll just end up in a Yankee prison. Find out what it's like firsthand."

"He's hunted you like a demon, and you never did a thing wrong to him." Tom longed to pound the man into a pulp. "It's time to end it, Terry."

The boy's shout for help resounded throughout the deck, causing bellows from the livestock.

"I was after the whelp this time," Talbot rasped. "Heard he'd run off to Bruinsburg when the Yanks crossed over. Didn't know you two were here 'til I seen you with your pretty missy this mornin'." He glanced at Sara, who scowled. "Saw your Arabian by the house at Wall's Bridge, where your buddy got me water."

Talbot appeared less anxious for a bullet.

Three muscle-bound men came running. A fourth loped behind with a rope.

Terry lowered his gun while the men tied Talbot up. "Tom, I couldn't shoot him. In a way, he saved me because I didn't want to be like him. It's strange."

Tom couldn't shake his head or nod either. He was flabbergasted, to use his grandpa's word.

Lieutenant Grayson met the group at the foot of the stairway. After hearing Terry's account of what happened, he viewed the bloody knife one of the soldiers had forced out of Talbot's hand. "Keep the lawbreaker tied up tight," he ordered the men. "Don't move things around."

The lieutenant turned to Terry. "Take your pistol and keep it unloaded in your stateroom. The captain will view the horse and knife and then hear the case when he has time today."

A sniffle from behind Terry caught the officer's attention as he started up the stairs. He stepped down and grabbed the boy's arm, dragging him forward.

"He's a freedman's child." Terry put his hand on the trembling boy's shoulder. "I met him at a widow's farm before I joined up with the Grierson Raiders. But I don't know how he got here."

"Speak up, boy." The lieutenant released Sam's arm. "How'd you come to be on the boat?"

"Mister Jerome let me come with him to go up north, suh." Sam could hardly speak he was shaking so much. "My family, they know. I be a wood chopper now. I carry the wood."

Grayson shook his head. "You're far too young to work on this boat. So, you'll have to find yourself a way back to your family."

"Sir," Terry cut in, "our fellow traveler, Mr. Pendleton, who you may remember from the captain's table, is lame and in need of a helper. He allowed his original companion to stay in San Francisco with a long-lost relative."

The lieutenant frowned. "He obviously wouldn't have a pass for the boy. Do you really think he'd pay for the boy's ride?"

"Yes, sir. And if he wouldn't, I would." Terry stood tall, a regular Rock of Gibraltar.

"So would I," Sara piped up.

"I would too," Tom said, regretting his slowness. His mind was still occupied with his brother's strange reactions.

Terry gave a final pat to the boy's shoulder. "As I said, I know Sam. His father and grandfather helped me and a friend after we escaped from the Confederate prison at Jackson."

"All right, *if* the captain approves and someone buys his passage. But you'll have to make room for him in your staterooms. There are no servants' quarters available on this ship."

"We can do that," Tom managed to say despite his amazement at what was still transpiring. Of course, God would begin to change his brother's heart, but it was inconceivable that anyone would spare an enemy like Talbot, who'd never shown one speck of mercy. And not only that, but the extent of his brother's devotion to the Black child still baffled him.

They found Mr. Pendleton in the saloon next to the dining room, talking with two of the off-duty officers, who had brought him a cup of real coffee from their private stash. He stood with the help of his cane and thanked the two men, who strolled away.

"Terry's horse was slain by Talbot," Sara burst out as soon as the men were gone.

Tom stared at her. Why had she spoken up before Terry? One look at Terry's struggle to remain calm and collected answered the question. His brother was well on his way to manhood, but who wouldn't be devastated over such a needless loss of a loyal animal? Tom could hardly hold back a sob himself as Sara continued her account.

Mr. Pendleton voiced what Tom still struggled to understand. "Why didn't you shoot Talbot, Terrence? No one would have blamed you. We are allowed to defend ourselves."

"He halted, sir." Terry had regained control. "He looked scared even though he spoke so rough. I knew he wasn't ready to meet his Maker. I still despised him, but the widow I told you about, she warned me that hatred would swallow me alive. It almost had. So, I turned Talbot over to God. I heard a minister talk one time about God's words, 'Vengeance is mine. I will repay.' Of course, it had just scared me then."

"Very wise, son. Very wise indeed." Mr. Pendleton closed his eyes for a second. Tom was sure it was in silent praise.

Of course, the saint of a man was all too happy to take Sam under his wing as his companion. Mr. Pendleton was almost salivating at the possibilities of educating the boy further in the Christian faith as well as in geography as they made their way to New York. Then to Tom's further amazement, Terry revealed he'd been teaching Sam to read—illegally, no less—and was anxious to continue the lessons. Sara joined in, offering to teach Sam about her country and the basic defensive moves of jiu-jitsu. Tom brought up the rear by offering arithmetic lessons.

When Mr. Pendleton asked Tom to lead them in a prayer of thanksgiving for Sam's deliverance from Talbot and for the Almighty to comfort Terry as only God could, he agreed to pray out loud before others for the first time. How could he not? His heart was full.

Three hours later, Lieutenant Grayson approached the group in the corner of the saloon they had reoccupied after their meal.

"I have a report for Terrence Ballard," he announced, standing stiff and proper.

He had their rapt attention.

Grayson cleared his throat. "The captain has found Mr. Matthew Talbot guilty of horse thievery and slaughter. Because of this heinous act as well as his unlawful presence on this boat and his association with Confederate irregulars, Mr. Talbot will be confined onboard. At Cairo, he will be transferred to the Union's Camp Douglas prison for the duration of the war."

"Thank you, sir," Terry said before the officer pivoted and strode away. He raised his eyebrows at Tom and Mr. Pendleton. "Won't bring Commander back, but at least he got justice." His voice quivered, and he brushed his cheek. "You know, I desperately wanted Talbot's death for months—sometimes could think of nothing else. But I'm relieved. It's like stones lifted off my back."

Tom nodded. "Actually, Dice, Sara, and I did something similar. We let the pirate Bolt have a second chance at life, instead of a sure hanging. We left him to live alone on the island with not much chance of escape—a kind of prison too."

"The inner prison of both men is worse than their circumstances," Mr. Pendleton said. "May they find the release all of us found."

Tom gave a half-hearted *amen*, the best he could muster for the moment.

"I think we're really on our way home, Tom." Terry's eyes had taken on a faraway look. "And Admiral won't have to share the space in our barn after all."

"I am sorry. I can hardly tell you how sorry I am." His brother's pain seemed to have invaded Tom's chest. If only Talbot had been repelled with the other guerrillas.

"It's all right. Commander was worn out, more than I wanted to admit. He may even have hurt some, but kept going anyway. He doesn't hurt anymore now. And I'm awful glad Talbot didn't get Sam." Terry looked at the boy perched on a lounge chair they'd borrowed from the deck. "I'd give more than a thousand Arabian horses to have one Sam with us."

Sam burst out crying.

Tom reached to pat him on the back at the same time as the other three leaned in to do the same.

"I be all right," Sam hiccupped out. "I'm just feelin' choked up an' kinda … kinda all warm inside."

When a smile found its way onto Terry's face, Tom felt the warmth too.

CHAPTER 31

Tom brought the surrey to a stop on their Albany home's drive. His heart beat like a tom-tom. "Here we are!" He thumped his chest while looking at Terry.

"I can hardly believe it." Terry, wide-eyed, stared at their house.

"Hope our folks are here." Tom kept his voice steady, though fear momentarily paralyzed him. The house seemed awfully quiet. Surely, both their parents still lived.

The next minute, Terry, as if struck by lightning, hopped down, causing Tom to follow. "Hope they got our Illinois telegram. Come on! I'm about to burst." Terry rushed around to the far side of the surrey to aid Mr. Pendleton.

Tom opened the surrey's side door next to him to help Sara and Sam out.

Remaining seated, Sara shook her head. "Thank you, but allow us to wait here a bit, please."

"We don't want to barge in on the homecoming." Mr. Pendleton glanced across Sara at the house and its still empty porch. "Fetch us when the excitement has died down."

"All right. I'll come back shortly." Tom followed Terry down the walkway, hardly able to stand the suspense. Would they be enthusiastically welcomed? Or greeted by a list of their transgressions, culminating with their signing on to the merchant ship? Like the parable's prodigal son, he had prepared his apology. But far worse—he swallowed hard—would be a cause for mourning.

All of a sudden, their home's door flew open.

"My boys! Praise God! Eunice, they're here!" Tom's father ran toward them. He swept Tom into his arms, then reached one hand for Terry. Their mother managed to embrace Terry first, smothering him with kisses, and then doing the same to Tom.

Their dog Tuffy circled them, yipping and wagging his tail ferociously.

Tom drew away after several minutes. "Father, I'm sorry." He felt the heat rise in his face.

"And I am too," Terry said from under their father's arm.

"You're both forgiven." His father smiled at them through tears.

"Yes, and you need not think of it again," their mother added, wiping her own tears. She cocked her head, staring at the surrey. "Are there people with you?"

"Our traveling companions. They're giving us a few minutes alone. They stood by us through everything." Tom peered toward the surrey, then leaned over to scratch impatient Tuffy behind his ears.

"They're a big part of why we survived," Terry said. "Two are continuing to the elder's relatives, who live in Boston now. I'm hoping the freedman's boy might stay in this town."

"Free is free, isn't it?" Their lawyer father rubbed his chin. "Without question, he can stay in the town, and we'll see what we should do to help. But right now, all I can do is rejoice at seeing your faces. Can't think about anything else."

"Yes," their mother said. "I can hardly wait to learn what has gone on in your lives. We'll have some refreshments and start by hearing the highlights of your travels. There will be additional days, won't there, to hear more and more details as you rest up?"

"We aren't planning to leave anytime soon, are we, Terry?" Tom chuckled.

Terry beamed at them. "Wild horses couldn't drag me away, like they say."

"We both are eager for more education," Tom went on. "Terry more than myself. But schooling and whatever the army requires are for much later discussions, I reckon."

"Oh, I thought this day would never come!" Their mother hugged herself. "Let's go ahead and have our company come inside with us. I'm sure they'll share our joy."

Their father strode to the surrey and invited Sara, Mr. Pendleton, and Sam to join them.

"Welcome, friends." Tom's mother stretched out her arms as the three walked up the pathway. "We're delighted to have you. As a girl, I wanted to travel and see the world, and now a little of the world has come to us." She wore one of her biggest smiles, reserved for the most special occasions.

The stableboy was called to take care of the surrey, and his father's manservant Peter helped with their valises and Mr. Pendleton's trunk. Soon they were seated around the dining room table, reminding Tom of the Evanses. He sent up a silent prayer for that family's safety. Then he launched into his and Terry's plight of coping with a ship full of bullies and their toilsome, perilous journey down the South American coast, around Cape Horn, and across the Pacific.

"I have to admit I made a terrible mistake on that ship." Tom drew in a breath, determined to admit the burr that had pricked him for so long. "It was really a sin. I stole a wine bottle, feeling I righted a wrong done to me, and I didn't admit my guilt. The captain's investigation of the theft turned up another sailor's minor wrongdoing. That man, who was whipped as an unexpected consequence of my theft, was a cousin of the first mate, named Talbot. He hunted Terry and me like animals and brought on the difficulties we're about to recount. So, one sin, which I thought was insignificant, resulted in horrors for Terry, Sara, and me and for the lashed man, who Talbot claimed lost his mind because of the unfair punishment."

Tom focused on his father's face and waited for his word. Mr. Pendleton had been a great help, but his father had tried to bring him up the best he could all Tom's life.

His father took a sip of coffee, then caught Tom's eye, "First, you are not responsible for that cousin's wrongdoing and punishment. However, your theft itself was wrong. Since Mr. Talbot was First Mate, any misbehavior by the crew affected and reflected on him. Perhaps you could write Mr. Talbot a note if you know where he is. You could state your regret for wrongfully stealing the bottle and for not admitting it. Then you could say you share his sorrow that the inspection revealed another man's wrongdoing, which was too cruelly punished. Just that. Don't mention the unknown person's responsibility in having given wine to the caught wrongdoer, and don't list any of Talbot's own sins in persecuting you and Terry."

"I can do that. He's got an address now—the Camp Douglas prison in Chicago." Tom gave a quick nod at his father's fleeting look of surprise.

"I'd like to point out an important truth related to this." Their father tapped the table in the manner Tom recalled so well. "We learned in your last telegram that both of you have believed in Jesus. You cannot imagine how your mother and I rejoiced." He gave them a look of affection joined by their mother's enthusiastic *yes, yes*! "The Scriptures make it crystal clear that *all* our sins are forgiven through Jesus Christ's sacrifice. Every one of them. If God says we are forgiven, we had better count on it, hadn't we?"

Tom's "Yes, sir, we had better" coincided with Terry's "I'll count on it, sir."

His father struck his forehead a second later. "Speaking of Chicago, a telegram for Terry arrived yesterday." Retrieving it from a pile of papers on the desk, he handed it to Terry. "Go ahead and read it, Son. It must be important. We'll wait."

Terry's hands visibly shook while he opened the folded paper and scanned the message. "It's really good news." His eyes sparkled. "From Joshua, my New York buddy, who you'll hear about when I tell my part."

"Maybe you could go ahead and share the news if it's not confidential." His mother gave a sheepish smile. "Assuage our curiosity."

"All right, I will." He reopened the telegram. "But first you should know that Joshua was badly injured in a battle after escaping with me from the Confederate Jackson prison. His leg was amputated below the knee, and I had to leave him while he was still in a field hospital in Rebel territory."

Their mother murmured, "Oh my."

"So here's what he wrote: 'The Confederates paroled me. I'm with my Chicago cousin. Got a Palmer artificial leg. Can move my ankle joint. Won't need crutches much longer.'" Terry looked up. "That's so great. He'll be able to ride a horse again— what he feared losing most. Then he says he hopes to see me mid-summer. Signs it, 'Trust in Jesus, Your faithful friend.'"

Terry gave a teary-eyed smile. "He's the best man I know besides each of you. He helped me believe too. Thank God he's recovering, and not just his body."

"Indeed," Mr. Pendleton said, "a great cause for thanksgiving."

Tom along with the whole group enthusiastically agreed.

"I'm glad too." Sam said, once everyone had quieted. He tilted his head at Terry. "He's a kind man an' called me a 'fine student.'"

"I remember. And it was true. You worked hard." Terry nodded at Sam, then faced their parents. "This may seem like too much to handle at first. I hope not. While continuing my education, I want to help with Sam's schooling too. In fact, I want to start regular classes for not only Sam but for any other freedmen's children in our town."

"As their teacher?" Their father asked the question on Tom's lips.

"Yes, but maybe not the only one." Terry looked at Tom.

"Sure, I'll pitch in." Pride for his brother welled up, bringing a whole new stream of happiness. "Having become an accomplished arithmetic tutor, I'll help with that and also with science if need be." He smiled at his brother's smirk.

"I think this is a grand project, worthy of our boys," their mother said. "You may be able to arrange for one or two rooms at our church, Terry. Failing success there, your father and I can discuss other options, maybe even our parlor here temporarily." From her twinkling eyes, Tom guessed she hoped to put her oar into the teaching too.

Sam sat still, eyes dripping tears, looking from one face to another.

"Nothing to discuss about the parlor. That's fine." Their father reached over to squeeze Sam's hand. "We can also host you in our extra guest room until something permanent can be worked out—as long as it takes—if you'd like that."

"Y-yes, suh," Sam stammered. "Nothin' I'd like better."

Terry beamed at the boy. "Even before the classes start, I'm going to help *you* write a letter to the widow's home, so she can read it to your folks."

"Thank you, Teacher Terry! Thank you!" Sam jumped up, then instantly sat down, as though remembering himself. "God's blessin' me more than I can hold."

The time around the table extended hour after hour. But when the cook poked her head into the room and asked about supper preparations, they agreed to take a break. Before everyone separated, however, Mr. Pendleton and Sara agreed to spend the night at the family's insistence.

Terry wasted no time in heading with Sam and Tuffy to see Admiral. Their mother left to supervise their maid Betsy's preparations of the guest rooms. Their father had a document he had to deliver before the day was out. Mr. Pendleton excused himself to freshen up in the downstairs powder room and its adjoining water closet. Thus, Tom was alone in the room with Sara, who still sat opposite him at the table.

The two of them hadn't been by themselves since they'd boarded the Mississippi steamboat. Here at last was his golden opportunity—to speak his mind before it was too late.

"I wish you weren't leaving tomorrow," he ventured. "I, uh, haven't been entirely honest with you. I need to tell you something. I mean, I want to share how I really feel." He couldn't seem to get the words out in a decent order. Maybe because there was a good chance she'd be shocked by his admission.

"Oh?" Sara set down her teacup and gazed into his eyes as though she sought the answer there.

He blinked, forcing himself to keep to his train of thought. "We've been very good friends since we stopped thinking of each other as barbarians on the island." He noted her smile. "But, you see, my feelings for you have grown beyond that. Way beyond that, even though I tried hard to restrain them for a long time. And now that we're separating, well, I'd like to talk about us— while we're still together."

"I wish we *could* stay longer, but Mr. Pendleton is eager to see his family. Perhaps you can visit us?" Sara had been speaking more and more boldly since arriving in America, but now a shyness came through.

"Definitely." He huffed a breath. "Sara, what I'm trying to say is that I care deeply for you, and not like a sister or just a girlfriend. Perhaps you've heard of the custom called *courting*."

She patted her chest. "I do know about courting. I read about it while on the steamship, in a book called *Pride and Prejudice*." Her brow wrinkled.

"You're hard to keep up with, you know, but I want to try. You see, I'd like to ask you and Mr. Pendleton—since he's your guardian—permission to court you. It would have to be for at least a couple of years, until we both finish our schooling, and longer if the war goes on and I enlist. And then, I want to spend the rest of my life with you because ... because I *love* you."

She turned bright red and covered her mouth with her hand.

"Only here's the thing." Tom forged ahead, thankful she hadn't stopped him, but dreading to bring up the biggest issue. "You told me once you would marry only a Japanese Christian. I fulfill just one of your requirements." He made himself breathe though he felt as if he were teetering on an edge, worse than when he'd perched on the ship's sky-high platform in storms.

"I-I don't know what to say." She pulled out her fan and flipped it open. "I care for you too, in the very same way you care for me. But how can I face my people, and how can you face yours if we ... if we did marry ... after the two or three years?" She stirred the air with her fan, then lowered her eyes and set the fan in her lap. A tear stood on an eyelash.

Mr. Pendleton walked into the room at that moment.

Tom tried to hide his disgust. *He interrupts us at the perfectly worst times.*

"I'm sorry." Their elder gave a little bow. "But one can stay in the powder room only so long. I hesitated to enter, seeing you both in a serious conversation, so I waited in the hall. I'm afraid I overheard a little, my dears. Please forgive me."

"It's all right, sir." Tom kept back a sigh. He glanced at Sara, who held her fan in the middle of a wave as if transfixed. "Since you know our situation, and if Sara doesn't mind, perhaps you could tell us what you think. Advise us."

"Please, do help us." Sara began fanning again.

"Then I shall gladly do so." He took the seat next to Sara. "First, may I remind you that you are both citizens of the *same* country, whether other people acknowledge it or not."

Tom ran his hand through his hair while a vague memory came to mind. Mr. Pendleton had spoken about their heavenly citizenship sometime during their travels.

"Back in New Orleans," Mr. Pendleton said, "we discussed the fact that not only cruel slave holders, but the world itself is wrapped in darkness. As Christians, however, we've been transferred into God's kingdom of light—strictly by grace."

"I remember." Tom tapped his head. "It seems like years ago, instead of just a few months."

"I remember too," Sara said.

"Good." Mr. Pendleton folded his hands on the table. "Saint Paul's letters declare that you and I have been given the title of ambassadors for that heavenly country. We're ambassadors for *God's* kingdom." He pointed a finger at the ceiling. "The question becomes not whether it is permissible for an American gentleman to court and marry a Japanese lady. Rather, the question is whether you love each other and can carry out your mission of representing the King of kings together, effectively serving others."

"Since I care deeply for Sara, I want to court her and let our feelings grow, or even let them wither if that's how it turns out … although I cannot imagine mine will wither." Tom looked from Mr. Pendleton to Sara. "There is no one I admire more than Sara, no one I want to be with more, want to support more, love more." He stopped himself from saying *take in my arms more.* "But I don't know if we can represent God's kingdom to others." He wrapped a hand around his fist, gripping it.

"All right, let's think about that." Mr. Pendleton stroked his beard. "You've been in communities together already. How was it on the Pacific Mail steamer, where I heard there was no shortage of Americans vying with you, Thomas, for dances with Sara on the quarterdeck? How was it with Elijah and Jessy? With the Evanses? With the wagon train and the rest of the trip here? With Sam? Did your close friendship with each other cause rejection?"

"No, sir, but Sara felt uneasy at the Evanses' church." Tom raised an eyebrow at Sara.

"It seems the people who counted looked into your souls, not at the different tints of your skin or where you came from. Now, if you did find reason to marry, there would be aspects of each other's cultures that would irritate you. You'd have to remind yourselves that nations and their cultures are, in a sense, the *foreign* countries. While striving to share the gospel and improve people's welfare, we all have to remember where our true citizenship resides."

Tom's heart started the tom-tom beat again. "Then, may I have permission to court your charge, Mr. Pendleton, if Sara is willing?"

Sara was still fanning herself and looking from one to the

other, saying nothing as though their conversation had incapacitated her tongue.

"Let's allow Miss Sara and me a chance to discuss this privately, and, if possible, I'll give you our answer before we leave tomorrow. In the meantime, I suggest you also discuss this with your parents. And perhaps you should meet with that former girlfriend of yours right away, to be considerate, if by any chance she has been waiting for your long return."

"Yes, sir, I plan to talk this over with my parents even though I'm confident they won't object. As for Peg, she was a very good friend, but I've had my eyes opened to what real love is. She may have too. But if she hasn't moved on, I'll make sure she knows our relationship won't go beyond friendship."

Tom stood as Mr. Pendleton and Sara excused themselves a few minutes later and headed to their guest rooms. Tom moved into the parlor and sat in a familiar armchair. How good it was to be home. How often he'd dreamed of this moment. And now, how perfectly wonderful it would be to look forward to a home someday with Sara.

He leaned his head onto the chair's back cushion. It was going to be a long evening and a longer night. But in the end, he would accept the decision as from his Lord. He had to. No matter what, the Almighty knew best.

CHAPTER 32

The morning sun glittered on dust particles as Tom approached the parlor for the interview that could devastate him. Sara had avoided looking at him during the breakfast meal, keeping a conversation going with Tom's mother about flower arrangement and the Japanese tea ceremony. Mr. Pendleton had asked Tom's father question after question about President Lincoln and the war in the East. Neither Sara nor Mr. Pendleton had given any hint about the decision they'd reached. Telling himself to keep calm, Tom forced himself to walk into the parlor with a normal gait.

Mr. Pendleton half-rose, then gestured for Tom to take a nearby chair as he regained his seat. "I'll get to the point. Both Sara and I spent a period of protracted prayer. We sought more guidance from the Scriptures. We discussed how her parents and brother would react. Sara was convinced that her brother had left her marriage considerations in my hands since she could not return to Japan during what *her* countrymen consider a marriageable age. She was less certain of how to proceed with her family if faced with an actual marriage proposal."

"I see." But he really didn't see. Was his elder reluctant to give him bad news? Was that why he wasn't getting right to the point?

"Now, as I promised to get to the point, my answer is *yes*. You may court one of the loveliest young ladies I've ever been privileged to know."

"I may?" Tom jumped up and shook Mr. Pendleton's hand, who had also stood. "Thank you, sir. I assure you I will be a gentleman throughout."

"Yes, I am counting on that, young man." He drew out his fob watch. "And now, you may have twenty minutes alone with Miss Sara. We have a train to catch, so that's all the time I can give you."

Tom swallowed a lump in his throat as Mr. Pendleton, on his way out, held the door for Sara to enter. Dressed in her deep green kimono, his favorite, she was what people, such as his mother, would term a "vision of loveliness."

He took her hand after the door closed, and to his surprise, she put her other hand on his shoulder and looked into his eyes.

"Thank God, I can court you." Tom had the strongest urge to kiss her. If not mistaken, she had the same desire.

"I *have* truly thanked God." She stepped back, but left her hand in his. "Only, it will be hard to be so far from you. But I will faithfully write. Also, there is an express train on the Boston and Worcester Railroad, connecting this city and Boston. The fare is not too high."

"Mr. Pendleton told you the fare?"

"No, I asked the station master." Her eyes sparkled.

"Like I said, how will I keep up with you? But oh, am I ever happy to get a chance."

She smiled up at him.

He took her face in his hands and kissed her gently on the lips. When her lips responded, he drew her to himself and kissed her again, fervently, treasuring the feel of her in his arms—at last. A warmth spread throughout his body.

She drew back and pointed her finger at him. "You stole a kiss."

"I stole two," he corrected.

"Just one. Mr. Pendleton told me he'd allow you one kiss."

"Well, since I'm already a thief." He leaned in.

"No." She turned her head aside. "I know when many kisses should come. It's at the conclusion of the courtship."

"Oh, phooey on those novels. Authors don't set the rules."

"I think we must follow Mr. *Pendleton's* rules."

Tom sighed. He had promised her guardian to be a "gentleman," which included the man's definition of proper behavior. He'd learned the hard way what a tremendous amount of trouble could result from breaking agreements.

"Then, that's what we'll do." He ignored the ache that urged the kiss, reminding himself he could claim another kiss at their next meeting.

Her eyes expressed happy relief as she faced him again.

Tom ran his finger down her cheek, thankful he hadn't broken her trust. "Do you know the first time I desperately wanted to take you in my arms but obeyed your brother's stringent rule?"

"I could make a guess or two, but might be wrong." She gazed into his eyes.

"That time I pulled you out of the island's quicksand, and you collapsed next to me. Almost on top of me." He grinned.

"My brother would have made jiu-jitsu moves that you wouldn't have liked had he caught you … and me."

"That went through my mind, but really it was because I cared about your friendship too much to wreck it."

Her smile reminded him of the sensations he got from

sunsets, hunting with Tuffy, fresh bread—but ever so much better.

"Do you know when I wanted you to hold me and never release me, but feared the consequence?" Her face had turned bright red.

"At that same time? After I'd pulled you out of the glop?"

"I was too upset then. But I did thank God later that you had cared about me. No, it was when we waltzed together. I knew I was in love with everything about you, even your 'foibles.'"

"I believe that could be a *backhanded compliment*." At her concerned look, he added quickly, "But I like it. And it's good you're not entering our courtship with your eyes closed."

All too soon, Mr. Pendleton knocked at the door while Tom told of yet another time when she'd kindled his deep affection. She kissed his cheek and sped into the hallway. The whole household was gathering at the home's entrance. There were quick farewells with phrases of *don't be a stranger* and *come to visit*.

Before Tom could get his mind out of a daze and his feet firmly on the ground, he'd escorted Sara to the surrey. "Dearest—I hope you don't mind my calling you that." He interrupted himself for her response.

"Not a bit," she whispered.

"I told myself you were like an angel when we first met." He shook his head. "I had no idea how true that would be for me. You really are dearest to me, next to the Lord."

A smile lit her face. "Well, on that same day, I knew in my heart you couldn't be a barbarian." She giggled. "And now, you are the best and dearest gentleman I know."

"I love you," he said as Mr. Pendleton flicked the whip and the surrey's wheels turned.

She waved goodbye and blew a kiss.

Terry thumped Tom on the back as they watched the surrey disappear around a corner. "Congratulations, elder brother. I take it you received a *yes* to courting Sara."

"Yes. Yes, I did." Tom studied Terry's glad face. "But as giddy as that's made me, nothing can take away the wonder of being home. Being with you. Being with our folks." He turned toward Sam, who was watching them. "And having Sam here."

Terry grinned. "We. Are. Home! And you know what?

"What?"

"There's a new, exciting adventure beginning right before my eyes."

"I've had enough adventure for a while."

"This one is called *romance*. From what I've heard, the lovers are exhilarated, then depressed, soulmates, then misunderstood. Up and down and all around. Watching you and Sara will be better than the best of stories."

"Think so, huh?"

"Yep. And you know what else?"

"I have no idea."

"I'm rooting for you and Sara to make it. Know why?"

Tom shook his head.

"That's what brothers are for. And you're the best."

Tom teared up.

Terry smiled.

And Sam laughed for the pure joy of it all.

EPILOGUE

So, did Sara and Tom marry?

Until August of 1863, Tom rode the train every weekend to court Sara in Boston, staying with the Pendleton family. Benefitting from Mr. Pendleton's schooling and recommendation, he attained a certificate of completion from the preparatory academy in which Mr. Pendleton had formerly taught. On his twentieth birthday, Tom signed up as a civilian volunteer with the U.S. Navy. He was assigned as an Acting Ensign to the Navy Department in Washington D.C. due to his experience as a sailor and his extraordinary mathematical expertise. During most of his service, he calculated tidal effects and charted ship movements for the blockade. By the end of the war, he'd been promoted to Acting Lieutenant.

Sara, also under Mr. Pendleton's coaching, graduated from the Girls' High School in Boston. Then she completed the two-year college program at the Boston Normal School.

Weekly letters—even sometimes daily ones—flew back and forth during Tom and Sara's war-time courtship, although the postman usually delivered the letters in bunches.

Their Albany wedding took place in the home church of Tom's family on a glorious day in early July, 1865. Terry was best man, and Amy Pendleton, the oldest granddaughter of Sara's guardian, was the maid of honor. The garden reception took place at the Ballard's home. As expected, all in attendance affirmed they had never seen a more radiant bride, and in addition, neither had they seen a more joyful-looking groom.

For their first year as a married couple, Tom and Sara helped with Terry's Albany school for freedmen's children. Tom taught all levels of mathematics, but felt a special love for the fourth graders, remembering Robert and his family, who survived the war with their farm mostly intact. Sara taught geography, sharing the adventure of exploring new places and the wonder of God's beautiful creation, seen even on uncharted isles.

Joshua paid four visits to Albany during that year. He showed the school children his prosthetic leg and demonstrated how he could beat even Terry in a horse race.

When Mr. Pendleton returned to Nagasaki, Japan, after the wedding, he made contact with Daisuke, who at first refused to give his approval to his sister's marriage. But Mr. Pendleton's account of the couple's devoted courtship and his emphasis on a Christian's citizenship in God's kingdom finally persuaded Daisuke that his approval and blessing of the marriage were necessary. Once Consul John Cardiff informed the Nagasaki governor of the young man's potential value in the nation's shipbuilding efforts, the governor spoke to the Shōgun on Daisuke's behalf. A pardon for his foreign travel resulted.

After their first year of marriage, Sara and Tom, desiring to strike out on their own, took the railroad to Junction City, Kansas, and from there rode a stagecoach to Colorado City. Tom worked initially as a surveyor, but it was after he became an Indian Agent for the Colorado Territory that he and Sara found their greatest satisfaction. They hosted dinner parties, mountain treks, forums, and church gatherings that fostered sensitivity to the different cultures, which led to genuine friendships among the native Americans and pioneer residents alike.

In 1871, rail travel became possible from Colorado Springs, the town adjoining Colorado City, all the way to Albany in just nine days. Because Tom's family was dear to both Tom and Sara—and eventually to their expanded family of five sons and daughters—they carried out a tradition of extended visits to New York almost every summer.

Above all, Sara and Tom prized their position as ambassadors of God's kingdom—together and in love.

HISTORICAL NOTE

Although *Fields of Shadow and Glory* is fiction, it mirrors the Civil War's actual history wherever I found known facts intersecting the story. Here are just a few examples, selected out of many: Beyond the Florida panhandle, New Orleans was the only deep-water Union port in the Gulf in which a damaged mail ship, loyal to the North, could find refuge in 1863. As for the Mississippi River, Confederate forces fully controlled navigation between Port Hudson and Vicksburg, where the townspeople dug caves into the high bluff and survived by eating rats and almost anything else that moved during the Union's siege. The Union Navy had made a withering attack on Baton Rouge as described in the story, and Union troops occupied the city.

The Confederate prison in which Terry suffered deserves special mention. A dilapidated covered bridge outside Jackson, Mississippi, served as the jam-packed enclosure for 399 Union captives. A back part of the bridge had already fallen into the Pearl River beneath it. Even in the cold months, the prison administrators did not allow any fires for warmth inside the bridge for fear it would burn down. Almost every day, two or three captives died, due to the lethal conditions.[1]

Finally, plotting a realistic escape for Terry and Joshua through miles of Rebel territory presented a huge problem. The famous Grierson Raiders historical expedition provided the answer. Designed to take the Confederate forces' attention away from the movements of the North's Army of the Tennessee, the Grierson Raiders' cavalry swoop through the heart of Mississippi was a roaring success. Grierson himself reported that during the

---

[1] Jerry Korn and the Editors of Time-Life Books. *War on the Mississippi.* The Civil War. Alexandria, VA: Time-Life Books, 1985, p. 117.

expedition, lasting less than sixteen days, they marched 600 miles behind enemy lines, tore up more than 50 miles of telegraph lines and railroad, destroyed an immense amount of arms, and captured approximately 1000 mules and horses. They took about 500 prisoners, whom they paroled, while they wounded or killed about 100 of the enemy. Only three of their own men were known to have been killed and seven wounded.[2] The expedition ended in Baton Rouge with the parade in the city, actually cheered by the citizens. Their encampment at the nearby Magnolia Mound Plantation provided the ideal location for the brothers' reunion.

Aware that the book's readers could include dedicated Civil War history buffs, I debated the wisdom of setting the story within the Mississippi River campaign, an unfamiliar part of the conflict for me. However, conducting the necessary research frequently turned out to be an enjoyable challenge, turning up fascinating historical events and personalities.

---

[2] Referenced in Timothy B. Smith, *The Real Horse Soldiers: Benjamin Grierson's Epic 1863 Civil War Raid through Mississippi*. El Dorado Hills, CA: Savas Beatie, ©2018, 2020, p. 298.

A NOTE FROM ELIZABETH ANN

Thank you for taking time to read *Fields of Shadow and Glory*. If you enjoyed this story, please take a minute to review it on Amazon. Even offering just a sentence or two can have a big impact. Reviews are a story's lifeline!

If you began with this third book of the *Brothers in Peril Trilogy*, wouldn't you like more? The first two stories in the series not only provide a myriad of insights into Tom, Terry, Sara, and Daisuke, but also dive into their struggles and victories leading up to the Civil War's crucible. Both are available on Amazon.

Book One, ***Entrapped—1861: The Journey Begins,*** traces the brothers' risky ventures from Albany, New York, to their grandparents' farm, then as sailors traveling through Havana, around Cape Horn, into the Galapagos Archipelago, and across the Pacific all the way to an uncharted island. Sara and Daisuke make a stunning appearance too.

In Book Two, ***Isle of Darkness and Light,*** Tom's enemies have left him on the uncharted Pacific island. He has to deal with far more than loneliness, earthquakes, a deep cavern, and pirates. Earning the trust of Sara and Daisuke is difficult enough, yet confronting life's ultimate questions demands his whole heart and soul. Meanwhile, Terry risks everything to find help for Tom, only to be entangled in the schemes of treasure hunters with deadly intentions.

How about visiting the years directly preceding the *Brothers in Peril Trilogy*? The **Dragonfly Trilogy** reveals Consul Cardiff and Sumi's astonishing stories, in which they shine as the stars. Also, the delightful Mr. Pendleton shows up as their indispensable counselor and friend. The fascinating, but treacherous setting of 1859-1861 in Nagasaki, Japan, waits the reader in the series' three novels, also available on Amazon

My author newsletters, emailed about every two months, contain insights and anecdotes related to my stories as well as notifications of special offers. If you would like to receive these occasional, brief letters, please let me know at ann@elizabethannboyles.com. I hope we can stay in touch. You are greatly appreciated!

DISCUSSION QUESTIONS

Spoiler alert: These questions should be discussed only after finishing the story.

1. Tom and Sara are close friends at the beginning of the story. What indications are given in the first few chapters that their relationship could progress beyond friendship?

2. How does Terry feel about Tom and Sara's friendship before his capture? Is his feeling at all justified? He comes across as disagreeable at times. Does he have good qualities too?

3. Was Tom entirely foolish to try to rescue Terry alone? Did you see anything admirable about Tom during the failed attempt?

4. Did the descriptions of the former slaves' dilemmas and the Southern culture of that time come across as a realistic and balanced treatment?

5. What part of Terry's captivity and escape did you find most gripping? What do you think caused Terry to have that first hint of happiness while he was teaching Sam? Have you had a similar experience during a difficult situation or heartbreak?

6. Four strong Christians—Mr. Pendleton, Joshua, Sam's grandfather, and the widow—especially impacted Terry in this story. What qualities in these persons' characters, or which of their actions, would have had the greatest influence on you if you had been in Terry's situation?

7. Sara was described as having the strength of steel girders. How did she demonstrate the strength of the "daughter of a samurai"? What did you like best about her personality?

8. Which character changed the most in this story? What were that person's biggest transformations?

9. Were you satisfied with Talbot's sentence?

10. What did you find most likable about Tom? If you read the first two books of the series, you probably grasped Tom's deepest desires. In what ways were his underlying needs satisfied by the end of the series?

11. What occurrences give evidence of divine Providence in the story?

12. Did Mr. Pendleton's statements about Tom and Sara's citizenship in God's kingdom strike you as a strong enough solution to their concerns?

ACKNOWLEDGMENTS

Throughout my years of writing, numerous people have kindly offered suggestions and encouragement. Here, I'll mention those who contributed improvements specifically for *Fields of Shadow and Glory* although I deeply appreciate every bit of help I've received.

Thank you to these members of the ACFW critique groups who read the story as it progressed and offered valuable suggestions: Savannah Allbritton, Lee Carver, Kerry Dreher, Martha Ladyman, and Kay Learned. Additionally, I'm grateful to Landie Holgate's contribution to the manuscript's final proof. All of you have been a tremendous blessing!

And last of all, a big thank you to you, cherished reader, for you make my effort truly worthwhile!

ABOUT THE AUTHOR

Unique historical settings have always intrigued Elizabeth Ann, especially ones that feature a mix of American and other countries' cultures. Those settings provide a treasure chest for her fictional stories of adventure and discovery, often including a strand of romance.

She developed a love for the Far East when she lived in Japan, where she met and married her husband. She also spent many years teaching and building relationships with her international students at a Christian university in Dallas, Texas.

After her husband of fifty years took his final step into heaven, she moved to Colorado. She cherishes spending time at the foot of the gorgeous Rocky Mountains with her daughter and son, while entreating her grandchildren to visit often.

Elizabeth Ann won the ACFW national Genesis award and the ACFW Virginia Crown award for historical/historical romance.

She would love to stay in touch through her newsletters, which you can sign up for by emailing ann@ElizabethAnnBoyles.com

Another way to stay in touch is at
Facebook.com/elizabethannboyles

Of course, the welcome mat is always out at
ElizabethAnnBoyles.com

www.ingramcontent.com/pod-product-compliance
Lightning Source LLC
Chambersburg PA
CBHW031122210626
46816CB00016B/1756